MURDER IN
THE MOUNTAINS

Previously published Worldwide Mystery titles by
HELEN GOODMAN

MURDER IN EDEN
TOXIC WASTE
THE BLUE GOOSE IS DEAD
MURDER AND MISDEEDS
VALLEY OF DEATH
MURDER AT THE LAKE

MURDER IN THE MOUNTAINS

HELEN GOODMAN

W🌐RLDWIDE®

TORONTO • NEW YORK • LONDON
AMSTERDAM • PARIS • SYDNEY • HAMBURG
STOCKHOLM • ATHENS • TOKYO • MILAN
MADRID • WARSAW • BUDAPEST • AUCKLAND

Recycling programs
for this product may
not exist in your area.

Murder in the Mountains

A Worldwide Mystery/October 2016

First published by Alabaster Book Publishing.

ISBN-13: 978-0-373-27960-9

Printed in U.S.A.

MURDER IN
THE MOUNTAINS

ONE

LEONA WHITLEY'S BODY lay crumpled at the foot of the basement stairs. Her forehead rested on the cement floor, and both her head and the floor were stained with blood. One foot was twisted under her while the other one dangled from a low step, her shoe halfway off.

The narrow basement windows let in only a smidgen of afternoon sunlight. The open door at the top of the stairs, though, allowed the kitchen's fluorescent beams to filter down the steps and bathed Leona in an eerie light. There were only two witnesses to her plight. One was a long-legged spider too busy spinning a rope ladder to pay her any heed, and the other was a tiny lost field mouse who'd crept under the outside door seeking refuge from the frigid cold. But the mouse was more interested in gnawing at a sweet, red apple than getting acquainted with the motionless woman.

Silence reigned in the small room, interrupted only periodically by the oil furnace trying to combat the North Carolina mountain winter.

The upstairs rooms were quiet, also, except for the sound of opening and closing of drawers, the shuffling of papers and the muttered, "Damn. Damn. Where in the world is it? Where did she hide it?"

LATER THAT EVENING, nearly two hundred miles to the east, Allison and Fred lounged in matching recliners, laughing together at a favorite Tuesday night TV sitcom. They were both in their pajamas and were wearing the purple slipper-socks they'd gotten for Christmas—looking like a middle-aged, longtime married couple who were now empty-nesters. But as any of their friends could explain, they were actually still newlyweds. Allison Aldridge, a single mom with two kids in college, had met Detective Fred Sawyer, a bachelor, during a murder investigation. He'd taken a liking to her almost at once, even though she was awfully nosy and kept butting in while he was busy looking for clues. It wasn't until she'd almost become a second murder victim that he'd realized how much he did care for her. It took him several months but he finally got around to popping the question, and the June wedding was the talk of the town.

Fred retired from the sheriff's office, left the detective work to younger officers, and took a job in school security—in the same school district in which Allison taught.

Her middle school students still called her Ms. Aldridge since she'd decided to keep Allison Aldridge as her professional name, but she loved being Mrs. Fred Sawyer. Now with Valentine's Day approaching, she was secretly searching for the perfect gift to give the man in her life.

THEIR QUIET EVENING came to an end with the chirp of Allison's cell phone. Scrambling out of her chair, she snatched the phone from under the newspaper, answered with a cheery, "Hello," while Fred muted the TV.

The voice on the other end of the line was somber, "Allison, this is Sam Babcock."

A shiver went through Allison as she realized immediately the call had to be bad news. Sam Babcock was the sheriff in the county where her Aunt Leona lived, and Allison had often worried about her aunt living alone on the isolated apple orchard farm. Taking a deep breath, she tried to sound calm. "Sheriff Babcock. What's the matter?" When he didn't answer immediately, Allison went into a panic mode, "Sam, has something happened to Leona?"

As she waited for the answer, she noticed Fred lowered the footrest of his recliner and gave her a questioning look. She put the phone on speaker. Whatever the news was, she wanted him to hear it, too.

The sheriff didn't waste any words. "Leona is dead. She accidentally fell down the basement stairs, struck her head."

Allison gasped, tried to take in the enormity of his words. Her aunt was dead, her only living relative on her mother's side, the person she loved more than anyone except for her immediate family. She knew she had to say something, anything, make some acknowledgement. "When? How did it happen?"

"This afternoon. According to the coroner, she died between two and four. I have no idea how it happened. I assume her foot must have slipped or she lost her balance somehow." He paused. Allison wondered what was coming next. When the sheriff continued, his voice was softer, "If it's any comfort, I don't think she suffered. The trauma to her head when she hit the cement was pretty profound. If she didn't die right away, at least she was unconscious."

Allison brushed back the tears streaking down her face. "Yes," she lied, "that helps." But of course it didn't. Nothing would help the pain of losing someone she'd always thought of as her big sister. Struggling, she managed to ask, "Who found her?"

"Harry Roberson. About six. They had plans to go out to dinner, but when he arrived, she didn't answer his knock. He tried the door, found it was locked, and he used his key to get in."

Interrupting him, Allison burst out, "He had a key to Leona's house?"

"Well, yeah. She must have given it to him. Didn't you know they were seeing each other?"

It took a moment for Allison to gather her thoughts. "Sure, I knew they were dating, but I didn't know it'd gotten to the exchanging keys stage." She glanced over to Fred and thought he had a half-smile on his face. Turning her back to him, she added, "Don't get me wrong. I know Harry. He's a good guy and I like him. But…oh, never mind. Go on. What did he do when he got in the house?"

"Kept calling for her with no answer. The lights were on in the kitchen and den and he could see that the basement door was open. He went over and looked down, but it was dark. When he flipped on the light, he saw her at the bottom of the stairs, ran down to her." Sheriff Babcock's voice trembled slightly. "He could tell she was dead and he called 911."

When Allison made no response, he went on, "I know this is really hard on you. Leona was only a few years older than you and she told me she thought of you as her little sister. That's why, after Dick died, she told me if anything happened to her, I was to call you. You know you're her next of kin—and her heir."

"I know," she managed to say through her tears. "She and Dick wanted children but when that didn't happen, we became even closer. Then when Dick died she told me I was to have the property. But that should have been years from now. She was only in her fifties, in good health, active. I can't believe she's gone." Trying to gain control of her emotions, Allison choked out, "I'll be up there in the morning, make the funeral arrangements, do what I have to do. Thanks for calling, Sam. I'll check with you in the morning before I leave."

"Good. But don't worry about the house. I made sure everything was locked up before I left, and I got her key back from Harry. You can pick the keys up at the station."

Allison ended the call, slipped down onto Fred's lap, and sobbed.

WANTING TO EASE her pain, Fred pulled Allison close, cradled her head against his shoulder and let her cry it out. When she seemed to be slowing down, he reached out one hand to the tissue box on his right, grabbed a handful and started dabbing at her cheeks. She sniffed, nodded her thanks. Taking the tissues, she wiped her eyes and blew her nose.

She kissed him on the forehead, whispered, "I'm so glad you're here."

"Me too." Shifting a little to get more comfortable, he said, "I wish I had gotten to know her better. I remember her from the wedding. We didn't get to talk much, but she seemed like a wonderful person. She said if we'd come up in apple picking time, she'd put me to work. I told her we'd try." He pushed some matted strands of hair back from Allison's eyes. "I'm so sorry we didn't make it up there. It just seemed as if we were too busy."

"I know. Now it's too late. But I have such precious memories of the times I did visit. When I was in my teens I spent most of my summers there. My dad had died and Mom had to work and she didn't want me to be alone all day—probably thought I'd get into trouble. Leona and Dick hadn't been married long, and we all had a great time together. And I ate so many of their apples, it's a wonder they made any profit from the orchard."

Fred felt Allison give a sudden jerk, a look of panic on her face. "Fred, what am I going to do with an apple orchard?"

He pulled her closer. "Nothing right now. You're going to bed and you're going to remember all the good times you had with Leona. Okay?"

"Okay. But I've got to call the kids. They visited there, too, and were very fond of both Leona and Dick."

"Of course, you'll call them, but not tonight. In the morning will be soon enough."

"You're right. No use upsetting their evenings."

She sniffed, blew her nose again. "They went with me to Dick's funeral two years ago. I told you about him having had heart problems for years so his death wasn't completely unexpected."

"I remember."

Fred wanted to keep her talking as it seemed to be calming her down, so he went on, "I heard you mention this fellow that Leona was dating. Harry somebody. Did you know him well?"

"Not too well, but he seems nice enough." Allison pulled herself up, grabbed some more tissues. "Oh, Fred, Sam said Harry's the one who found her."

Not wanting her to go down that path again, he attempted a bit of levity, "You must be pretty well acquainted with the sheriff to call him 'Sam.' Is there something from your younger days I should know about?"

She favored him with a slight grin. "Nothing for you to worry about. Upton is a small town in a small rural county. Everyone is on a first name basis."

"Same as where I come from. I like that." Fred gently pushed her off his lap, got up, and led the way into the bedroom. "You need to get some sleep now. We'll talk more in the morning." She nodded and crawled under the covers.

But long after Allison had drifted off, Fred's mind was still in turmoil. He ached for her pain but even worse was the fact he couldn't be there to share it with her. He was scheduled to fly to Dallas the next day to attend a national seminar on school safety and security. Part of his job as the liaison between the schools and law enforcement was to keep abreast of new information. He'd been asked by county officials to attend the two-day conference, and since they were paying all his expenses, he'd gladly agreed. And now he saw no way to get out of it. The funeral of an aunt in-law would hardly qualify for bereavement leave.

IT WAS ALLISON who brought up the subject of Dallas the next morning. "You have to go. I'll be fine. Don't worry about me."

Allison knew she was trying to reassure herself as well as Fred. She'd coped on her own before he came along and she could do it again. But, she had to admit to herself, it wasn't going to be easy.

She started that coping by making the necessary phone calls. Madison Middle School was first on the list. The principal told her not to worry, to take as much time as was needed, that there'd be no problem in getting a substitute teacher.

Connie and Dave were next. She wanted to catch each of them before either went to class. Both her children had loved their great aunt Leona, had enjoyed visiting the farm, had picked and eaten their share of apples. As expected, they said they wanted be with her and to attend the funeral.

Allison appreciated their concern, but being a practical person, she vetoed their coming. She knew they were loaded with class work and missing several days would put them behind. She told both of them the same thing, "I wanted you to know, but I don't want you to miss any classes. I'll be fine by myself. I know everybody around there—the neighbors, Leona's friends in her church and in the town of Upton. And I'll call you every night."

Each finally admitted it would be difficult to get away, but they would be there in spirit. The calls ended with rounds of, "Love ya," that made Allison feel both blessed and empty.

She then phoned the only funeral home in Upton. It was difficult, but she had to get started on the arrangements. Mr. Knotts, the funeral director, was expecting her call, got the information he needed for the obituary, said he would have time to put it in this evening's paper. Allison knew *The Upton Messenger* was published three evenings a week with local news, ads, and gossip. Anyone wanting real news subscribed the Asheville paper.

Mr. Knotts also said Harry Roberson had already called and suggested the funeral be on Thursday since there was a storm predicted for Friday.

"But that's tomorrow," Allison said. "Isn't that awfully soon?"

"Not really. Since she passed away on Tuesday, a Thursday funeral is acceptable." He hesitated. "But, of course, the final decision is up to you. Harry said he'd spoken to the pastor of their church and he agreed to Thursday."

Allison closed her eyes, took a deep breath. She tried to remain calm, but her mind was screaming, *What right did Harry have to make such a decision? I'm the next of kin. Couldn't he have at least consulted me?*

Then her rational mind took over. Harry was probably trying to make things easier for her. And what difference did it make when the funeral was held? She was going to be saying goodbye to someone she loved. Delaying it wouldn't make it any easier. "I guess Thursday probably would be better," she said, "since a storm is on the way. But there won't be any visitation at your funeral home. I want just a short public viewing at the church prior to the funeral." She went on to tell him she would be in that afternoon to pick out the casket.

She thought briefly about calling Harry, but simply didn't feel up to it. Putting Leona's boyfriend out of her mind, she made one more call. She wanted to tell Sam about what time to expect her as she needed to stop by his office before going to the farm. Allison recognized Marie Walker's calm voice when the dispatcher answered. Marie had worked for the sheriff department since forever and was known for being a grandmother figure to every cop in the area.

When Allison identified herself, Marie's voice oozed with sympathy, "I'm so sorry for your loss. Leona was such a fine person. We're all going to miss her." It took a few exchanges before Allison could make her request to speak to the sheriff and to learn he wasn't in. "But he left your keys with me," Marie said.

She ended the call with relief. Now, she thought, I've got to start packing. It wasn't long before she and Fred were hugging goodbye. She promised to call when she got to Upton; he promised to call when he got to Dallas.

Soon she was on her way. The day was clear and the traffic light as she headed west on Interstate 40. Wanting to dwell on happier times instead of the reason for her trip, Allison's mind drifted back to mid-June when she'd last seen her aunt. Leona had driven down a few days before the wedding, accepted Allison's invitation to stay at the house, while Fred's clan consisting of his brother's family, his sister, and assorted cousins filled most of the rooms at the newest motel. Leona seemed to have fitted right in with the Sawyers, and at the rehearsal dinner, she was the object of good hearted teasing by some of them that she should be the next bride in the family. She'd countered with, "It's hard to find a man my age that still has all his hair, all his senses, and plenty of money. But if I ever do find one, you're all invited."

And from what little she knew about Harry Roberson, he qualified on all three counts. He owned the only hardware store in Upton and it seemed to do a brisk business. His hair was graying but there was still plenty of it, and despite being a little pushy about making the funeral arrangements, he probably was a sensible man. However, if there was anything serious going on with Leona and Harry, her aunt had never hinted at it during their frequent phone calls.

The thought of Harry naturally brought Allison's mind back to Sam Babcock's call the evening before. Bits and pieces of the conversation forced themselves into the forefront of her brain. Sam had said that Leona had accidentally tripped while going to the basement. Why? Something left on the steps? She was in a hurry? Maybe had a dizzy spell? Allison knew her speculation was pointless, but still she wondered.

Then she recalled what the sheriff had said about Harry coming in. The kitchen light was on and he

TWO

FOR THE NEXT couple of hours, the sun rode right along with Allison, its rays shining in the rear window and bouncing off the rearview mirror. It certainly didn't look as if any storm were coming in the near future. She knew, though, that weather in the high country could change very quickly. By Friday, the mountains could be adding several inches of the white stuff. When she stopped for gas, she could tell the temperature had dropped several degrees.

Over the years, nearly all her trips to the mountains had been in the summer, so she wasn't very confident about driving in snow. The few snow storms they had in the middle of the state were usually minor and short-lived. Even a few inches of snow was enough to close schools for the day. Being a teacher, she could stay home just like her students did—but instead of lazing around the house or playing in the snow like the kids, she always seem to have papers to grade or classes to prepare.

She did remember a couple of ski trips up there during her college Christmas breaks, but those were with a group of friends, and she never did the driving.

As she got back into the car, Allison knew her worries about the weather were only a cover so she wouldn't dwell on how much she was going to miss Leona. Both of them had grown up pretty much alone except for each other. Leona's only sibling, Fern, was already grown and married when Leona was born. A few years later Fern gave birth to Allison, who turned out to be her only child. Aunt and niece bonded into their own form of sisterhood.

Swiping back some tears at the memories, Allison tried to focus on the road ahead. Several miles before reaching Asheville, she veered off from the main highway onto a two-lane rural road that led to Upton. As she drove into the small mountain town, good memories of past visits floated through her head. Upton had grown and modernized in the thirty some years she'd been coming, but it still maintained that certain small town essence. Duncan's Diner competed well with the hamburger and chicken franchises; the corner soda shop was now an ice cream parlor, but one could still get an old-fashioned chocolate malt. The new hospital was as up-to-date as it was possible to be, but the emergency room nurses still called most of their patients by their first name.

Before going any further, she pulled off into a parking lot to call Fred and report her safe arrival. She got his voice mail, left a brief message, ended with, "Will talk to you later."

As she drove on, Allison brought her mind back to her tasks at hand. Her first stop was the county sheriff's department. It was located just outside the city limits on the other side of town.

Allison smiled as she recalled her first visit to that office. It was on one of her college ski trips. Leona had made room for her and her three friends, but had declined the invitation to go skiing. Late in the afternoon the skiers decided to get in out of the cold and party a little. None of them thought they had much to drink, including the driver, but the officer that stopped them thought otherwise. He took them all in, had the car towed, and called Leona. No charges were brought and they were released to her aunt's custody with the warning it had better not happen again. It hadn't. This was before Sam's time as sheriff, but Allison made friends with Marie, the dispatcher, and always dropped in for a visit when in the area.

It wasn't long until Allison pulled into the parking lot. Marie must have seen her coming because by the time Allison had gotten through the swinging door, the dispatcher, her gray hair as shiny as a silver dollar, was waiting with a hug.

"It's so good to see you again, but I hate that it's under these circumstances. I'm so sorry for your loss. Leona was such a fine person."

Allison responded with a nod. She knew this would be only the first of many such encounters and she had to steel herself to accept the sympathy of others who knew and loved her aunt.

Marie stepped back, looked behind Allison. "You alone? I was looking forward to meeting that new husband of yours."

"He couldn't make it now—had to attend an important conference in Dallas. His job, you know. But he'll be here this weekend."

"Good. Bring him by. I want to tell him what a prize he got when he married you."

Allison laughed. "Oh, he already knows that." Then her face sobered again as she asked, "Sam in?"

Picking up a packet, Marie handed it to Allison and explained, "I'm sorry. The sheriff wanted to see you but had to go back out. Some ruckus at the high school. Here are Leona's keys, and he made sure everything was all right when he locked up." After a pause for breath, she added, "Was there anything special you wanted to ask him?"

Allison shook her head. "I just thought he could give me a few more details about the accident. But that can wait."

"You going out to the farm now?"

"Not now. I have to stop by the funeral home first."

"Of course. And since you don't have to worry about the dog, there's no hurry."

"Dog?" Allison clamped her hand over her mouth, then let out a slow moan. "Oh, I forgot all about Elmer. Leona loved that shepherd. How could I forget him?"

"Well, like I said. Not to worry. Harry took him to his house. He'll take good care of Elmer."

Allison felt an instant resentment. Like he took care of the funeral date, she thought, like he took care to let himself into Leona's house, like... Her thoughts and her anger drifted away. Harry was simply being helpful. She had to stop being so touchy. But, she vowed to herself, when I leave Upton, Elmer is going with me.

The station phone rang and Marie rushed to answer it. Allison waved to her, slipped out the door, and headed to her next appointment.

She knew the location of the Knotts Funeral home but had never been inside and wasn't acquainted with any of the family that ran it. It was Mr. Albert Knotts she'd spoken to on the phone, and when she gave her name to the receptionist, the girl acknowledged it with a nod. "Mr. Knotts is expecting you." The young girl rose, smiled. "Right this way."

Mr. Knotts looked and dressed just as Allison imagined all undertakers did: dark suit, neatly trimmed hair, somber visage, carefully modulated voice. He gave her a limp handshake and a weak smile. "Would you like a few minutes to view Mrs. Whitley?"

Unable to make any words come out of her mouth, she simply nodded. He led her to a table in the back of a small, dimly lit room. "She's all prepared. As soon as you supply us with the clothing you want her to wear and pick out the appropriate casket, we can complete her presentation."

Allison blinked back tears, her thoughts in turmoil. *Presentation? What kind of word is that? It isn't as if Leona's here for a job interview or that she's going to make a speech.*

Willing herself not to fall apart, Allison stood rigidly as Mr. Knotts pulled back the sheet covering Leona's face and front torso. Her aunt's beautiful face appeared before her, eyes closed as if in peaceful slumber. The makeup had been carefully applied; her dark hair, streaked with gray, was combed over the left side of her forehead. Allison suspected it was covering the area that had struck the cement, and she was grateful for the way the wound had been hidden. Leona's arms were crossed over her chest; her hands, usually so busy, lay in quiet repose.

Mr. Knotts had been standing a short distance away, giving her the privacy she needed. Then he stepped forward, motioned to Leona's hands and asked, "Do you want us to redo her nail polish?"

Jerking around, Allison stared at him. "Nail polish?"

"Since her polish was smudged on a couple of her nails, I took the liberty of ordering it all removed. However, if you wish, we could apply it again."

"No. That won't be necessary. She only wore nail polish on special occasions."

A little voice inside her head seem to mock her. *Don't you consider your aunt's funeral a special occasion?* Of course, she wanted to answer herself, but nail polish is for special joyous events—not sad ones.

She took a deep breath, turned around. "Your staff did a beautiful job. Thank you. Now I guess I'd better finish up here and select the casket."

As Allison left the funeral home, she began to feel faint and realized she hadn't eaten since early morning. Not wanting to chance meeting anyone she knew in the diner or a restaurant, she opted for a drive-thru chicken meal and drove to a nearby park. The air was too cold and the breeze too brisk to eat at one of the inviting picnic tables. She stayed in her car, devoured the nuggets and fries in record time, and washed it all down with a Diet Coke.

Feeling refreshed, she was ready to tackle the next job of meeting with Leona's pastor. She knew and liked Reverend Pierson, had accompanied her aunt to church on several occasions. The meeting was short but pleasant. He made suggestions regarding the music, scriptures, and pallbearers, but left the final decisions up to her. They agreed to an open casket prior to the church service and, in deference to the frigid temperature predicted, there would be only a few words at the graveside.

"One more thing," he said as she started to leave, "the ladies of the church want to bring some food by the house before the service. I know you probably won't feel like having people in, but you'll need something for yourself."

"That's very nice of them, but not necessary."

"Allison, it's what we do whenever we lose a member. And Leona was a beloved member here."

"Of course." She reached into her purse, pulled out an extra key the sheriff had left for her. "They can let themselves in if I'm not there."

A measure of peace settled over Allison as she left the church and headed toward Mount Vista Road. That peace was shattered as soon as she saw the sign in Leona's front yard, *Whitley's Apple Orchard.* In times past, the sign had greeted her with a promise of fun, laughter, and all the apple pie she could eat. But now it meant the end of all those good times. She would have to have it removed as soon as possible.

She let herself into the house by the kitchen door, flipped on the overhead light. The afternoon sun was low over the western slope and Allison shivered

slightly at the thought of the coming night. Looking around the room, she marveled at how normal
everything seemed: the kitchen table with a bowl
of apples in the center, the counter with an opened
cookbook, the magnet on the refrigeration holding
a grocery list. It was if Leona would come out from
the den any second with a welcoming hug.

She shook the image out of her mind and pro-
ceeded to her aunt's bedroom. There was no way
she could spend the night here—not until after the
funeral. Maybe then it would be easier, but for now
she would get the clothes she needed to take to the
mortuary and then find a room in the nearest motel.

As she made her way back through the den, the
blinking light on Leona's house phone caught her
attention. Could someone had not yet heard of her
aunt's death and had called to chat or to remind her
of an appointment? How spooky would that be? Feeling like an eavesdropper, Allison pushed the 'play'
button. She was surprised to hear her own name.
"Allison, this is Molly Kirkman. I don't have your
cell number, but I figured you'd be staying at Leona's,
and I just wanted you to know if there is anything I
can do for you, just give me a call. Leona was such
a dear friend to me. Ted and I will be at the funeral,
but call me anytime, even if you only want to talk."
As she rattled off her phone number, Allison grabbed
a pencil and a piece of newspaper from the coffee
table and scribbled it down. She crammed the paper
in her coat pocket. It was sweet of Molly to call, but
Allison had no desire to talk to anyone now. It was

going to be hard enough tomorrow when she would be surrounded by her aunt's friends.

Going through the kitchen, she again noted the open cookbook on the counter, stopped to see what Leona may have been planning on cooking. She stared at the picture of an apple pie with a lattice crust. Something about the picture seemed strange, but she couldn't take time now to think about it. She wanted to get back to town before it got completely dark.

The sun slipped behind the mountains as she pulled out into the driveway. Turning on her headlights, Allison headed toward Upton. She'd gone only a short distance when headlights came up behind her. Since she wasn't driving very fast she expected the car to pass. It didn't. The road was curvy, but every time there was a straight section, she slowed down enough so the driver behind could safely go around, but whoever it was seemed to prefer to stay on her tail. Was she deliberately being followed? Or was the driver just too timid to try to pass?

Allison became increasingly nervous as she neared the town limits, but as the two cars approached Upton High School, the one behind abruptly turned left and swerved into a parking lot. She could see it was a dark sedan, but couldn't get a look at the driver. Lights were on in the gymnasium, and she let out a sigh of relief as she realized it must be kid going to basketball practice or some such thing. She scolded herself for being so skittish. She didn't know what had gotten into her. It wasn't like Allison Aldridge Sawyer to be afraid of shadows.

THREE

ALLISON WOKE UP Thursday morning at the Country Inn Motel and wondered how she was going to make it through the day.

While checking in the evening before, she'd gotten a momentary respite from her grief when her schoolmarm persona fumed about the name of the establishment. She wanted to tell the desk clerk that its nomenclature was erroneous and redundant. The building was in a town, not out in the country, and it could be called either an inn or a motel, but not both. Of course, she hadn't said anything about it and had meekly accepted the key card.

When she got to the room, she had to admit there was a touch of country in the décor. The scene on the wall opposite the beds was definitely rural, a timeless farmhouse. The paint on the white clapboard was peeling in places, the tin roof was rusty and patched, but the wraparound porch exuded an air of welcome with its rocking chairs and a tub of old-timey petunias.

Allison had turned away from the picture. It was too peaceful. Its serenity only made her inner turmoil more painful.

Talking to Fred later she told him where she was staying, joked about the name, but didn't mention the picture. She tried to sound upbeat although she knew Fred wasn't fooled.

"I can ditch this whole conference, hon. Probably catch an early morning flight and be there in time for the funeral. Just say the word."

But she couldn't or wouldn't say the word. Fred had his duty and she had hers. Allison knew his offer had been genuine and she loved him even more for it, but she'd gone through tougher times than this alone and she could do it again.

Then when he told her he might not call her in the morning, she began to falter. "The conference starts with an early morning breakfast," he said, "and goes straight through until five. I'll call you if I get a break at lunch, but, if not, it'll be late in the afternoon. Okay?"

"Sure. We're both going to have a busy day."

Trying to put last evening out of her mind, Allison opened the shade, stared out at the sun glistening off a snow bank, at icicles dangling from the end of a gutter, at a fellow traveler scraping frost off his windshield. The world was moving on and she had to, also.

Grabbing her lifeline to her kids, she spoke to each of them. Connie sent her love and prayers and some practical advice. "Don't bother with proper funeral garb, Mom. The weather channel says the wind chill will be in the twenties. Wear your heavy slacks, a sweater under your coat, and a scarf over her head."

Allison smiled. In the past year her little girl had made the transition from needing advice to an expert on giving it. Maybe advice giving was included in the med school curriculum. As far back as Allison could remember Connie had wanted to be a doctor. Although Allison applauded the decision, she'd been a little fearful Connie's first year of medical training might be overwhelming to her rather reserved daughter. Those fears proved to be completely unwarranted.

Her mind fast-forwarded a few decades and imagined Connie saying, *"Now, Mom, you have to stop doing wheelies in your wheelchair. It's too dangerous."*

On the other hand, in that faraway time, Dave would probably be promoting a wheelchair race with her fellow nursing home residents. His parting advice to her today was, "Be sure you don't run out of Snickers."

She ended each conversation with, "Don't worry about me. I'll be fine." She hoped she wasn't lying.

Knowing she needed to eat something, Allison bundled up and went to the motel lobby for their continental breakfast. She gulped some orange juice, enjoyed the tiny box of Frosted Flakes, nibbled at a glazed doughnut. On the way out, she snatched a banana. That would do for her lunch.

Back in her room, she decided to make lists. It was one of her coping methods she'd developed through the years. It didn't matter if the items of the lists were ever done or if they were completely ignored. The important thing was that the making of them kept her mind busy for a little while.

She jotted down items as they came to her mind. Call Dewey Vernon, attorney re: will. Call a real estate agent. Put farm on market, need appraisal? Inspection? Check on Leona's taxes—has she filed for last year yet? Who does her taxes? Do I have to pay inheritance tax? If so, when? What to do with clothes? Furniture?

The last item stopped her. Leona had some lovely antique furniture, but Allison had very little space left in her house. Would Connie or Dave want some items for their future homes? But what about the orchard? In a couple of months spring would be here; the trees would start budding. Who could she get to look after them if she couldn't sell the property right away?

Stifling the panic that started to rise, Allison told herself to forget about everything until after the funeral. Time enough then to take care of the details.

She did make one decision, though. She would stay at the farm tonight. Her aunt had lived there alone for nearly two years after Dick died. There was certainly no reason why Allison couldn't spend a few nights there alone.

THE AFTERNOON CAME; she made it fine through the church service. Several of Leona's friends and neighbors scooted into the pew with her, smiled encouragement or briefly squeezed her hand. Allison appreciated the support. The organ music was soothing, the hymns familiar, the eulogy consoling. Mr. Knotts ushered her out of the sanctuary to the waiting limo.

It was at the cemetery her walls started to crumble. Maybe it was seeing Harry. He was inconsolable. As soon as he saw her exit the funeral home limo, he staggered toward her, wrapped his arms around her and sobbed. Mr. Knotts kindly extricated her from his embrace and led them both over to the burial site. The resentments she'd harbored against him melted away at his obvious pain. Perhaps there had been more to their relationship then she'd realized. He was certainly acting more like a bereaved mate than a causal boyfriend. She held his hand while Reverend Pierson gave his final comforting words.

As she turned to leave, he clung to her, cried out, "I don't understand. How could this have happened?" He swiped at his tears. Allison could tell he was trying to control himself. Taking a deep breath, he shook his head in puzzlement. "She hadn't been sick. She was fine at church Sunday. Leona was active, healthy, never complained of any dizzy spells. What could have made her fall down the stairs?"

Allison felt as if an electric shock had gone through her body. Those were the exact thoughts that had hovered around in the back of her brain the day before, but she'd tried to dismiss them.

Molly Kirkman came up to them, placed a sympathetic hand on Harry's arm. "You're right that she never complained. But she could have had problems. Leona was a very private person in many ways, and she didn't like people to fuss over her. Even if she hadn't been feeling up to par, she probably wouldn't have said anything."

Allison had to agree with Molly. Leona was not one to complain, but as a woman only a few years away from sixty, she was bound to have some aches and pains, probably hot flashes, and maybe even dizziness.

Trying to turn the conversation in another direction, Allison said, "I appreciated the message you left, Molly. I didn't call back, just didn't feel like talking, I guess."

"I understand. But maybe we can get together while you're here. I don't know what I'm going to do without Leona to talk to. She always had time to listen to my troubles."

Allison wondered briefly what troubles Molly could possibly have. Her husband, Ted, was a very successful business man. She had the body of an athlete, and looked years younger than her age—which Allison suspected was the result of a facelift.

That thought was interrupted as Molly went on, "I dropped in on her the day before she died. She was in the middle of cleaning out the desk drawers in the den, but she stopped what she was doing, made tea, and we chatted a bit."

"And was she all right then?"

"She did seem a little perturbed about something, but she cheered right up and we had a nice visit."

Allison saw several of Leona's other friends coming toward her. She remembered most of them, greeted them by name as they gave her hugs and their condolences. Many said much the same thing. "Her death was such a shock."

"She was always so full of life."

"She never said a word about not feeling well."

Hanging back from the others, Allison spotted Jerry Howe. Jerry was an Iraq War vet who couldn't keep a steady job. He apparently had suffered some brain damage during the war and had been given a medical discharge. He still had the build of a marine, but seemed to have the manner of a child. He had done seasonal work at the orchard for years and after Dick's death, Leona had hired him to also do odd jobs around the house and farm. Allison motioned him to come over, but he gave her a shy smile, shook his head, and quickly fled to the safety of his old black Ford he'd driven for years.

Harry stopped his sniffing back tears long enough to offer an explanation. "He's gotten awful skittish around people lately. He still did some work for Leona and does other jobs around town, but he doesn't have much to say to most people."

Molly came closer to Allison and lowered her voice. "I never did like the idea of Jerry being around Leona. You know he isn't exactly right in the head. I warned her he might be dangerous."

"Dangerous? That's hard to believe. He always seemed so harmless."

"You haven't been around him lately. Mark my word—that man is a time bomb waiting to explode."

Molly's husband, Ted, came up as they were discussing Jerry, and he joined in the warning. "I agree with Molly on that one. As much as I like Jerry, I have an uneasy feeling about him. I just don't think he can be trusted."

The cemetery was emptying and Mr. Knotts made little motions as if he, too, was ready to depart. Allison had driven to the church and left her car there to ride with him to the cemetery. She nodded to him, said her goodbyes to those around. She'd only taken a few steps, when she stopped and hurried back to Harry. "I appreciate you taking care of Elmer, but I'd like for you to bring him home this afternoon. I'm going to be staying at the farm and I'd like him with me."

Harry bobbed his head. "Sure. I'll go home and get him. But I've got to tell you, he's not much of a watchdog."

She bristled at his statement. "I don't need a watchdog—just some company."

Mt. Knotts was holding the door for her when Allison heard another voice, "Allie, just a minute."

It'd been years since she'd heard that nickname, and Allison knew immediately who'd uttered it. She abandoned the limo, ran to meet Claire Reilly. The two embraced each other like long-lost friends, which is exactly what they were. Claire spoke first, "I'm so sorry I missed the funeral. I just got back in town from a business trip."

"You're living back in Upton now?"

"Yes. And I just have to have some time with you, catch up on the past years. But not now. You staying at your aunt's house?"

Allison nodded. "Come by in the morning if you can."

"I will." She hugged Allison again. "See you then. Got to go now."

Thrilled to see Claire, but puzzled by her abrupt manner, Allison walked back to the waiting Mr. Knotts. She gave him a timid smile and let him assist her into the rear seat of the limo. He wasted no time in leaving.

After retrieving her car, Allison headed back to the farm. Fluffy snowflakes accompanied her on the narrow, twisted road—not enough to pose any hazard, but enough to give the ground a new, clean cover—and to give Leona a new soft blanket. The thought pleased her. Her aunt was now at rest.

Entering the kitchen, she noted the table was covered with bowls, casserole dishes, pies. A note informed her of other dishes in the refrigerator. Allison decided she could survive several days, if not weeks, on the offerings, and since cooking was not one of her favorite activities, she sent up a silent prayer of thanks. The house key she'd given the pastor lay on the table.

Leona's coffee maker sat on the counter and Allison soon had it perking. As she reached for a mug, the pecan pie beckoned to her, and she pulled out a plate. She would start with desert and work her way through whatever else appealed to her.

She was munching on a chicken leg when she heard a car drive up and then a short bark. Elmer had arrived. Quickly wiping her hands on a napkin, she went to the door. Surprised that it was already getting dark, she turned on both the kitchen light and the outside one. As soon as she opened the storm door, Elmer bounded in, looked her over, then started searching the room for a more familiar face.

Allison knelt down, called the dog to her, put her arms around his neck, stroked his beautiful fur—the color of soft butter. "I know you're going to miss her just like I will, but we'll get through this together." Glancing up she saw Harry still standing by the door, looking as if he was going to start crying again. She jumped up. "Won't you sit down? Join me? There's more food here than I'll ever need."

Harry shook his head. "Guess I better be going. Talk to you later."

He was gone before Allison could think of anything else to say. She turned back to Elmer. "Well, boy, it's the two of us then. Let me find your bowl and food and you can join me. This will be our farewell meal for Leona."

Allison spent much of the evening with phone calls to her loved ones, telling them briefly of the funeral, of Leona's many friends, of the frigid wind chill. She mentioned a few people to Dave and Connie they'd met on visits in the past and how the neighbors hoped the whole family would visit again.

She even teased Dave a little about all the delicious food the church ladies had brought. "Too bad you can't share the chicken dumplings or taste the Coconut Supreme Cake."

"Mom, I'm drooling so much on my phone, I'm going to have a major cleanup job. Can you get the recipes?"

"Of course. I'll add them to my file of other recipes I never cook."

With Fred, the tenor of the conversation was more serious. She admitted to being lonely, of feeling somewhat like an orphan with the last link of her family gone.

"But," Fred countered, "you're forgetting about your in-laws. I'll gladly share my crazy family with you."

Allison appreciated his efforts to lighten her mood—and it did help some.

"And speaking of crazy," he said, "let me tell you of some of the crazies I met today." The talk then went from her day to his, and she could feel herself relaxing little by little. By the time they said their goodbyes, she felt much better.

The rest of the evening was spent prowling the empty rooms with Elmer at her heels, and making more lists. After the late TV news, she let the dog out for his last evening stroll and got ready for bed. She headed for the front bedroom she'd always used on her visits here, and Elmer headed for his cushions in the utility room.

When she snuggled under the covers she realized how exhausted she was—physically and emotionally. What she needed now was a good night's sleep.

Her dreams took her back some thirty plus years when she and Claire would climb the apple trees to get the biggest, reddest ones on the top limbs or take their shoes off and splash in Cider Creek that ran east of the farm.

In her dream, they were hiding from each other in the spooky barn when some kind of noise stole her sleep. Allison lay motionless—listening—waiting. Then a creak, a slight crackle. She took a deep breath to still her jangling nerves. She told herself it was just the old house groaning in the cold. Nothing to worry about.

Pulling the warm quilt over her head, she tried to go back to sleep. It was no use. Fingers of bitter cold air slithered through the window panes while moonlight cast eerie shadows on the drawn shades.

She shivered, stared at the bedside clock with its illuminated dial. Twelve fifteen. She crawled out of bed, ran her fingers over her short, dark hair. Now fully awake, she went to the hallway, slipped into her boots and parka, grabbed a pair of mittens.

Not bothering to turn on the porch light, she opened the door; Elmer was right beside her. She gave him a pat and they stepped outside. The world seemed to be in a clean, pure state of suspension. The carpet of snow glittered in the light of the moon as if elves had been busy scattering jewels. Allison studied the stars and thought she saw what looked like a springtime kite. But taking a breath of the icy air, she knew spring would be a long time coming. This had been a bad winter for North Carolina and especially for the mountains. There had been no usual January thaw, February had already broken low temperature records, and another snowstorm was predicted for tomorrow.

As she stood on the porch she heard a faint tinkling sound, almost like a Chinese wind chime, but there was no wind. Was something or someone disturbing the ice that clung to the tree limbs, the fences? A nocturnal creature getting his exercise?

Elmer must have heard something, too. The shepherd's eyes seemed to search the yard as he minced down the steps. His weight broke through the crusty surface of the snow and each step sounded like the crunch of dry cereal. She could see his breath very faintly escaping like puffs of a steam engine.

Then his head jerked up. His ears stood at attention. He admitted a low growl. And Allison froze in place.

FOUR

NOT DARING TO MOVE, barely breathing, Allison peered into the darkness. The cluster of pine trees in the front yard blocked most of the moonlight. In the scattered patches where some of the light filtered through, she could see no form, no movement. Extending her range of inspection, she tried to see around the holly bushes, under the chinaberry tree, out toward the apple orchard. There appeared to be nothing and nobody around. Should she go back inside and get a flashlight? Turn on the porch light? Venture out into the yard? The last thought sent a tremor through her body that wasn't caused by the cold. If there was someone out there, she had no desire to come face to face with him. But, she realized, if such a person existed, then he had a good view of her. She needed to call Elmer back and get inside.

But where was Elmer? He'd let out one slight growl and then nothing else. Had something happened to him? Before she could go further with that scary idea, she again heard him crunching his way back to the porch. She sighed in relief.

When he climbed the steps and nuzzled her mittens, she let out a soft laugh. "I guess we were both spooked, boy," she said. "Maybe it was just some twigs breaking under the weight of too much ice. Let's go in and get warm."

A cup of hot chocolate later, some sweet thoughts about the coming reunion with her husband, and with Elmer's soft snoring by her side, Allison felt relaxed enough to go back to bed. She slept soundly, dream-lessly.

She awoke with a bang—a loud bang on the kitchen door. Elmer answered with a warning bark and scurried toward the noise.

Allison pushed back her quilt, jumped to her feet. "Coming," she called out. Still half asleep she opened the door and a blast of freezing air preceded Claire into the room.

"Thank goodness you're all right," Claire gasped.

Allison stared at her friend as Elmer squirmed by her to get outside. She slammed the door shut and motioned for Claire to have a seat. "Why wouldn't I be all right?"

"The footprints! I saw deep footprints in the snow in front of the house. Looks like someone may have been spying on you."

"Spying on me?" A shiver of fear went through Allison's body as she remembered the noise that woke her, the breaking ice, Elmer's reaction. At the same time, she tried to think of a more benign expla-nation of the footprints, and said, "The prints could be from the women who brought food up yesterday."

"Allie, it snowed after the funeral. Remember? It would have covered any old tracks. I'm telling you these are fresh—had to be made last night—and they were made by a man. You've got to call the sheriff's department."

"You're right," Allison conceded. "But let me put on a pot of coffee first. And tell me why you're here so early."

"It's not really early. You slept late. It's after nine. But never mind that. Get your coat. While the coffee's perking, I'm going to show you those footprints."

Allison grinned at her old friend; she'd forgotten how bossy Claire could be. But for now, it seemed so good just to have someone with her who cared.

"At least give me a chance to get some clothes on."

Allison dashed to her bedroom and jumped into some old jeans and a sweatshirt. She slipped on a pair of fuzzy socks, crammed her feet in her boots, grabbed her parka and followed Claire out the door. She'd expected Elmer would be waiting at the door to get in. He wasn't, and she soon found out why. He, too, had discovered the footprints, or rather the boot prints, and was busy sniffing around them.

"See. I told you. Some man was lurking around here last night. Spying on you. This can't be good."

Allison had to agree. It hadn't been her imagination. She and Elmer *had* heard someone out here. She'd stood on the porch, clad only in her pajamas and parka while some man stood in the shadows watching her. A chill went through her. She bolted back to the house, calling Elmer as she went.

Shedding her coat, she called the sheriff's department. She was disappointed when Marie didn't answer but explained to the dispatcher on duty about hearing someone in the yard last night and about the footprints. She was told an officer would be out shortly.

When Allison ended the call, Claire exploded. "You heard someone in the yard last night and you didn't call for help then?"

Pouring a cup of coffee, Allison motioned to Claire. "Sit. Drink. I'll tell you all about it."

She gave a thorough account of the noises, her trek to the porch, Elmer's reaction, and ended with, "So I concluded there was no danger and I went back to sleep."

Claire shook her head. "You always were too brave for your own good."

Allison didn't tell her friend she hadn't been feeling at all brave lately, but rather she changed the subject. "Enough about me. Now explain why you didn't attend my wedding, didn't even make an excuse."

"I didn't get the invitation."

"But I sent it to your Atlanta address."

"I know. It was forwarded to me later, but not in time to attend, and please forgive me, but I couldn't explain then." She reached across the table, covered Allison's hand with hers. "I was hurting too much."

Instantly concerned, Allison asked, "What happened? Were you sick? Lose your job?" When Claire didn't answer immediately, Allison took both of her friend's hands in hers. "You can tell me. Remember? We could always tell each other everything."

Claire sniffed. "I remember, but at the time all I wanted to do was to crawl into a hole and pretend it hadn't happened."

"What hadn't happened?"

"Dale left me. Ran off." Claire took several deep breaths. Knowing her friend was trying hard to control her emotions Allison kept silent. After several moments, Claire went on, "He ran off with another woman. He'd already stopped making payments on the condo—which I didn't know until I got a letter from the bank. I found out later he'd been having an affair for months."

"Oh, Claire, I'm so sorry. But you should have called. Maybe I could have helped."

"Nothing helps except time and keeping busy. Thank goodness we didn't have any kids and that I have a career I love. Anyway, I moved back here, got a tiny apartment, travel a lot in my job, and am waiting out the year until the divorce is final."

"I'm going to be here a few days getting the legalities taken care of, arranging for the sale of the farm. There's plenty of room. Bring your pajamas and we'll have some sleepovers like we used to."

"Sounds great, but I'm scheduled for a Saturday meeting in Charlotte tomorrow, leaving tonight. Maybe Sunday?"

"Absolutely. You'll get to meet my husband. He's flying in from Dallas in the morning. He's been attending a mandatory conference or he would have been here with me."

"But I don't want to intrude."

"Don't be silly. Friends can never be intrusions."

"And on that note, I'm leaving before the police get here. You can explain about me seeing the footprints but otherwise I'm completely innocent."

"Oh yes. You were always completely innocent, no matter what kind of trouble we got into."

One more hug and Claire was out of sight only minutes before a brown and white police cruiser drove into the yard.

Allison rose, greeted Sam Babcock at the door. "So glad to see you. I didn't know if you'd come out yourself or send a deputy."

The sheriff's grandfatherly face smiled down from a foot above her head. "I was in the office, wanted to see for myself what was going on."

She opened the door wider, and the sheriff stepped into the house. Allison hadn't noticed the young man standing behind him until then, but she motioned him in, too.

The men stomped their boots on the mat and took off their hats. The young man was nearly as tall and as husky as the sheriff. He brushed back his acorn colored hair, the same shade as his brown leather jacket, and gave her a quick smile. The sheriff hastened to introduce him. "I'd like you to meet the newest deputy on the force, Andy Cox." He turned to the officer. "And this is Allison Aldridge Sawyer."

Allison held out her hand. "I'm glad to meet you."

The deputy hurried to remove his gloves, crammed then into his pockets, and gave her hand a strong shake. "The pleasure is mine, Mrs. Sawyer."

His smile deepened, and she was reminded of her son who had that same kind of smile—one that charmed every female he ever met, young and old.

Putting Dave out of her mind and remembering the reason the cops were here, Allison became all business and grabbed her parka. "I'll show you the boot prints I called about."

"No need for you to go out," the sheriff said. "Andy and I will look around."

"But I want to go." Allison opened the door and stepped out. She blinked as the sun bounced off the snow. "Warming up a little. Hope the prints aren't melting away."

She went down the steps to the clump of pines where the prints started—or rather, ended. Andy hunched down and studied them. "Big man, heavy, long stride. Looks like a hunting boot, deep cleats."

"Like most of the men in this area wear," Sam said. He lifted one foot to show the bottom of his boot. "Same, same. Not quite as heavy as I am, though. He didn't sink in as far as I do." He turned to Allison. "You told the dispatcher that you heard something during the night. What exactly did you hear?"

"I don't really know. Something woke me up, and then when Elmer and I were standing on the porch, I thought I heard a tinkling—kind of like ice cubes in a glass. Then the dog took off in this direction. He growled once, and then in just a little bit, he came back. I never saw anybody. I wouldn't have known about the tracks except that a friend came by this morning, saw them and told me. That's when I called you."

Andy stood up straight and brushed against the drooping limbs of a pine tree. Tiny fragments of ice fell around his feet. "The noise might have been falling icicles."

The sheriff nodded. He walked back a few steps toward the house. "Here are the dog's tracks. He came this far. You said he growled once, then turned around."

"Yes. I assumed maybe he saw a squirrel in the tree or something. Seems as if he'd seen a man, he wouldn't have returned so quickly."

"Or he may have recognized the man and decided he was not a danger."

Allison gasped. "You mean it was someone I know?"

"Maybe. Or at least someone your dog knew. It hardly seems plausible a complete stranger would traipse up here through the snow. A stranded motorist or someone looking for help would come up the drive and knock on the door. This man wanted to see while not being seen."

While Allison and the sheriff were talking, Andy went back to the trees and stared at the house. "From here," he said, "the prowler had a good view of the porch and the west side of the house." He faced Allison. "Where's your bedroom?" His soft voice held a note of concern.

She stared at him a moment before answering. "West side, front." She swiveled around and gaped at her bedroom window. The blind was down and nothing in the room could be seen, but the thought of a man that close to her window sent shivers down her spine. "I always keep the blinds down, but someone could tell if the light was on or not."

Andy asked, "Did you turn your light on when you got up?"

"I don't think so. No, I didn't. I remember now. I went out to the den, but I didn't turn a light on there either."

The sheriff nodded his head. "So our friend was surprised when you and the dog appeared on the porch. If he had plans to go any further, that must have made him change his mind."

"Do you think he was planning on breaking in?"

"Don't know."

"But why?"

"Don't know that either," Sam said. "But we're sure going to try to find out. Now you go back in, get warm, and put on a fresh pot of coffee while we see what direction these tracks came from."

Allison did as instructed, her mind caught up of in a whirlwind of emotions. She was worried, scared. Someone had been spying on her. Who? Why? Did it have anything to do with her aunt's death? Would he be back?

Her second pot of coffee of the morning started to perk. If she drank much more, she wouldn't be able to sleep for a week. Not that she'd do much sleeping anyway until the footprints were explained.

She wondered if Leona had ever been afraid living here alone after Dick died—out in the country with no close neighbors. She immediately rejected the idea. Leona had been a strong, courageous woman, just as Allison had always considered herself to be. She may not sleep much tonight, but she was determined to stay here.

ANDY WALKED BEHIND the sheriff as they followed the tracks away from the house. He took several pictures even though the tracks were scuffed and blurred and not likely to be of use for identification. Instead of leading to the road, the boot prints veered off to the west and headed for a fence partially buried in the snow. When the prints continued over the fence, the two officers did also. They stopped when the tracks stopped in a narrow lane where a car had been parked.

"Looks like he pulled up into this lane," Andy said, "then took off across the field to the house. He probably didn't park in the road in case there was passing traffic that might see him. What do you make of it, Sheriff?"

Sam squatted down by the car tracks. "I'd say his boots are in better shape than his tires. Tread marks are pretty shallow. Kind of dangerous driving on slick tires in the snow."

"Maybe he's not from these parts."

"Oh, he's local, all right. Has to be to know this lane was here. With the snow cover, he wouldn't be able to see it from the road. It goes to the apple orchard, and it's only used during picking season." He stood up and shook his head. "Wish I could figure out what the fella was up to."

"Do you think Mrs. Sawyer could be in any danger?" As he asked the question, Andy hoped fervently the answer would be, "No." When he'd met her a few minutes ago, she'd reminded him of his mother—smart and a little sassy, but still vulnerable.

"We have to assume she's in danger until we know otherwise. It could be simply someone wants something from the house, maybe thought it was empty.

FIVE

THE MEN HEADED back to the house. Allison heard them on the porch and dashed to the door. "Did you find anything?"

Sam grinned. "If you invite us in for some hot coffee, we'll let you know."

"Of course. Where are my manners? Coffee and cookies coming up."

Elmer came up and sniffed at the officers as they made their way to the table. Allison smiled as Andy stooped down to pat the dog's head, and speak to him, "Hi, boy. How's it going? Taking good care of the lovely lady?"

Elmer responded with a soft bark.

"Good boy."

She motioned them to the bathroom down the hall. "You can wash up there if you like."

The sheriff's report was brief and blunt. "A man was standing in your front yard after midnight, staring at your bedroom window. We don't know his motive, but we do know he was local." He went on to explain about the car being parked in the lane where only people in the neighborhood would know about or perhaps some seasonal worker who remembered the lane. "So," he said, "Marie told me about your husband being in Dallas, and that being the case, I don't think you ought to stay here alone at night."

"But I'm not alone," she argued. "I have Elmer here with me."

"Elmer isn't a guard dog. He's just an overgrown pet. He makes friends with everybody. Why he even likes Andy which shows how indiscriminate he is."

Andy said, "What's not to like? He knows a good guy when he sees one."

Sam went on, "I know you have friends in town you can stay with while you're in the area."

"Yes. But I really don't think that's necessary." Allison decided she wasn't going to let some phantom in the dark scare her away. "Whoever it was probably won't come back, but I'll make sure every door and window is locked, and I'll sleep with my phone by my pillow, and I'll even change bedrooms, and I'll have Elmer sleep at the foot of my bed." Following her recitation, Allison took two deep breaths and smiled at the sheriff.

He didn't smile back. "Well, if you insist on staying here," he said, "I'll have a deputy do frequent drive-bys during the night. Roberto Flores is on duty tonight. If you need anything, call 911, and he can be here in a manner of minutes."

Allison rose and poured them all another cup of coffee. "Good, but before you go," she said. "I have some questions about the day Leona died."

Both men stared at her. She hesitated, "I was just wondering...."

Stirring sugar into his coffee, Sam frowned. "Wondering about what?"

"When you called me that evening, you said that Harry had found her at the bottom of the stairs—that she must have fallen while going to the basement."

"That's right. He said he'd come to pick her up for a dinner date, and when she didn't answer the door bell, he let himself in. Then like I told you, he saw her at the foot of the stairs. He hurried down to help her but realized she was dead. He called 911."

"Yes. I know, but it's just that...." She paused, took a quick sip of her coffee. The men across the table waited for her to go on.

Allison wondered why she was being so hesitant to voice her suspicions. Was it because she simply didn't want to think someone actually meant to harm her aunt?

In any case, she had to tell the sheriff about her doubts. "Well, in the many times I visited Leona here I don't remember her locking the doors during the day. She'd lock up at night but never during the day. This is a safe neighborly community. It wasn't unusual for people to drop by. And since she was expecting Harry, why would she lock him out?"

"I see your point," Sam said. "Anything else bothering you?"

She nodded. Once she'd started, she was determined to air all her questions. "There are a couple of other things. You said Harry didn't see her until he'd turned the basement light on. But why would she go into a dark basement? That doesn't make sense."

The sheriff rubbed his chin but didn't say anything. Andy broke the silence that hovered over the table. "Unless she was trying to hide from someone."

Sam held up his hand. "Let's not get carried away in speculation. Remember Leona had lived in this house most of her adult life. She would know every corner, every cranny, where everything was stored. Maybe deciding to make an apple pie, she dashed down to get some apples without turning on the light."

"What made you think she was going to make a pie?" Allison asked.

"Because the cookbook on the counter was opened to an apple pie recipe."

"Yes, it was," she said. "I noticed it myself last night—and that's another thing that struck me as wrong. Leona had made every conceivable kind of apple pie, apple cobbler, apple strudel, even apple bread. She didn't need a recipe for any of them." Allison paused. "And she always kept a bowl of apples on the table or the counter." She pointed to the apples in front of them. "These apples were on the counter when I got here. There's plenty there for a pie. Why would she need any more?"

Shaking his head, Sam slid his chair back and paced the floor for several seconds. He came back to the table and flopped down. "But I didn't question the coroner's report. He placed the time of death between two and four that afternoon and concluded her injuries were consistent with a fall. Cause of death was head trauma resulting from hitting the concrete floor." He ran a hand through his graying hair. "And Dr. Franklin is a darn good coroner. I've never had any doubts about his findings."

Andy tapped his fingers on the table. "It's possible someone made it look as if she'd fallen down the stairs. Maybe the cookbook was opened to give a reason for her going down to the cellar." A few more taps of his fingers and Andy added, "And doesn't it seem odd she would be baking a pie or cooking anything if she was going out for dinner?"

"We could talk all day about *maybe* and *someone* and things that seem odd," the sheriff said, "but if it wasn't an accident, we need to think first of why anyone would want to harm her. Leona had a lot of friends, and as far as I know, no enemies." He picked up another cookie and waved it at Allison. "Can you think of anybody who might have been mad at her, or jealous, or owed her money, or she owed money to, or that she was blackmailing, or...."

"Blackmailing? Remember who you're talking about here. My aunt was a good, honest woman."

"I know. She was the finest. I'm just saying that if she was killed, there had to have been a reason."

"Then you're going to investigate?"

"Yes, but not only because of your suspicions. Mainly because of your midnight visitor. He's got me worried."

FRED TRIED TO keep his attention on the lecturer who was explaining advance security systems being installed in some middle grade and high schools throughout the country. They were innovative, admirable, and expensive. He doubted, though, that many small counties, like the one he worked for, would be interested in such high-tech equipment— or could afford it.

His mind kept wandering to the love of his life. He was worried about Allison. The death of her Aunt Leona had seemed to hit her harder than he'd realized. One of the things that had attracted him when he first met Allison was her spunk, her courage, her resourcefulness. And although she kept trying to put up a brave front during their telephone calls, he could tell those attributes were ebbing. Sometimes she sounded like a lost child trying to find her way home. Maybe he could skip out for a few minutes between speakers and give her a call.

Glancing out the window to his far right, he was surprised to see snow falling thick and fast. On the morning news the weatherman had predicted snow flurries throughout the day, but this looked like more than a flurry. Thank goodness, the conference would be over this afternoon, and he had a flight booked for Asheville in the morning. By this time tomorrow he'd be holding Allison in his arms.

ALLISON CLEARED UP the table as she watched the patrol car drive out. Sam had promised to investigate Leona's death. She hoped the sheriff would find logical explanations for her questions—and for the footprints. But at the moment, Allison couldn't even imagine what those explanations would be.

If only she could talk to Fred, put his detective mind to work on the mysteries. But that would have to wait until tomorrow. Today, though, she had work to do and she was glad for that. Focusing on her many tasks would keep her mind from thinking of a possible murderer spying on her.

She found the local telephone book and called a realtor whose name she recognized. She remembered that for a brief time after her husband's death, Leona had contemplated selling the farm and Brice Hauser had been her realtor. After a couple of months, though, her aunt decided she could run the orchard herself by hiring out much of the work. Allison hoped Mr. Hauser had kept the records of any appraisals he'd done. It would be a starting point in listing the property.

She found the realtor to be most helpful and encouraging, and he did have all the records. The house and acreage had been appraised separately from the orchard equipment. That way, potential buyers could be given the option of buying the whole package or just the house and land. If the buyer hadn't wanted the equipment, it could have been auctioned off along with any furniture Leona didn't want to keep.

"We could do the same arrangement for you," he said. "However, you understand I can't do anything until Mrs. Whitley's will is probated and you have clear title to the property."

Pounding a fist against her forehead, Allison groaned inwardly. What must Mr. Hauser think of her—trying to sell property she didn't even legally own yet. She tried to explain, "I didn't mean to be jumping the gun. It's just that I have so much on my mind, I was trying to get a handle on affairs."

"I understand, but these things take time. I doubt, though, you'll have any problem in finding a buyer once we get the property listed. Just give me a call when you're ready."

Ending the call, Allison felt the beginnings of a

headache. She had no problem diagnosing the cause: too much stress, too much coffee. The cure was also easy to prescribe. She needed to get out of the house, exercise her body, free her mind. One look out the kitchen window was enough to convince her that the predicted storm for the area was nowhere in sight. The sun was high, the clouds were light and fluffy, and the temperature must have risen because some of the snow was melting and forming puddles in the yard. She pulled on her boots, grabbed her parka, and slipped her cell phone into a pocket. Elmer met her at the door. "Let's check out the barn, Boy. I haven't been out there in a long time."

The barn had been used by previous owners to house dairy cattle. There were stalls for calves, stanchions for the milk cows, and a huge loft for hay. Now it only housed farming equipment needed to care for the orchard. The big double doors in front were padlocked, but Allison knew of a small side door that was never locked. She pulled open the creaky door and went in with the dog right on her heels. Dust covered everything, and cobwebs hung down from the ceiling like gossamer drapes. The thought occurred to her that this would make a marvelous setting for a spooky movie. Waving her hands in front of her face to make a path through the cobwebs, she entered the milking parlor. She'd always thought it was comical to call the room where cows were milked a "parlor." She and Claire joked about it, inviting each other to, "Please come into my parlor."

She circled the feed troughs and entered the main section of the barn. Sunlight poured in through windows on both sides. Tractors, wagons, and sprayers were all lined up ready to start another season of fruit growing. She felt a moment of sadness that there might not be another season. Maybe, she thought hopefully, some young, ambitious farmer would buy everything and continue producing delicious mountain apples. That would be a good outcome to a terrible tragedy. At the same time her practical mind told her that small orchards, just like small farms, were often being squeezed out of business. Huge commercial conglomerates with thousands of acres were now growing much of the nation's food supply. Would this orchard soon be just a memory?

She looked up to the haymow. The loft had not held any hay for years, but she and Claire would climb up and swing back and forth on the huge rope that hung from the rafters. The rope was positioned through a pulley with one end tied to the back of the loft. Its original purpose was to hoist bales of hay from the barn floor into the loft. They'd modified it to act like a pendulum so they could push off, swing out, and come safety back.

Was the rope still there? Was she too old to be playing Peter Pan? She had to find out. Studying the ladder nailed to the wall, she decided it was still sturdy enough to climb. "Sorry, Elmer," she said as she mounted the first rung, "you'll have to stay down here."

Allison was halfway up the ladder when she began having second thoughts. The loft seemed a lot darker than she remembered, and she thought she heard a scratching sound. What could that be?

It took a few seconds to bolster her courage before she could continue climbing. It was the thought of relating the details to Claire and the two of them laughing about old times that helped her make it up the last few steps. And it would give her something to tell Fred when he called this afternoon. She knew he worried about her and this story would reassure him that she was doing just fine.

At the top step she paused a moment to savor what Connie's appalled response would be to the escapade. She could almost hear her daughter's voice, *"Mom, you climbed into a barn loft and swung on a rope? What were you thinking?"* It was with a light heart she climbed over the top of the ladder and jumped to the floor. A cloud of dust swooped up to hit her in the face, brought tears to her eyes, and produced a sneezing fit. She yanked off her gloves and grabbed a tissue out of her coat pocket to wipe her eyes and blow her nose. It was hard to believe so much dust could have accumulated in one place. Her first reaction was to get out as fast as possible and back into the fresh air, but then her stubborn streak took hold. She'd made the climb to the loft in order to swing on the rope—and if it was still there, that was exactly what she intended to do. For a few moments she wanted to feel young and foolish, to forget her loss, her fears.

Her eyes searched the room. As she became more accustomed to the murkiness, she found what she was looking for—the twisted, braided twine nearly as thick as her wrist. She walked toward it slowly, not wanting to stir up another dust storm, but also to relive the anticipation she'd always had just before taking off on the daring ride. As she moved forward, she again heard the faint noises she'd heard earlier, almost as if someone—or some thing—was in the loft with her. She hesitated. She didn't remember there ever being any noise up here except for one old owl that used to scold them for intruding upon his solitude. But this noise seemed to be coming from the corners of the floor, not from the beams above. Now that she'd come this far, though, she had no intention of running away.

Hurrying her steps, Allison grabbed the rope and gave herself a running start. She closed her eyes, felt the sensation of flight, the excitement of soaring, and the exuberance of youth. The rope swung back and forth, back and forth, each trip losing momentum until it came to a stop. Her trip was over, but it had been enough to satisfy her. She let go of the rope— along with the past. It was great to escape momentarily to the days of her youth, but she didn't want to live there. She had a wonderful life and a wonderful family. It was enough.

Dropping to the floor, Allison lost her balance and toppled forward. She put out her hands to stop her fall. One hand landed on the dusty floor. The other one landed on something soft. When that something moved, she looked down—and screamed.

SIX

ALLISON JERKED HER hand away from the mega-rat she'd fallen on and tried to scramble to her feet. She didn't move fast enough, though, to escape his revenge. Sharp nails clawed at her hand and even sharper teeth nipped at the end of her middle finger. In desperation she swung one leg around, smacked the rat with her boot and sent it spinning across the floor. Without looking back, she ran to the ladder, took the steps two at a time, slid down the last few and ended up in a heap on the barn floor. Her little adventure had suddenly lost all its glamour.

Her flight down the ladder was accompanied by Elmer's anxious barks and followed by his relieved sloppy kisses. Putting her arms around the shaggy dog, she let out a ragged half-laugh, half-sob. "It was only a mean, old barn rat, Elmer, but he scared me out of my wits. And how did a rat get up in the loft? I didn't know they could climb ladders." As she hugged her companion, Allison wondered what was happening to her—spooked by one critter and pouring her heart out to another. She had to pull herself together and quit messing around.

Hurrying back to the house, her left hand began to ache and tiny tendrils of blood seeped from the scratch marks. The finger the rat had attacked was red but the skin didn't appear to be broken. She remembered she'd had a tetanus shot last summer when she'd stepped on a piece of broken glass, so that wasn't a concern. The possibility that the rat might be rabid skidded across her mind momentarily, but then she remembered rabid animals attacked without provocation which hadn't been the case here. She had provoked the animal big time by falling on him. He was only lashing out in revenge.

Her reasoned decision, therefore, was not to go to the emergency room, but to get out of her filthy clothes, have a good shower, and put a bandage on her hand.

Before going into the kitchen, she tried to brush off as much of the offending dust as possible. As she was brushing, she noticed it wasn't just dust clinging to her coat and pants. There also seemed to be some kind of chaff. Where did that come from? As far as she knew the loft hadn't been used for any kind of grain storage. She slipped off her parka, shook it vigorously, and let the brisk breeze take away the dust, the chaff, and the awful sensation of the rat biting and scratching at her.

Allison came out of the shower clean and hungry and feeling rather foolish. Maybe telling her family about the barn loft adventure wasn't such a good idea after all. There were some things that were meant to be kept private—maybe this was one of them. She didn't want Fred or her kids to think she was completely irresponsible. The noon hour had come and gone and she was so ready for lunch. She dressed hurriedly, applied antibiotic cream to the scratches and wrapped her hand with gauze to keep it clean. Then she headed for the refrigerator.

The church ladies had outdone themselves. There was still enough food here to last all weekend. She and Fred would be able to gorge themselves while they pooled their detective minds to solve the many puzzles that swam around in her head.

Having planned ahead, she had two plates in her good hand. She filled one with cold foods: potato salad, sausage balls, deviled eggs, veggies and dip. The other one would go in the microwave to heat up the green bean casserole, the Swedish meatballs, and a smidgen of chicken dumplings. If her stomach had any room left, she would find a third plate for the Mississippi Mud Cake.

Thirty minutes later, she was stuffed and satisfied. Glancing at the still bright sunlight out the kitchen window, she decided to watch the weather channel. Maybe there would be news of what had happened to their predicted snowstorm. There was. The somber weatherman was pointing out the storm that had left the Rockies two days ago heading east had stalled over the state of Kansas, dumping close to two feet of snow there. Now it was on the move again but was veering to the south. Allison's smile of relief was short-lived as she noted the snowstorm was now covering much of Oklahoma and parts of Texas. Even as she stared, the map was displaced to show heavy snow piling up at the Dallas-Fort Worth airport. The weatherman's voice continued in the background, "The northern section of Texas may get as much as a foot of snow out of this storm."

A wave of nausea swept over Allison. Bad news never sat well on a full stomach. And this could be really bad news for Fred. He was booked for an early flight out of Dallas in the morning. Even if the storm was over by then, would the airport be cleared in time?

She grabbed her cell phone, punched his name, hoping against hope that he would be able to answer. But it didn't happen. She tried to keep her panic from creeping into her message. "Hey honey, just saw on the news about your storm. Think you'll make it out tomorrow? Call me. Love ya."

It was strange, she thought, in the short time they'd been married, how much she'd come to depend on Fred—his companionship, his sturdiness, his common sense. She'd been counting on him to steer her through the quagmire surrounding Leona's death, as well as the comfort of his arms around her.

She tried to put a good spin as possible on her situation. If Fred couldn't make it here until after the weekend, then at least Claire would be here on Sunday. Maybe her old friend could be a listening post for her. They'd always been able to talk things out—come up with solutions to their problems. Admittedly, their problems during their halcyon days were limited mainly to boys and clothes, but she was a good listener and that's what Allison needed now.

Allison corrected herself. What she really needed now was to forget about storms and keep herself busy. She did that by making some more important phone calls. The first went to Dewey Vernon's office and she made an appointment to see the attorney Monday morning. Leona had told Allison about naming her as heir, so the will shouldn't offer any surprises.

The next call went to Madison Middle School to check on how things were going without her, and to tell the secretary, she might be out some days next week. The school had several excellent substitute teachers so Allison knew she needn't be concerned. The call ended with the words she expected, "Take all the time you need, Allison."

Dropping the phone on the coffee table, she stared at the heavy oak desk across the room. It reminded her of what Molly had said at the funeral about visiting Leona on Monday, the day before she died. Molly said when she arrived Leona was cleaning out the desk and that she'd seem perturbed.

That added two more questions for Allison to toss into her pile of unknowns: Why was her aunt cleaning out the desk? And why was she perturbed?

The desk had always been Dick's station alone. Allison recalled him sitting there many evenings making entries into his ledgers and then carefully filing the receipts in the drawers below. When his health started to fail, Leona took over the bookkeeping chores, but she didn't use pen and paper or record anything in the ledgers. All her records were on her laptop and the receipts in shoe boxes on a closet shelf. She even joked about the desk and ledgers being dinosaurs and that she may have to donate them to the Smithsonian.

Walking over to the desk, she picked up the last ledger in the row and flipped through it slowly. Her

Uncle Dick's handwriting was neat and precise just like the man. He'd recorded the orchard's every expense as well as the number of bushels of apples sold, given away, or kept for household use. The "given away" entry didn't surprise her as she knew he kept the local children's home and several nursing homes supplied with the fruit.

Returning the ledger to its place, Allison opened the right top drawer. She expected to see neatly inventoried receipts and paid bills. What she saw was a drawer crammed with pieces of paper stuffed in any which way. She pushed back in her chair. What had happened here? She tried to think of possible explanations. Maybe Leona had pulled the drawer out too far and it had fallen to the floor, spewing out its contents. And being in a hurry, she had just dumped everything back into the drawer. Possible, but unlikely. Her aunt was too neat to leave such a mess.

The other explanation that leapt to mind was unnerving but more plausible. Someone else had been rummaging through the desk. And whoever it was didn't bother about being neat.

She slowly shut the drawer and opened the one beneath it. The same condition existed. Sam had said if Leona had been killed, then there had to be a reason for it. Maybe this was it. Maybe Dick's files had some damaging information about someone. And perhaps Leona had accidentally found it. Had the knowledge made her a threat to that unknown someone? As always there were too many questions and no answers.

Allison shut the drawer and picked up her phone.

The dispatcher said she would give the information to the sheriff.

It was nearly an hour later when Sam called back. "Now tell me exactly what you found," he instructed.

Allison explained the best she could about Dick's desk. In the process, however, she began to feel rather silly. "Maybe I just overreacted. I shouldn't have gotten so upset about the messy drawers. I'm sorry I bothered you."

"You did the right thing. Andy and I can't come out right now though. There was a break-in at Lou's Gas Station last night. He didn't notice the merchandise missing until a short while ago. We're going out there and look into it. You just relax, take a nap, read a book or something. We'll be by later this afternoon."

"All right," she said, but Allison knew there was no way she was going to do any of the things he suggested.

She was about to end the call when he added, "And lock your doors."

LOOKING AROUND THE ROOM, Fred could tell many of his fellow school security people were getting as anxious to as he was for this conference to end. It had been interesting and worth while, but now with snow blanketing the windows and no one knowing how high it was piling up outside, they were ready to make their exits. He knew many were planning on driving home tonight even though home might be a couple of hundred miles away. In his case, he wanted to call the airline and check on his flight, and then phone Allison and let her know the situation.

It was close to three when the powers that be came to an agreement to end the meeting early. The announcement was made along with a reminder for them to pick up the evaluation forms they were asked to complete. It didn't take long for the room to empty. Fred hurried to his room so he could talk to his sweetie in private.

It wasn't until he went to make the call that he noticed he had a message. He smiled at the sound of her voice, "Hey honey, just saw on the news about your storm. Think you'll make it out tomorrow? Call me. Love ya."

The smile quickly vanished. The storm must be really something if it was making the national news. Before calling, he turned on his TV, found a weather channel and his heart plummeted. How could the weather have gotten this bad without anyone at the conference knowing about? It was one thing to be wrapped up in your work as the conference leaders definitely were, but one also had to be aware of the outside world. And that world right now seemed to be in bad shape.

The airline representative confirmed his fears. The last plane out of Dallas-Fort Worth left a few minutes ago. There would be no more flights allowed out this evening and probably not in the early morning. After that it depended on whether or not the snow stopped and when the runways could be cleared.

He slumped down on the bed, called Allison. It

was not a happy conversation. He kept apologizing as if he had personally dumped a foot of snow on the airport; she kept assuring him she was all right and for him just to stay inside and keep warm.

After the last, "Love you," he kept the phone in his hand, rubbed it down one cheek and pondered. Something was wrong and Allison wasn't telling him about it. Her voice was too chipper, her words too careful. He recognized it because he had used the same ploy in the past—trying to protect the person you love by keeping back bad news or scary news or.... He didn't even want to finish the thought. Besides he was probably way off base. Allison was tired and lonely, and since she took pride in her self-reliance, she wouldn't want to admit to any human frailties. That was all there was to it. But he would call her again later just to be sure.

ANDY FINISHED UP the paperwork on the gas station break-in. Lou said, as far as he could tell, the burglar had taken only cigarettes, snacks, and a couple of cold drinks. No money was ever left in the store overnight.

"Probably a kid," the sheriff said. "It's a short walk from the Westside Apartments. Lot of kids there without much supervision. Looks like he smashed a window in the store room to get in. The surveillance video might give us an ID. We'll let you know what we find out, Lou."

Andy climbed behind the wheel, turned to the sheriff, "Think we ought to go back to the Whitley place now? See if Mrs. Sawyer is all right."

"Naw. She's fine. We'll check on her later. Let's go back to the office and look at the tape. Maybe we can nab this kid before he gets into any more trouble."

Andy gunned the engine a little more than was necessary and Sam gave him a questioning look. "You worried about Allison?"

He shrugged. "I just have this gut feeling. Something's just not right."

Sam didn't say anything for a minute. Then he nodded. "Yep, I've had those gut feelings before, and there's been times I was glad I paid attention." He twisted in his seat, and seemed to make up his mind. "Tell you what, you take me back to the office and then you follow that gut feeling. Call me if there's anything I should know."

ALLISON MADE THE rounds of the house, checked the locks, tried to calm her nerves. It'd been silly of her to expect Sam to drop everything and rush to her side just because some desk drawers had been riffled. On the other hand, she thought, a gas station break-in didn't sound awfully important either, since he didn't say anything about a shooting or injuries. On her second round of the rooms, she made sure the lock of each window was secure. As she finished up, she heard a car coming up the drive and soon the beautiful brown patrol car pulled up to the back door.

Elmer welcomed Andy with a joyous bark and a lick to his hand. Allison was a little more reserved. She liked the young deputy, but she would have preferred the old sheriff.

As if he'd read her mind, Andy hastened to explain. "Good afternoon, Mrs. Sawyer, Sheriff Babcock asked me to look into the matter and let him know what I find." He gave her a toothy smile. "So, lead me to the scene of the crime."

"Well, there may not have been crime at all, but it struck me as suspicious." She led the way into the den, pointed to the desk and pulled out one drawer and then the other. "This is what bothered me. Leona would never have left a mess like this. Someone else must have been here."

Andy sat down in the desk chair and peered into the top drawer without touching anything. "A wild search for an incriminating piece of paper?"

"Maybe, but I have no idea what it could have been, or who could have wanted it. What about finger prints?"

"I could get someone out to dust for them and keep them on file until we have a suspect to compare them with. I'll check with the sheriff, ask what he wants to do. Until then, let's just speculate a little. Maybe your aunt found something puzzling and mentioned it to someone. Who would she have told?"

"Molly Kirkman. Molly told me she had visited on Monday and that Leona stopped working at the desk and they chatted over tea."

"So if she'd just come across something unusual in the desk, it would be natural to mention it—that is, if Molly was a personal friend."

"She was. Molly was several years younger, but I think they both served on the public library board and perhaps other organizations."

"And since Molly loves to talk, she probably tells someone else about the mysterious paper."

"You know Molly?"

"Met her at the Arts Council Christmas party. Since I was a newcomer, she filled me in on all the gossip around the county. Like I said, she loves to talk, and since she's a good size woman, I didn't feel safe walking away from her. I could see her muscles bulge under her silky dress."

Allison's mind veered away from the task at hand, and she couldn't help but grin a little as she pictured Andy at the mercy of Molly's mouth and muscles. "I understand she has a home gym and works out regularly."

"I don't doubt it."

"But now you've got me curious as why you were at the Arts Council party. You an art lover?"

"Not really. Seems that every agency in the county had to send a representative. We drew straws to see who would attend." Andy lowered his eyes. "I lost."

Allison tried to keep a straight face. "So you bit the bullet and attended on behalf of your buddies. You're a brave soldier, Andy Cox."

Andy nodded his head in recognition of the facetious compliment. "Now back to my speculation. Molly tells someone about the puzzling piece of paper. This person understands its significance. It may be a threat to him or his business, and he has to recover it."

Pulling a chair up close to the desk, she nodded. "That might be it. So he comes here. Maybe Leona lets him in. Then what? While her back is turned, he searches the desk?"

"Or after her death."

Allison caught a quick breath and her eyes became teary. "You mean while she's dying at the bottom of the stairs, he's looking for a crummy paper? Could anyone be that callous?"

Andy shook his head. "I was simply speculating. I shouldn't have said anything like that. I'm sorry."

"That's all right. My imagination has been coming up with all sorts of wild scenarios. But what really worries me is that if he didn't find what he was looking for, he might come back. Maybe that's why he was watching the house last night." She closed her eyes, took some deep breaths. "I don't want to think about it anymore."

Andy reached over and started to pat her hands when he noticed the bandage. "What happened to your hand? Hurt yourself?"

"Not really. Some foolishness on my part." With some chagrin, Allison told of her trip to the barn, her swing on the rope, and her encounter with the angry rat. "It's just some scratches. Nothing to worry about. I've had a tetanus shot recently."

"That's good, but I think I'll get my flashlight and check out your barn—might find something interesting."

"Fine with me." She told him of the side door and how to get to the loft. "I'll put on a fresh pot of coffee. You'll need it when you get back if you run into my friend."

Andy wasn't gone long and Allison was relieved to see a slight smile on his face when he returned.

She poured him a cup of coffee while he removed his coat and gloves and waited for his report.

"The good news is there was no sign of human habitation."

"Human habitation? What are you talking about?"

"Tramps. It's not unusual for them to hole up in vacant barns during the winter months. We've found regular campsites in some abandoned buildings."

"Omigosh. That thought never crossed my mind." Pouring herself some coffee, she slid into the chair opposite the deputy. "And the bad news?"

"Your rat friend has a lot of company. When I shined my light in the corners, dozens of bright eyes stared back at me."

"I don't understand, Andy, how could rats have gotten to the loft, and what did they have to eat up there?"

"Rats can climb most anywhere, although I've never seen one climb a ladder. More likely they were stowaways in some crates or baskets. I'm thinking your aunt must have stored something up there. The important thing now is to get an exterminator. I think the Feed and Seed Store in town has a service. I doubt they would come out today, but they might be able to on Monday. Want me to call?"

"Yes, please. While you're doing that, I'll rustle up something to go with your coffee. Pie or cookies?"

"Both would be good."

He ended his phone call and grinned. "Not only did I get a promise of an exterminator for Monday, but Jake, the owner, also gave me an explanation for your trespassers."

"Really? Is he a buddy of yours?"

"I met Jake Garner last month when he had a break-in. Using my great detective skills, I rounded up the culprit the next day. Jake was impressed."

"So am I. How did you do it?"

"In all modesty, it didn't take any skill at all. The only thing the man took was a bag of horse feed. So I asked around as to who had horses who might be hungry, which led me directly to the thief. He confessed quickly enough. Said he was sorry but couldn't stand by and see his horse starve to death."

Allison shook her head. "Of course he had to feed his horse, but there must have been a way besides stealing."

"When I told Jake about it, he said he would have gladly given the feed away if only the man had asked. As it was, Jake refused to file any charges and set up a charge account for the horse—to be worked off by its owner."

"What a marvelous story. I'd love to hear more of your detective adventures. But right now, tell me what you learned about my rat infestation."

"Oh, yes. Jake said that last fall Leona ordered some grass seed. She wanted to replenish the riparian bank along Cider Creek by your property. She was afraid all the rain during the summer might have led to some run-off, and she didn't want any chemicals from the orchards to seep into the creek bed. Jake and a helper did the seeding themselves and stored the leftover seed in the barn loft. Now he realizes that was a mistake, and he apologizes. But he assured me your rats will all be gone by Monday."

"That's a relief." She refilled their cups and shoved a selection of sweets toward him. "Your reward for a job well done."

As Andy munched on coconut cookies, Allison talked. "I'm curious about something. May I ask a personal question?"

Nodding and swallowing at the same time, Andy waved his hand at her. She interpreted that as an affirmative and continued with her line of thought. "Sam introduced you as being new on the force. You're what? Twenty five? Twenty six?"

Andy took a couple of sips of coffee and managed an answer. "Twenty five. So what does that have to do with anything?"

"I was just wondering what you were in your previous life—before moving to Upton and becoming a sheriff deputy."

"The short answer is that I lived in the Sandhills area of North Carolina with my family—Mom, Pop, and two beautiful sisters known as Sissy and Sassy. Of course, the girls will claim their names are actually Shirley and Sandra, but that's never been proven. I graduated from a community college with absolutely no idea of what I wanted to do with my life. Opted for the army. After a couple of tours in Afghanistan, I figured a job as a cop would be safer. I aced the academy, moved here and Sam put me on his payroll."

"But why Upton? Didn't they need cops in your home town?"

"Two reasons. One—I love to ski so I came to the

mountains. Two—I didn't want to have to arrest any of my old buddies."

"Well, for what it's worth, I'm glad you came here and that Sam hired you."

"Why?"

"Because I have soft spot in my heart for law enforcement officers. In case you didn't know, I'm married to one."

"Lucky man."

Their camaraderie was interrupted by the ring of Andy's phone. Allison sighed. She'd been enjoying the young deputy's company. He reminded her so much of Dave and it was nice simply to have someone to chat with, share a smile or two.

Andy slowly rose from the table and turned his back. She could hear only part of his side of the conversation. He seemed to be filling the sheriff in on what they had discussed about the desk and then listening to further instructions. "Sure." Pause. "No problem." Pause. "I'll check with you tomorrow."

He sat back down. In answer to her unspoken question, he said, "The bad news is there's been some trouble at the ski lodge and Roberto has to go up there. That means he won't be able to do his drive-bys and keep an eye on you this evening. Sorry about that."

SEVEN

"OH," WAS ALL Allison could think to say when she heard the news about being alone with no protection. It would be getting dark in a couple of hours and she started getting a panicky feeling. Calling up her inner reserves and her positive thinking mantra, she sat up straight, squared her shoulders, and gave Andy her bravest smile. "That's all right. I don't need a body guard."

"Well, I forgot to give the Sam that bit of information. So the good news is that he asked me to hang around for awhile and escort you into town if you decide to stay at a motel."

"And if I decide not to go?"

"Then I would have to say that you're being foolish."

"Like I was foolish to go into a vacant barn that might have human habitation?"

"Something like that."

Allison noted there was not a hint of gentle teasing in Andy's voice now. He was serious about trying to protect her. She gave in gracefully; she'd had enough of trying to be brave. "In that case I'd be delighted to be escorted to The Country Inn Motel by such a competent officer of the law. I'll call and reserve my room."

"Phew, I was afraid I might have to handcuff you—for your own good, of course."

"That's the same line my son used to come up with when he tried to curb my reckless behavior. Did I mention you remind me of him?"

"No. But does that mean I can call you, 'Mom'?"

"Absolutely not. One pushy son is all I can handle."

"But 'Mrs. Sawyer' is quite a mouthful."

She couldn't help but smile as she came up with the perfect response, "From the way you devoured the rest of my pecan pie I would say you have a big enough mouth to handle it." Before he could protest, she went on, "But you could call me 'Allison' if you wish. That's what friends do."

"So we're friends now?"

"Seems that way."

Andy got a very serious look on his face. "I like being your friend, but you *do* remind me of my mom. And since your son's not here, I'll try my best to take care of you."

Allison wanted to argue she didn't need anyone to take care of her, but since Fred and the kids weren't here, a substitute son might do just fine.

Turning to the task at hand, she called the motel and made a reservation, said to Andy, "I'll go pack my overnight bag."

"We've got plenty of time," he said. "Mind if I inspect the basement? I've not been down there and I'm curious." He went on to explain, "I wasn't here on the initial call. That was Roberto." He hesitated. "Have you been down? I mean since…"

"No. I haven't been able to." She sniffed. "I may never be able to, but you go ahead. Do what you have to do while I get some things together."

Andy switched on the light at the top of the stairs and went into his detective mode. He inspected the steps and the railing. They were solid, smooth, no evidence of any spills or anything that might cause a person to slip or trip. On the bottom step he saw a small dark stain that might be blood. He made a mental note to read the coroner's report.

Roberto was the deputy who responded to the 911 call from Harry Roberson He'd then notified the sheriff and the coroner, Dr. Franklin, of an un-attended death. All of the officials were convinced Leona Whitley's death was an accident. Now, because of the footprints in the snow and Allison's questions, the sheriff was having second thoughts.

Andy decided he needed to talk to Roberto and have him go over exactly what he'd found. Something may come up that wasn't in the written re-port. And what about Harry's account? He wanted to hear that first-hand, too. Andy had seen Harry in the hardware store he owned. The man was friendly and helpful to customers—but what was he really like? Did he and Mrs. Whitley have any problems? Disagreements? Harry said he'd found her dead at the bottom of the stairs. Was there more to the story?

Looking carefully around the small cellar, Andy made his mental notes. It was neat and organized. One wall held shelves with Mason jars of canned to-matoes and green beans. Leona Whitley must have had a garden and canned her own vegetables. He knew many women in the area still did. It was a mountain tradition that continued on long after there was any need for it.

He opened a door in the far corner and realized this was the root cellar. There were three peck baskets filled with apples stored here to use until the next crop ripened. This was where she was headed, if indeed, the sheriff's theory was correct. He closed the door and scanned the room again. But if she came down for apples how was she going to carry them up? There was no bowl or container in sight. And it hardly seemed likely she came down to get a can of beans or tomatoes since she had planned on going out to dinner.

He shook his head in puzzlement. Was there any other reason for her to go down the steps? There were no storage boxes, no trunks, nothing but the canned goods and the apples. He studied the walls and ceiling. Everything was finished in plywood with no nooks or crannies for hiding places. There was a locked door in the back of the room. He assumed it led to outside stairs probably used when apples or any other farm produce was brought in.

Andy's head spun with questions and suspicions. He needed to find answers—for himself—for Allison.

He came back up the stairs, hunkered down in the den, stared at the desk. He recalled Harry's statement about letting himself in. Harry said the kitchen and den lights were on, but not the basement light. So maybe, Andy thought, the desk drawers were searched after Leona ran—or was pushed—down the stairs.

On the other hand, the desk may have been searched the next morning or even on the morning of the funeral. As he understood it, Allison didn't arrive until Wednesday afternoon and then stayed at the motel that night and the next morning. Sam said he'd taken Harry's key from him, but was there another key to the house floating around somewhere? Had Sam checked the doors and windows for any sign of a break in? He answered his own question that time. He did recall the sheriff saying after finding Leona's body he'd checked for any signs of unlawful entry and didn't find any. But, Andy argued with himself, that didn't mean someone couldn't have come back the next day to do his searching. He was going to have to talk to Sam about that possibility.

Before he could contemplate further, his phone rang again. Allison came out from the bedroom with a bag in her hand and a question in her eyes.

"Dispatcher," he said. "Roberto needs backup at the lodge and I'm it. Marie is going to find someone else to escort you to town."

"Tell her not to bother. It's still light out. I'll leave as soon as I let Elmer out for one last run. I'll be tucked into the motel before the sun sets."

Andy relayed the message, got an okay, hurried to the door. Before leaving, he held out his hand to Allison. "Let me see your phone."

"Why?"

"I'm going to put my private cell number in your phone book."

"Why?"

"Because you might want to call a friend sometime and I'm off this weekend if you run into any trouble—or need company."

He smiled as she placed the phone in his hand. He did his magic with the number and then was gone.

LATER, ELMER CAME back in the house as Allison went out. "Now you take good care of everything while I'm gone. I'll see you in the morning." The dog gave her a forlorn look and headed for his food dish.

A short distance down the road, a car pulled out from a driveway and started following her. She tried to remember who lived down that long drive and came up with the name of neighbors her aunt had told her were spending the winter in Florida. Oh well, it could be a relative keeping a check on the place.

As she drove on, she looked back again. The car seemed familiar, a black older model car, like the one that had followed her before. Allison told herself to stay calm. Maybe it's some kid going to the school again. After all, it was the height of basketball season, and school teams needed a lot of practice. Approaching the high school gym, she watched to see if the car turned in and when it did, she let out a sigh of relief. Then she sped up, anxious to get to the motel.

The desk clerk welcomed her back, asked if he could help with her luggage. She assured him she was very glad to be back and the only help she needed was the name of a good pizza place that delivered. He not only gave his recommendation but volunteered to call her order in.

"Great. Make it a large with everything except black olives." She felt a little guilty thinking how disappointed the church ladies would be she wasn't still dining on their beneficence. But, she reasoned, even if she'd stayed at the farm, she doubted she could've faced another serving of three-bean casserole.

Entering her room, Allison dropped her bags, marched to the TV, and turned on the weather channel. Snow-clogged streets, cars in ditches, and stranded airline passengers flashed across the screen. The announcer lamented the wintry conditions in Oklahoma City and environs, and added, "Airports across the southwest are dealing with delays and cancellations."

It wasn't what she wanted to hear, but she had to keep listening and watching. "Dallas," she nearly shouted to the young and sprightly weathergirl who was dressed more appropriately for a stroll on the beach than for facing a snow storm. "Tell me about Dallas."

Thankfully, her phone rang and curbed Allison's frustration. Now she could hear it from the man himself. She muted the TV, said in her most loving voice, "Hey honey, how are things?"

It was the wrong question. "Gone to hell in a handbasket."

She'd heard the phrase all her life and never had figured out the kind of basket it referred to, but she did understand the destination. Not good.

"Oh, Fred, I'm so sorry. Are you snowed in?"

"Snowed in. Snowed under. Snow everywhere you look and more on the way. No planes in or out for at least twenty-four hours. And then who knows?"

"But you're all right? The hotel hasn't lost electricity or anything like that?"

"Sure, I'm fine." Allison noted her husband's voice dropped a decibel or two. "Sorry I sounded off like that. It's just that I miss you so much, want to be with you."

"Me too. But it won't be long. Maybe you'll be able to get out by Sunday."

"Or I might rent a car in the morning and get to Upton in the afternoon."

"Don't you dare. You know the roads are treacherous. I don't want you ending up in a ditch."

"As usual, you're right. As long as you're okay, I guess there's no hurry." When Allison didn't respond immediately, he went on. "You are okay, aren't you? Nothing wrong?"

"Of course, there's nothing wrong." She hated lying to Fred, but she wasn't about to tell him all her troubles until he was by her side and was able to do something about them. Instead she told him half-truths about her day: her delightful visit to the old barn and swinging on the hay rope, the young deputy who just happened to drop by and how he reminded her of Dave, all the delicious food she'd been eating since the funeral. "But," she said, "it was so lonely at the farm, I decided to stay in town until you get here. I'm at the Country Inn Motel, warm and comfy." That seemed to satisfy him, and she almost convinced herself that maybe all her suspicions were nothing to worry about.

Long after she ended the call, Allison sat guru-style on the bed trying to crawl her way to nirvana. She was nearly there when a knock interrupted the process. Smiling, she flew to the door, quickly exchanged a fistful of dollars for a cardboard box emitting a heavenly aroma. Now she'd attained paradise—at least temporarily.

After gorging herself and licking her fingers, Allison felt up to facing whatever else might come along. She carefully placed the last uneaten slices in the tiny motel fridge, and since she also had a microwave in the room, her breakfast was already planned.

As she pulled up her cell's phone book to call Dave, she noticed Andy's name he'd entered. Maybe someday her son and her friend could meet. She was sure they would get along very nicely.

Dave answered after only a couple of rings in his usual boisterous voice. "Hi Mom, everything going all right?"

Again, Allison longed to blurt out the whole truth, but she couldn't put that kind of burden on Dave. "Pretty good. I guess you heard of the storm in Dallas. Fred's snowed in and won't be able to come up tomorrow."

"Bummer. I wish I could come, but, you see, I have tickets for the game."

Allison knew exactly what game he was talking about. State's basketball team was in the middle of the February Frenzy leading up to March Madness. She wouldn't think of asking him to miss a game.

"And I'll be watching the game. If the TV camera is ever pointed in your direction, give me a wave." Opting to change the subject, she said, "I spoke with the realtor today. He seems to think the farm will sell easily enough. I'll probably have to auction off most of the furniture, but that can wait awhile."

"I remember when I visited there, that Aunt Leona had some nifty antiques. You going to keep any of them?"

Allison grinned. Only a college kid would describe Leona's lovely antique furniture as 'nifty.'

"Probably. Some of the smaller pieces. And if you want anything for a future home, we can put it in storage."

"That sounds good. We can talk about it later."

Knowing that was Dave's code for 'got to go,' she quickly wound up the call.

Her call to Connie was much the same, except her exit line was, "better get back to my studying. Big exam next week."

Soothing herself with the knowledge that if she ever really needed them, they would both drop everything and rush to her side. But for now they had their own lives, and she respected that.

Dropping her phone for the remote, Allison flipped through the channels. She'd had enough pictures of snow for a while; what she needed now was an inane comedy. But before she found one to her liking, her phone rang again, and questions spun around in her brain. Had the kids forgotten to tell her something? Did Fred have more bad news? She glanced at the number on the screen and it brought no glimmer of recognition. Who on earth could that be?"

Her "hello" was soft and hesitant, but the voice on the other end was loud and confident. "Allison, Ted Kirkman here." Before she could even comment on his surprise call, he went on. "Ran into Brice this afternoon. Says he's handling the sale of Leona's farm. Just wanted you to know I'm ready to make a bid."

It took a few moments for Allison's brain to process what she'd just heard, and then instead of replying to the information, she blurted out, "How did you know my cell number?"

"Brice gave it to me. He thought you'd be thrilled to know you already have a buyer."

Some rather ugly thoughts whirled around in Allison's head. Was this the same Brice Hauser who'd told her he couldn't begin to represent the property until after she had a clear title? And when did realtors start giving out private phone numbers instead of handling all the details themselves?

She determined to deal with the realtor later, but right now she was going to get some details for herself. She knew Ted and Molly Kirkman owned and/or ran several businesses in the area, but he wasn't a farmer. "What on earth," she asked, "do you want with an apple orchard?"

"Investment. It's a beautiful piece of land. A lot of possibilities. I'd be glad to take it off your hands."

"Well, as right now, it's not in my hands and won't be until the will is probated. After that, if you're still interested, you may contact Mr. Hauser. He'll be handling the sale."

"Sure," he said. "No problem. I just wanted to give you a head's up."

Lowering her voice to near frigid, a talent school teachers learn early on, she replied, "I'll keep you in mind. Give my regards to Molly." Without waiting for a response, she ended the call.

The few times she'd encountered Ted, she'd never been particularly impressed. He was too smooth—too suave. He was probably a little over fifty, had the beginnings of jowls and his expensive overcoat couldn't cover up an emerging potbelly. Maybe it was his smile had made her uneasy; it seemed artificial, vacant.

She wondered what he had in mind for the property—probably something she wouldn't approve of: a housing development, a racetrack, a gambling casino? She didn't really want to do business with the man, but she had to be practical and would have to sell to whoever made the highest bid.

Since the evening's peace had already been shattered she might as well go ahead and roil the waters some more. As she punched in the call to Hauser Realty, she rehearsed her little speech to Brice. The recorded message felt like a slap in the face. "Hauser Realty. The office is closed now. If you will leave a message, I'll get back to you as soon as possible."

She glanced at the time and it was just a little after five. He probably closed the office early to get a good start on his weekend. Well, she didn't mind a bit about spoiling some of that weekend because she was in no mood to wait until Monday for a return call. Grabbing the phone directory from the dresser, she fingered the H's in the hope that Brice Hauser was old-fashioned enough to still have a listed landline number. He was.

When he answered, Allison, without even identifying herself, opened with, "I just received a call from Ted Kirkman wanting to buy the apple orchard." That's as far as she got before Brice cut in.

"Great. He said he would call. This may be the easiest sale I've ever made."

It took all of the self-restraint she could muster not to tell him that since she hadn't signed a contract yet, he had no right to start marketing the property.

Apparently that hadn't occurred to him as he rattled on, "He gave me a great bid and it didn't include the machinery so we can auction that off separately as we discussed earlier."

Allison decided to let the conversation flow on so maybe she could get an idea of Ted's plan. "Why would anyone want to buy an apple orchard without the equipment to tend it?"

"He doesn't want the orchard—just the land. My guess is he'll cut down the trees."

Allison felt a sudden sadness. Cut down the apple trees? She'd been hoping the orchard would continue. It would be legacy to her aunt for all the work she and her husband had done over the years. "But," she asked, "why does he want the land?"

"As a buffer zone for his Silver Lake Park condos north of your place. To keep anyone else from building nearby."

"He owns those condos?"

"A big chunk of them, anyway. I'm sure he has other investors, but he's the big cheese. He owns the property north of there and with your place, he'll have land to the south. With the road in front and

Cider Creek in back, he won't have to worry about encroachers on his domain."

Allison mulled over the information and finally muttered, "I see."

"So what do I tell him when he calls."

"Tell him I'll have to think it over."

"I wouldn't take too long if I were you. Ted Kirkman isn't accustomed to being toyed with."

She didn't like Brice's tone of voice. "I'm not toying with him. Remember, I don't even own the farm yet, so I can't very well be selling it. I'll talk to you next week." She decided, though, it might be after she found a more reputable realtor.

Just when she thought the evening couldn't get any worse, Allison's phone rang again.

EIGHT

WHEN SHE SAW Claire's name on the screen, Allison's spirits went up a few notches. It didn't last long.

"Allie, I'm so sorry, but I won't be able to see you Sunday."

"Don't tell me you're snowed in, too. I didn't see any news of snow in Charlotte."

"No. It's not the weather."

The ensuing silence was lasting too long to suit Allison, so she prompted her friend, "What is it then?"

"Dale."

Allison's response was immediate and loud. "Dale? The rat that ran off and left you? Who had an affair? Who traded your condo for a floozy? The man you're divorcing? What's he got to do with anything?"

"He's wants to talk. Says he made a mistake."

Trying her best to stifle her resentment against the man who'd hurt a dear friend Allison lowered her voice and asked, "Do you want to talk to him?"

"I'm not sure, but if I don't I might regret it." Another pause, but shorter this time. "We did have a good marriage, you know, before…"

"I know." Against her better judgment, Allison had to agree with Claire. Having lived with regret after her first husband had absconded, wondering what she'd done wrong, and if it could be repaired, she understood what Claire was going through. She said what had to be said, "Claire, if you think you should give it another chance, then go for it." Allison took several short breaths before continuing. "But be careful. I don't want you hurt even worse."

"I promise I'll be careful. He's coming to Charlotte tonight and we'll see how it goes. Thanks for understanding."

"I'll be thinking of you. Call me in a few days."

When she hung up, Allison's thoughts swung from Claire to herself twenty years earlier. If her husband had asked for a second chance she would have gladly given it to him. But he never asked. He left and, apparently, never looked back.

In retrospect, Allison knew the marriage had never been a good one and never would have been. But she was continually thankful for the two sweet kids that came of it. And she was so grateful for the marriage she had now.

For the second time that evening, Allison traded her phone for the TV remote. This time she knew exactly what she wanted to watch and turned to the horror movie station. It would be a relief to watch someone whose life was in more turmoil than hers.

After a while, Allison had had enough of screams and mayhem and was thrilled when Fred called to wish her sweet dreams. Turning off the TV, she curled under the covers, and slept like a baby.

Saturday morning streamed in through the motel

window on a sunbeam, danced on Allison's eyelids, promised her a beautiful day. She believed it.

A quick shower, a cup of coffee from her room's miniature coffee pot, and a few long-distance lovey-dovey words from Fred was all she needed to get the day off to a good start. Remembering the left-over pizza, she nuked it for thirty seconds, scraped the topping off the soggy crust and washed it down with dregs from the coffee pot. Not bad for the first meal of the day. She was eager to get back to the farm and start making lists: what to give to Goodwill, what to save for herself and kids, what to auction. She had a smile on her face as she headed toward Mount Vista Road.

On the other side of town, Andy woke up Saturday with a sore back and a fat lip. His call to the ski lodge the evening before hadn't gone too well, and ended with a tussle with an out-of-control party animal. Some of the men in a ski group had decided they'd rather spend their time in the bar than on the slopes. As a consequence, they had gotten into a brawl. He and Roberto had to haul three of them off to the county jail. It hadn't been an easy task.

After doing their required paperwork last night about the brawl and the arrests, Andy had a chance to update Roberto on the sheriff's doubts now about Mrs. Whitley's death. The other deputy knew about the footprints in the snow where someone had apparently been spying on the house, but he hadn't been aware of all the questions that had arisen since then or about the riffled desk drawers.

Andy took his time, gave Roberto all the details.

When he finished, Roberto shook his head, "That doesn't sound good."

"No, it doesn't," Andy agreed. Then he said, "You're a good cop, Rob. And you didn't think there was anything suspicious about her fall when you responded that night?"

Roberto rubbed the dark stubble on his chin and studied the ceiling a bit before answering. "Not really, but...."

"But what?"

"But when the coroner did his examination, I thought he was rather quick to say it was an accident. Then when the sheriff concurred—well, I didn't say anything. After all, they've been at this game a lot longer than I have."

Andy stared at his fellow officer. "Roberto, this isn't a game. But I know what you mean; you felt intimidated."

"Yeah. I was going to point out one little thing, but then I decided it would sound silly."

"Nothing's silly if it helps get at the truth of what happened." Andy propped his chin in his hand and waited a little before asking, "Want to tell me about it?"

Roberto shrugged. "Guess I better. Like I said, it's just a little thing."

"Little things can sometimes shed light on bigger things."

"Yeah. Well, it's just that I noticed that her nail polish was smeared on a couple of her fingers. Like maybe, the polish wasn't quite dry when she decided to go down to the basement."

Andy let that bit of knowledge sink in. Leona Whitley had applied finger nail polish because she was going out to eat with her boyfriend. That sounded logical. What wasn't logical was going to the basement before they had time to dry thoroughly. He voiced the thought to Roberto.

"That's what I wondered, too," Roberto said. "What could have been so urgent she would risk messing up her nails." He grinned at Andy. "I have two sisters who love to paint their nails. And when they do, they go around the house not daring to touch a thing until the polish is dry. They won't even answer the phone. So why was Mrs. Whitley in such a hurry to go downstairs?"

"I can think of at least two reasons. One, she may have been trying to get away from someone who was threatening her." Andy ran a finger across his sore lip. "Or, two, someone pushed her down the stairs."

Roberto put his head in his hands. "I really messed up, didn't I? I should have told the sheriff."

"Which is what you need to do first thing in the morning."

"Yeah. I'll do that. He can't do more than fire me."

Andy tried to smile and ended up grimacing. "He's not going to fire you. Of course, he might keep you on the night shift for the next six months so you'll never be able to get a date. But he won't fire you."

All the way home the previous night, Andy kept thinking of the nail polish dilemma and kept coming up with the same answer. There was no way the woman went down those basement stairs on an innocent trip to get apples.

And in the light of day, he knew he'd come to the right conclusion, but it wasn't his story to tell. The sheriff would be in the office this morning catching up on paperwork and Roberto promised to talk to him about what he'd noticed. Sam would consider the new information and form his own conclusions.

For his part, Andy intended to enjoy his day off—after he got so he could move without wincing. He could hold his own in a fair fight, but wrestling with a drunk was a different matter. He climbed into the shower and let the hot water work its magic on his aching body.

Since the sun was shining, Andy figured he would start his day with a long jog. He was tying his running shoes when he got the phone call summoning him back to work. It seems the sheriff had found an important task for him to do. Changes in schedules were common in the department. They were chronically short staffed and work assignments changed frequently. It was part of the job and Andy had no problem with it. He quickly switched from sweats to a clean uniform and headed out.

As was common with him when he was driving, Andy's thoughts went to his girlfriend, Millie. He pictured her getting up, facing whatever the day would bring without a doubt that she was in the right place at the right time. And at that time she was in Africa using her skills as a nurse to help the native people. He missed her terribly which was why he never minded working extra hours. It kept him busy and made the time go faster until she got back. Knowing she had only a couple more weeks to go on her commitment, he was in a good mood. He darted into the station with smile on his face and waved to Marie. The dispatcher played mother or grandmother to everyone in the department under forty. To the older ones, including the sheriff, she was a big sister. Her sixty some years, her gray hair, and her homemade cookies gave her the right to give advice, orders, and reprimands.

As he started to sail past her desk, she called out to him. "Whoa there, Handsome, come back here and get your assignment for the day."

He whirled around and obediently went back. "Yes'um, Boss Lady, what can I do for you?"

"First you can try one of my peanut butter cookies—new recipe—I need your opinion."

Andy pretended reluctance. "If you insist." He took a nibble of the cookie and frowned a little. "I dunno. Maybe a tad too much soda."

Marie swatted him with a magazine. "Just for that, I'm going to bury you in work. The sheriff wants you to review the video from Lou's Gas Station, then nose around the Westside Apartments. He made some stills of the culprit—see if you can find him."

He grabbed another cookie along with the package she handed him. "I'm on it."

At his desk, he leaned back in his chair and studied the tape. The back of the boy was in full camera view. The kid was maybe five-six or seven, probably skinny since the gray hooded jacket seemed to hang on him. The boy, at least Andy assumed it was a boy, must have been aware of the camera because he kept his back to it. Occasionally there was a glimpse of his faded jeans, but nothing of his shoes or boots. He wore black gloves which eliminated any chance of seeing his skin color or of any fingerprints.

Part of the front window was visible on the film showing the outside lights. He stopped the film when he spotted the outdoor thermometer and squinted to read the temperature. Twenty-one degrees. Cold. He looked back at the boy wearing only a fairly light jacket. Where was his coat? Sam had suggested the thief might have walked to the gas station from the nearby apartments. But still, even the three or four blocks would be enough to chill a body without a heavy winter coat. The Westside Apartments were for low income families. Maybe the poor fellow didn't own a coat.

Andy shook his head. He didn't need to start feeling sorry for the kid. But he would like to find the boy before he graduated to bigger crimes.

Something else outside the window caught his attention. Was that a shadow? A man's shadow? He restarted the film, rewound a section, and this time instead of focusing on the boy inside the store, Andy stared at what was outside. It definitely was a moving shadow—a man or another boy. Did our thief have an accomplice?

He picked up the phone, called the gas station, identified himself. "Lou, don't you have a camera outside the station, too?"

"Sure."

"Why didn't you give us that film?"

"Cause you didn't ask."

"Well, I'm asking now. Be there in a little bit."

Lou's Gas Station was actually a neighborhood convenience store and he did a fair amount of business. He kept a limited supply of groceries, snacks and drinks, stayed open long hours and weekends, and let regular customers run up a tab. He wasn't a chatty person, but he was liked and respected.

He greeted Andy with a question. "Found the scamp yet?"

"Not yet. Got a picture, though, for you to look at. See if you recognize the kid."

Lou studied the picture of somebody's back in a hooded jacket. "Not much to see."

"Afraid not. Any ideas?"

"Could be any of the kids who come in here for a cola or candy bar. They usually pay with a crumpled up dollar bill or a handful of change. Nobody's rich in this part of town, you know."

"Yeah, I know. Well, let me have that other tape and see what I can come up with."

Back at the station, Andy reviewed the new tape. The outside camera was aimed only at the gas tanks. It showed no one approaching the front of the station. It did show the hood of a dark car parked near the road, but there wasn't enough to tell the make or model. It only proved that a car was in the area at the same time the store was being robbed. Was the occupant of the car an accomplice? A lookout?

He looked at the time recorded on the film. 12:40 a.m. Not long after someone stood in the Whitley front yard and spied on Allison Sawyer. Was there a connection? Lou's Station was only a few miles from the farm. But according to his boot prints, that prowler had been a grown man, whereas this burglar was a young kid. Two separate cases.

Leaving the station, he drove to the Westside Apartments. He knocked on several doors, showed the picture, asked his questions. No one was able to identify the hooded thief. He hadn't expected them to. He was sure some of the residents had suspicions of who it might be, but they weren't about to tell the law.

ALLISON KEPT BUSY most of the morning, going through her aunt's dishes, her kitchen gadgets, her pots and pans, her knick-knacks. She set aside what she wanted to keep for herself or what she thought either Dave or Connie might want in the future. Everything else would either go to Goodwill or to a charity shop in town.

When she came to Leona's clothes, she knew nothing would fit either Connie or herself. Everything, except a few scarves, went into plastic bags to be given away.

She was in the process of going through the linen closet when the house phone rang. She didn't much want to talk to anybody, but the thought of hearing her aunt's voice on the answering machine was more than she could bear. She snatched up the phone, said a quick, "Hello."

A man's low, hesitant voice, asked, "Is this Allison Aldridge?"

"Yes," she answered, not bothering to explain the change in her last name.

"This is Jerry Howe. You may not remember me, but I've been doing odd jobs around the farm for your aunt and uncle for years."

"Yes. I do remember you, Jerry. Aunt Leona used to tell me how helpful you were." Allison wasn't sure where this conversation was going, but she wanted to be polite. "What can I do for you?"

"Well, that's just it. I was wondering if I could do anything for you. Leona, that is, your aunt, used to call me to shovel snow, or fix things, or...."

It sounded to Allison as if Jerry had lost his train of thought. She broke the ensuing silence. "I appreciate you calling, but I really don't need any help now. I'm only staying for a few days."

"All right then. Well, Good-bye." She heard the click on the other end of the line. She shivered a little as she replaced the receiver. It was nice of Jerry to offer help, but Molly's words from the cemetery echoed in her mind, "a time bomb waiting to explode." There was no way she'd asked him to do any odd jobs for her.

She reached for her "to do" list and added a note to have her aunt's phone disconnected.

Going back to her sorting tasks, she worked another hour before feeling the need for a change. The sun was bright, the snow was melting, puddles were forming in the yard. Forgetting all the work she still needed to do, she yielded to the temptation to get out in the fresh air, maybe a take a walk through the orchard. She pulled on her boots, grabbed her parka, and slipped her cell phone into a pocket. Elmer must have sensed an adventure coming up because he waited for her at the door.

As she started toward the orchard, her eyes gazed at the bare apple trees only weeks away from starting a new season. She could picture the pink and white blossoms painting the hillside like icing on a cake—to be replaced in a few weeks with the tiny green fruit. Would there be red ripe apples again in the late summer, or had Whitley's Orchard seen its last harvest?

Putting that thought out of her mind, Allison zigzagged through the trees, paying scant attention to the direction she was heading. After a while, she found herself nearing the banks of Cider Creek which ran along the east side of the Whitley farm. She recalled again summers when she and Claire would wade and splash in the clear, nearly colorless water as it rippled over the rocky bottom.

Since she was this close, perhaps she should check on the grass her aunt had asked to be sown on the bank to prevent runoff. Allison made her way from the trees toward where the land began to slope. The twigs and broken branches she'd been walking over or sidestepping disappeared. Matted, brown stubble peeked through where the snow had melted. Before long the stubble would be transformed to lush grass. She hoped the sides of the creek bank looked as good.

She reached the brink of the ridge and peered down. Most of the snow here was gone, and she was pleased to see that the ground had a good covering of grass. Her gaze went down further to the stream, and she shook her head in puzzlement. The water seemed streaked.

She climbed down the bank to get a closer look. When she got to the water's edge, she couldn't believe her eyes. There were splotches and blobs of faint yellowish and whitish discoloration. Maybe no one else would see anything wrong with the water, but she remembered how perfectly clear the stream had always been. What had happened to their lovely, pure creek? Could Leona have seen this and thought it was chemical runoff from the orchard? Is that why she'd ordered the grass seed? But this contamination wasn't coming from the orchard. It must be someone upstream who was polluting the creek. Allison knew there were laws about dumping chemicals or whatever this was in creeks or any body of water, and she intended to report it.

Kneeling cautiously by the water, she bent down, dipped in a finger, and brought the finger to her face. She detected a slight acrid odor. Allison had no idea what chemicals or toxic wastes were in the water, but she was furious with whoever had committed this horrible offense against nature.

Elmer bent his head toward the water to get a drink, but Allison grabbed him by his collar and hauled him back. "You're not drinking any of that poison. Come on. We've got to get to the house and call the EPA or somebody."

She scrambled back up the bank with the dog right behind her and headed back the way she'd come. She stopped abruptly as a sharp cracking noise echoed in the air. Her sudden halt took Elmer by surprise, and he bumped into her left leg. She grabbed for his collar, held him still, looked toward the orchard. All was quiet now, but she *had* heard the noise of a breaking twig or small branch. She'd stepped on several on her way through the orchard and knew the sound. Could a branch have simply fallen from a tree?

Or was someone stalking her?

She held her breath and listened intently for any further sound. After a few moments, her breath escaped like a deflating balloon. She bent down and petted the dog. "Guess my imagination is working overtime. How can I let a breaking twig send shivers through me?"

She headed back into the trees, but had gone only a few steps when she heard another snapping sound. This one was closer, louder, and she saw something brown moving among the apple trees.

Someone was in the orchard with her—hiding— watching—stalking.

NINE

FRED SPENT THE morning going over the notes he'd taken during the conference and scanning the material he'd received. After deciding which safety and security procedures could be applicable to his school district, he detailed a plan to present to the school board and the police department. Since it was a job he would have had to do anyway when he got back home, he decided he might as well utilize the hours he was held hostage by the snowstorm.

It was well in the afternoon before he wandered down to the restaurant for a late lunch. He sighted several other captives and joined them in mutual commiseration. When one of them suggested a poker game for the evening entertainment, there was instant accord. There ensued some loud dickering about where to have this game until Jake somebody announced that he had booked a suite expecting his girlfriend to accompany him, but she'd backed out at the last minute. "So come on up, boys, bring your money, and leave your phones behind."

Fred knew he had to do three things before the game started: get some cash from the desk clerk and bill it to his credit card, change into the most comfortable clothes he had, and call Allison. The first two went smoothly, the third—not so good. He felt a flash of irritation when her voice mail came on. "What can she be doing," he muttered, "that's more important than answering my call?" His message was short. "Still snowing here. What's happening there?"

ALLISON HEARD HER phone ringing but couldn't stop to answer it. She was running for her life. At least that's what it felt like. Terrified at the sight of a man among the apple trees, she made a flying U-turn and raced back toward the creek bank. Once there, she kept running at top speed along the ridge. She knew if she followed the creek, it would lead her away from the orchard, and eventually to the barn where she could hide from her stalker. Her only plan was to escape from the threatening figure.

Or would she be going from one threat to another? The rats were still there and their range was probably not limited to the loft. Wherever she hid, one of those monster rats might be there to greet her.

She tried to block that thought out of her mind and concentrate on getting away. She was a pretty good runner, but what if her pursuer was a better one? Don't think about it, she told herself. Just keep going. Elmer ran on ahead, probably thinking they were playing a game. But Allison knew this was no game. A man had been watching her, following her, and even now could be gaining on her.

Her breaths started coming in short gasps. A sharp stitch attacked her right side; she bent over in pain, but she wouldn't stop. She couldn't stop. She had to get away.

The end of the orchard was within sight. Just a few more yards, then a short distance to the relative safety of the barn. She could dash into the side door as she had yesterday, then pull some piece of machinery or boards or something to bar the door. And she would find some kind of weapon to deal with the rats if she had to.

Allison was beginning to feel some confidence when, without warning, her left foot dropped into a chuckhole. She sprawled forward, spread her hands out in front to protect her face. When she was able to right herself, she gaped in fear at the shadows dancing in the apple trees. She couldn't make out any human form, but she could sense the man was there—staring at her.

The sun that had been so bright earlier now hid behind darkening clouds. It was getting late in the afternoon and there wouldn't be much more daylight. She had to keep going.

Elmer came back to her, gave a short bark. He wanted to continue their race. She reached up and used him for a crutch to help her stand. She got to her feet, but when she tried to walk, the agony in her ankle made her forget about the pain in her side.

She had no choice. She had to call for help. Pulling her cell phone out of her pocket, her thumb vacillated between two numbers. Taking a deep breath, she bypassed 911 and punched in Andy's number.

ANDY'S PHONE RANG as he was leaving the Westside Apartments. His heart constricted when he heard the low plea, "I need help."

He raced to his patrol car, fearing for Allison's safety. He knew his new friend was a proud and independent woman and wouldn't call for help unless she felt really threatened. He kept his voice calm. "Where are you?"

"Between Cider Creek and the orchard. A man's hiding in the trees. I can't see him, but I know he's watching me." Andy waited for her to go on. He had a hundred questions, but he couldn't waste time now getting details. He heard her take a deep breath. "I was running away when I tripped. I may have sprained my ankle."

Andy jammed in the key, started the engine, spun out the drive. "I'm on my way. How do I get to the creek?"

"Left of the barn. You'll have to park there. No road. I'm going to try to get to the barn, but my ankle is throbbing with pain. Hurry."

"Five minutes—tops."

"Be careful. The road's so curvy."

"Will do. I'm putting the phone down, but yell if anything happens."

He skidded around Lou's Gas Station and barreled onto Mount Vista Road.

ALLISON SLIPPED HER phone back into her jacket pocket, but she didn't disconnect the call. She balanced on one foot while her eyes searched the orchard area closest to her. Nothing. No noise. No shadow. Her panic started to subside. If her stalker had wanted to catch her, he'd had ample time to do so. If there had actually been a stalker. Maybe she imagined the whole thing. Maybe she was getting paranoid.

She hobbled forward, touching only the toes of her left foot to the ground, wincing in pain with each step. What if she'd broken her ankle in her stupid dash to escape a phantom?

The barn was in view when she also sighted Andy. He was sprinting toward her so fast she wondered if he'd be able to stop.

Elmer ran to meet him as if he were a playmate. The deputy ignored the dog, scoured the scene with his eyes, and steadied Allison with his left arm. "Easy does it. Let's get you to the house and have a look at that ankle."

She shook her head, pointed toward the trees. "But maybe he's still there. Maybe you can catch him." If only Andy could get a glimpse of him, she thought, it would prove that I'm not going crazy.

"I doubt it. I'm sure he was gone the instant he heard my car coming. The important thing now is to be sure you're all right." Allison nodded and limped toward the car.

Once in the kitchen, he led her to a chair and dropped down to remove her boots. "Now let's see what damage you've done." He slid off her sock and gently examined the injured ankle: palpating, moving, rotating, gauging her pain reaction.

Allison smiled between grimaces. "You seem to know what you're doing."

"Had some medic training in the army. It comes in handy at times." He nodded his head in satisfaction.

"No broken bones. Ice and an ace bandage should take care of it."

"Good. Ice pack in freezer, and I think you'll find an ace in the hall bathroom cabinet."

A few minutes later Allison was iced, wrapped, and propped up in the recliner in the den. Andy handed her a bottle of ibuprofen tablets. "Your aunt had a well-stocked medicine cabinet. Take two now and keep the bottle handy. You'll probably need more. Now you rest. I'll be back shortly."

Feeling a burst of irritation toward her rescuer, Allison blurted out, "You're leaving me? I can't stay here alone. And besides I have to tell you what happened and about the creek and…."

Smiling, Andy shook his head. "I'm not leaving. But I have to do some investigation before it gets dark. I'll lock the door behind me and take the key. When I get back you can tell me the whole story."

After Andy left, Elmer came up to her and sniffed around her bandaged ankle. Allison stroked the top of his head. "You may not be a guard dog, but you're a good friend. And I hate leaving you all alone here, but as soon as Andy gets back, I'm hightailing back to the motel, staying there until my hubby gets to town." She kept scratching behind his ear, tried to think of an alternative, and came up with a possibility.

She picked up her phone to call the Roberson Hardware Store. She planned to ask Harry if she could bring Elmer to his house for a day or so. It was then she noticed she had a message and remembered her phone ringing while she was in flight.

Going to her voice mail she heard Fred's terse message. "Still snowing here. What's happening there?"

Tears sprang to her eyes, and she wasn't sure why. Was it because Fred sounded angry with her? Or because she missed him so much? Or because she was going to have to lie to him when they did talk? She absolutely couldn't tell him what was happening here, since there was nothing he could do about it. Later, when they were together, she would tell him everything—but not now. And she would have to wait until she got her emotions under control before calling him back.

She went ahead with her original plan to call Harry at his store.

A bored voice answered. "Roberson Hardware. How may I help you?"

"I'd like to speak to Harry, please."

"I'm sorry. He left early this afternoon. May I take a message?"

That's odd, she thought. Leona had told her Harry was always at the store whenever it was open.

"No," she said. "But I really need to talk to him. Could you give me his home or cell number?"

Allison grabbed the paper and pen from the coffee table that she'd been using to make her lists earlier. The woman sounded even more bored as she rattled off a number. "That's his home, doesn't have a cell phone."

Even as Allison thanked the store clerk, she was surprised at getting the information so easily. However, it didn't do her much good as Harry wasn't home to answer. The answering machine asked for a message and she explained about her sprained ankle, asked if she could bring Elmer by this evening. She left her cell number and asked him to call.

"Don't know what I'll do," she told Elmer, "if he doesn't call back before I leave."

Resting her head on the back of the recliner, Allison closed her eyes and tried to sort out her tangled thoughts. Had someone followed her? Or had she imagined it? And what about the pollution in Cider Creek? She hadn't imagined that. She wished Andy would hurry back. She had to tell him everything. Her thoughts were interrupted by the ring of her phone. Thinking it was Harry calling back, she answered without looking at the number.

A booming voice blasted her ear. "Allison, Ted here. I know you talked to Hauser about my offer. I understand you want time to think it over, but I'd love to stop by and see if you have any questions for me. I'm at Silver Lake Park right now and could be there in a couple of minutes."

She shuddered. He was the last man she wanted to see right then. Managing to control her anger, she answered politely, "This isn't a good time, Ted, and any questions will have to go through the realtor. Being a businessman, I know you understand. Have a good evening, now."

"Well, Elmer," she said to the attentive dog, "That should put Mr. Big Man in his place."

She hoped Andy wouldn't be gone much longer because she wanted to leave as soon as possible.

Knowing Ted, he might stop by even without an invitation, and she didn't want to be here if he did.

GRABBING HIS FLASHLIGHT and camera, Andy leapt from the car. He'd driven as far as he could behind the barn and now headed toward the spot where he'd found Allison. He followed her footprints backwards in the matted grass, shining the flashlight as he went along. At one point, the prints became shallower. He reasoned that up until that point she'd been walking slowly, and when she started running, the impressions of her boots were deeper. So maybe this is where she thought she'd seen or heard someone in the orchard. He veered to his left and marched into the shadows. Keeping the light on the ground, he canvassed the area as quickly as he could. There were plenty of sticks and twigs on the ground broken off by winter winds and snows. He was looking to see if any had been recently disturbed, and hoping he'd really luck out and find a boot print.

Darkness was falling quickly. His flashlight was powerful, but it only illuminated a small section of ground at a time. He looked back at his own boot prints and saw that they were barely detectable. He didn't expect to find a distinguishable print, but he really wanted to find some kind of evidence to prove Allison's assertion that she had been followed. More snow was predicted for tonight. If he didn't find anything now, tomorrow would be too late.

He didn't want to leave her alone for too long and was about to turn back when his light picked up a patch of darker brown. He grinned. Lady Luck was with him tonight. He bent down and scrutinized the distinct heel print in a dab of mud. He pulled his camera around and captured it on film. It probably wasn't enough to match with any particular boot, but it verified that a man had stood in this spot and from here he had a clear view of where Allison had been walking.

She *was* being stalked.

He took several more pictures around the area even though he couldn't make out any other prints. Maybe the film could be enhanced to show something else. He doubted this print could be matched to the pictures of the prints in the front yard, but Andy was convinced they were made by the same man.

It was time to get back to the house with his news. And it was time to get Allison somewhere safe.

TEN

WHILE SHE WAITED for Andy, Allison's mind remained on Ted Kirkman and his bombastic persona. He obviously wasn't accustomed to having his wishes denied. She wondered what kind of marriage he and Molly had. According to Leona, Mrs. Kirkman wasn't any slacker when it came to getting what she wanted. Although Molly was her aunt's friend, she knew Leona didn't always agree with the way she commandeered committee meetings and pushed through her own agendas.

Allison's mind flitted to Silver Lake Park. It'd been finished last fall, and in one of her calls, Leona had mentioned something about the luxury apartments and amenities. It would be interesting, she thought, to have a look at the place Ted was so anxious to keep from any encroachments.

She heard the kitchen door open, heard Andy scrape off his boots and shed his jacket, and then his rugged face appeared in the doorway. "The good news is that you were right." He paused. "The bad news is that you were right. A man *was* following you. I found a print, got a picture of it. Now you've got to tell me exactly what happened and I'll write up my report."

"I will. But not now. Not here. Can't we go to the

station and do that? I don't want to stay here any longer."

Andy nodded. "Sure. That'll work."

"Good. Then if you'll help me hop into the bedroom, I'll change into something a little less muddy and get my overnight case. And since I won't be able to get by boot back on this foot, I'll find my old tennis shoes and wear them."

"All right."

"And I need to take Elmer with me." She explained about her phone call to Harry. "He hasn't called back yet and if he's not at home, I'm not sure what I'll do."

"No problem. I can take him to my apartment. They allow pets."

Andy walked around and made sure the house was secure before they left. "I'll take your things out and come back for you. Sure you can drive?"

"I'm sure. No problem with my right foot." Then she added, "But you stay close behind me." She felt a little foolish saying that, but she was in no mood to see a black car following her again—even if it was a kid going to the high school gym.

"I intend to and I'll take Elmer, along with his dish and food in my car."

Andy steadied her as she hobbled to the door. "Now here's the plan," he said. "That is, if it meets with your approval. We'll go by Harry's first, and since I don't know where he lives, I'll follow with Elmer. If he's there and agrees to be a dog sitter, we'll leave Elmer, after which we'll go to the office where I'll take your statement about the stalker."

"And the pollution," she put in.

"What pollution?"

"That's the part I haven't told you yet. Someone has been polluting Cider Creek and I have to report it to Sam so he can call the EPA."

"Fine. And by that time, we'll both be famished, and we'll go to Duncan's diner for their Saturday night special. Then I'll escort my weary adopted mother to the motel."

Allison was too tired to argue with him about any of his plans—or his verbiage. She just wanted the evening to get over so she could call Fred and tell him how much she loved him. That part of their conversation, at least, wouldn't be a lie.

She led the way to Harry's house. His pickup drove into the yard just before she pulled in followed by Andy in his patrol car. A yard light illuminated the entire area. Harry exited his truck holding a rifle. Frowning, he headed in her direction, and Allison felt a moment of uneasiness. What did she really know about this man who had courted her aunt? Who had a key to her house? Who had found her dead?

She swallowed her misgivings, smiled as he came up to her car. "I'm glad you're home," she said. "I brought Elmer if you could take care of him for a couple of days. I left a message on your house phone, but I guess you haven't gotten it yet."

Harry leaned down and glanced in the back seat. "Where you hiding him? In the trunk?"

"Sorry. I meant to say the deputy brought him."

Still clutching the rifle, Harry straightened up and

stared at the patrol car. "Since when do you need a police escort to visit me?"

Allison felt her nerves fraying like a piece of old flannel cloth. The grieving boyfriend she'd seen at the funeral seemed to have disappeared and had been replaced by a hostile stranger. If Harry was teasing her, she was in no mood. "I called the store, but you weren't there."

He nodded. "Left early to get in some hunting. Thought I'd get me a rabbit or two. Nothing like good rabbit stew on a cold day."

Thankfully, Andy came up before she had to comment on rabbit stew. He let the dog out of the car and stretched his hand out. "Don't think we've officially met, sir. I'm Andy Cox." At the same time, Elmer greeted Harry by nuzzling his pant legs encased in mud-splattered boots.

Harry shook Andy's hand briefly. "Pleased to meet you." He then bent down and petted the dog. "And I'm especially pleased to see you."

Allison stole a look at Andy's face. Had Harry just insulted the officer? If so, it didn't seem to faze Andy, who just grinned. "Guess you've got a guest for a while, then. I'll get his food and bowl, and Allison and I'll be on our way."

Harry seemed to remember his manners. "Won't you come in? I'll put on a pot of coffee."

"We can't now," Allison said. "I was hoping we'd have time to talk, but we'll have to make it later. I'll probably be here for a few more days. She looked from Harry's rather haggard face to his rifle. "Leona didn't tell me you were a hunter."

He gave a rueful smile. "I'm not surprised. It was one of the things we disagreed on."

One of the things? She wondered what other disagreements they'd had.

Andy interrupted her thought as he asked the hunter, "How many rabbits did you bag?"

"Actually, none. Couldn't see their tracks too well with so much snow melted. Should have known better than to try."

Yes, Allison thought, a good hunter *would* have known better. She glanced from his brown hunting jacket to his muddy boots and as she drove away, she wondered just what woods he'd been hunting in.

By the time they reached the county police station, both Allison's ankle and her head were throbbing. She parked as closely to the door as possible and dragged herself out of the car. In an instant Andy was by her side and helped her inside.

Marie gave her a worried look. "What happened to you?"

"It's a long story. Right now I just want to sit where I can prop my leg up."

"Sure, honey, we'll get you fixed up," and Marie started issuing orders like a drill sergeant. "Andy, take her to the break room, let her sit in the easy chair and prop her foot on a stool."

"But I have to take her statement."

"So? You can do that in the break room as well as at your desk." The dispatcher called across the room to Roberto. "Rob, use some of those quarters you're saving and get the lady a coke." She turned to Allison. "Or would you prefer coffee?"

"A coke would be wonderful—and a glass of water so I can take some more pain pills."

"Coming up."

Andy and Roberto both jumped to their tasks and soon Allison was leaning back in comfort, her ankle cradled on a pillow, a cold cola by her side. She dug the ibuprofen out of her bag, swallowed two of the pills, and then announced, "Now I'm ready to make my statement."

"We have to wait for the sheriff. I radioed him on the way and he wants to hear your story."

"My story? You make it sound like a fairy tale."

"Sorry. Your statement regarding the events of the afternoon. I know it's not a fairy tale because I have a picture of a boot print to prove it." He hastened to add, "Of course, I would have believed you even without the proof."

Her eyebrows rose in amusement. "Really? For a while I doubted myself."

The break room door opened and Sam Babcock came in. "Heard you had quite a day, ma'am. Suppose you start at the beginning and tell us all about it."

She did. Starting with wanting to get out of the house, she told of wandering through the orchard, of checking the creek bank where the grass seed had been sown, and then of going down to the water's edge. When she mentioned the pollution, the sheriff stopped her.

"Are you sure? Melted snow can be pretty dirty at times."

"It wasn't dirt. I'm sure it was chemicals of some kind. Hasn't anyone else reported a problem?"

He shook his head. "Not that I know of. But it probably wouldn't be noticed downstream. When Cider Creek leaves your property, it veers east and goes through some pretty rugged country—no houses. By the time it empties into the New River, it'd be clean."

"So that means," Andy said, "we have to go up-stream to find the contamination."

"Not this department. On Monday we'll report it to the proper authorities, and they'll investigate. We have enough on our plate without getting involved in something that has nothing to do with us."

Allison wiggled in her chair. She was tempted to argue that the pollution might tie in with her aunt's death, but she knew the theory was pretty far-fetched. Better put it out of her mind. Right now all she wanted to do was complete her statement and get something to eat.

The two officers listened closely as she spoke of hearing someone among the trees and of her panic to escape. "I could feel his eyes on me." A shudder went through her body as she relived the terror that had gripped her.

Andy then told of finding the boot print in the mud. "The picture may not be of much help, but it proves someone *was* following her."

Sam looked at his deputy in surprise. "I never doubted that for a minute. Now all we have to do," he said with a grimace "is line up every man in the county with mud on his boots."

Allison understood what the sheriff was saying. Knowing someone was following her was a lot different than knowing who. A picture of muddy boots zipped across her brain—boots she'd seen only a few minutes ago. There was Harry—standing in his drive, holding a rifle, with Elmer sniffing at his muddy boots. She shook her head. The pressure of the last few days was really getting to her. She had to back away, stop letting her imagination run wild.

"Is that all for now?" she asked. "I need to get something to eat and then collapse."

"That's it. Tomorrow's Sunday. Why don't you just stay at the motel, relax, and do the monster crossword puzzle in the Asheville paper. That should keep you out of trouble."

"That's exactly what I intend to do and listen to the weather news. Have you heard if air travel is getting back to normal yet?"

"Nothing much is moving. It'll probably be Monday before your husband can get here."

Approving of Andy's plan for them to eat at the diner and then for him to escort her to the motel, the sheriff walked with them to the door. "By the way, Andy, make sure this last call of yours goes on the books. Marie told me she didn't know anything about it."

"Yes Sir, I'll take care of it. See you Monday."

As Sam headed back to his office, Andy held out his hand to Allison. "Give me your keys and I'll pull your car up so you won't have to walk so far. And if you want, we can stop at the drug store and rent you some crutches."

"Yes to pulling the car up. No to the crutches." She handed over her car keys. "I'm not going to get

in the invalid mode. My ankle will be fine by tomorrow."

Andy shrugged. "Just as I thought, you're as stubborn as my mom. But when we get to the diner, pull
up to the door and I'll park your car."

"Gee," she said with a grin, "I've never had my
very own valet."

"Enjoy it while you can."

When she arrived at Duncan's Diner and noted
the very full parking lot, Allison really did enjoy the
idea of a private valet. She even waited for Andy to
open her door and assist her out. Might as well play
it for all I can get, she thought. She only regretted
she wouldn't be able to tell Fred about it tonight. If
she mentioned her sprained ankle, she would have to
go into the scenario behind it, and she wasn't ready
for that yet.

Upon entering the restaurant, Allison was dis-
mayed to see two familiar faces heading her way.
The chubby cheeked man had a wide smile, while the
thin, wrinkled old lady wore a forbidding frown. Wes
Snyder and his mother, the formidable Mrs. Cornelia Snyder, had been frequent guests at her aunt's
summer barbeques whenever Allison had visited.
Wes was her age and had somehow gotten the idea
that they were best buds, an idea that Cornelia tried
to her best to squash. Wes was a CPA, never married, and seldom went anywhere without his mother.

Now as he drew nearer, he stretched out his arms
toward her. "Allison, how delightful to run into you
here."

She avoided a hug by reaching out her right hand

and grasping his. "Nice to see you, too, Wes." Allison turned toward his mother with what she hoped was a pleasant smile, "Good evening, Mrs. Snyder. How are you doing?"

The older woman hesitated. "Not bad considering...."

Allison didn't want to know what ailment was at the top of her considerable list and said quickly, "You're certainly looking good. The cold weather must agree with you."

"Not really, but it doesn't help to complain. I do my best to bear up under the burdens the good Lord has seen fit to send my way." She then gave Allison a look that had disapproval written all over it. "But, my dear, I'm surprised to see *you* out this evening. So soon after the funeral, that is."

Allison stopped herself from rolling her eyes in just the nick of time and replied sweetly. "Like you said, Mrs. Snyder, we all must bear up under our burdens. And I seem to bear up better when there's people around."

"Mother!" Wes sounded embarrassed. "There's no reason why Allison shouldn't get out. No need for her to sit all alone in an empty house."

Mrs. Snyder patted her arm. "Of course, dear. I understand. If it wasn't for Wesley, I don't think I could stand living in that big old house of mine."

Allison glanced to her side at Andy who seemed to be enjoying the scene. "Mrs. Snyder, Wes, have you met Andy Cox? He's with the county police department and a friend of mine."

They both shook their heads. Allison finished the

introductions. "Andy, this is Mrs. Cornelia Snyder, an old friend of my aunt's and her son, Wes, Upton's top CPA."

When everyone had made the proper acknowledgements, Andy started inching away. "We'd better find a seat, Allison. The place looks pretty crowded."

"Yes," she said. "It was nice seeing both of you." But before she could make her getaway, Wes placed his hand on her arm.

"Wait a minute," he said, "I've wanted to talk to you—to offer my services."

"Services?"

"For your aunt's taxes. Tax preparation after a death can be pretty complicated and I'm an expert in the field. I'd be glad to go over her accounts for you."

The offer surprised Allison. "That's very thoughtful of you. That part of settling the estate hadn't entered my mind yet." Actually, it had occurred to her to find out if Leona owed any taxes but she hadn't done anything in that direction yet.

"Well, there's absolutely nothing for you to worry about. I can take care of the whole thing. When would you like me to come and do it?"

"But Leona had an attorney. It could be that he did her taxes. I'll have to check and see."

"Some attorneys are all right for the usual tax returns, but not for anything complex. Better let a professional handle it."

Allison backed away. "I'll give it some thought. Talk to you later."

"Here. Take my card and give me call. What are friends for, anyway?"

She shoved the card in her coat pocket and sighed with relief as Wes and his mother walked away.

When they were seated, Andy voiced exactly what Allison was thinking. "What was that all about? Is Wes so short of work he has to go about drumming up business?"

"I noticed he didn't give *you* his card. Cops have to file tax returns, too."

"But mine is a simple form. Like he said, death taxes are more complicated." Andy took a sip of water. "You know, Wes might be just a nice guy wanting to be helpful—but on the other hand, he might have a personal reason to want to pry into at your aunt's accounts. You'd better be careful with him."

THE POKER GAME had been going on for hours; a couple of the men had already left saying they'd lost all they intended to for one evening. Fred was getting close to that point, too. He blamed his losses on the fact that he kept getting distracted in thinking about Allison. As instructed, he'd left his phone in his room and then wondered throughout the game how many times his wife had called and not gotten an answer. He worried too about the abrupt message he'd left for her earlier. He should have called back, apologized, and told her about the poker game. After losing another hand and a goodly amount of cash, he decided to call it quits.

Back in his room, he snatched up his phone to see

how many messages Allison had left for him. When he saw there were no messages, he threw the phone on the bed, closed his eyes and shook his head. "Oh, man," he said to the vacant room. "She must be really mad at me."

He decided he needed some nourishment before he called and wallowed in repentance.

ELEVEN

AFTER THE WAITRESS took their orders, they kept their conversation light. Andy started it off with, "Tell me about this son of yours that I remind you of."

Allison was delighted with the request and was glad to oblige. She loved to talk about her kids. "Dave's a few years younger than you, a junior at NC State, thinks he wants to be a teacher like his old mama, has a wild sense of humor, and has a different girl every month or so."

"You didn't mention him being handsome and brilliant."

"How did you know?"

"Has to be since he's like me—or I'm like him."

Allison gave her companion the expected laugh. "But, unlike you, he's only slightly conceited. Although he does brag a little about being on the wrestling team," she added. "Do you wrestle, Andy?"

"Not unless you count trying to arrest a drunk who doesn't take kindly to being handcuffed. That turned out to be quite a match."

"Of course, you won."

"I guess so, seeing that he spent the night in jail and all I got was a fat lip." He rubbed his upper lip. "Hope it didn't spoil my good looks too much." Taking a sip of water, he said, "But enough about

Dave. What about your daughter? Is she a duplicate of you?"

"Not at all. Connie is tall, willowy, gorgeous, and deeply dedicated to her calling."

"Which is?"

"Medicine. She's in her first year of medical school and loving it."

"Sounds like someone else I know."

"Oh, who is that?"

"My girl."

Allison slid back in the booth, shot her eyebrows up. "If you have a girl why isn't she here with you tonight instead of me?"

"She's away."

"Oh, where?"

"Zambia."

Leaning forward, Allison asked, "Zambia as in Africa? Thousands of miles from here?"

"'Fraid so. And before you ask, I'll explain why."

"Good. This is a story I want to hear."

"Millie's a nurse, a RN, works in the hospital OR. She took a leave to donate two months to the charitable organization, Doctors Without Borders."

Allison nodded. "I've heard a lot about them. They do some wonderful things."

"Yeah, they do. Right now they're doing surgeries that aren't usually available in many of the African countries, making a big difference in a lot of lives."

The rest of his recitation was delayed while their meal was delivered and they started eating. After a bit, he continued, "I'm mighty proud of Millie, of what she's doing—but man, I do miss her."

"So, do the two of you have an understanding?"

"Sure do. We plan to be married this summer. But before we could come to that decision, we both had to understand about giving each other space to be ourselves. She'll continue working, probably go on other mission trips, and I have to accept that. But on the other side of the scale, she'll be marrying a law enforcement officer and will have to accept the danger that goes along with it."

Allison reached across the table, touched his arm. "I'm proud of both of you, and with that attitude, you'll have a marvelous life together. I hope I get to meet her someday."

They finished the meal in silence. Allison knew Andy was thinking of his Millie, while she was thinking of the law enforcement officer she'd married, who'd been shot in the line of duty only months before their wedding.

She knew the young couple would have difficulties, but hoped they would be as happy as she and Fred were. At least they'd been happy up until now and would be again once they were back together. This separation was hard on both of them.

As was the plan, Andy followed Allison back to the motel, helped her inside, wished her a good evening.

Hobbling over to the nearest chair, she removed her sneakers. She was glad the pant legs of the jeans she had on were long and loose and did a good job of hiding her footwear and the ace bandage around her left ankle. Her ankle, although still a little painful, didn't seem to be swelling much. Hopefully by morning she would be able to wear her boots again.

She climbed up onto the bed, her phone in one hand and the TV remote in the other. First the weather channel and then her sweetie pie.

The perky, suntanned weathergirl pointed out all the high and low pressure areas bringing in record precipitation and low temperatures. The only glimmer of hope was that the snowfall in the southwestern states was expected to wane over the next hours even though the temperatures would remind below freezing.

As she punched in Fred's number she hoped he had good news on the local weather front. But more important than the weather was the fact she had to apologize for not calling him sooner.

He answered with, "Hi hon, I'm so sorry."

At nearly the same time she said, "Honey, I'm sorry I didn't call earlier."

Seconds went by as each waited for the other to go on. Then with a laugh, Allison gave in, "Okay, you go first. Explain yourself."

It took several minutes but he apologized for his terse message and for not calling back. He told of playing poker and losing the equivalent of a Caribbean cruise. "But, hon," he said, "I had to do something to keep from missing you so much."

"That's all right. I'm not much of a cruise person, anyway." Taking a deep breath and crossing her fingers, she went on, "And the reason I didn't call earlier was because I spent the afternoon with a tall, dark, and handsome young man."

"O-k-a-a-y."

Allison could tell he was trying hard to come up with something indignant or sassy to say. To end his misery, she explained. "I told you about Andy Cox, the deputy who reminds me of Dave."

"Yes."

"He was helping me with some things around the farm. It seems that there are rats in the barn and he called an exterminator for me. And he took Elmer, Leona's dog to a friend's house to stay since I can't keep him here at the motel. And some other little chores..." Her voice trailed off.

"I see. Well, that's good. I'm glad you had some help since I wasn't there, and it looks like I won't get out of here tomorrow either."

"I heard the weather report. It said the snow was slacking off."

"Yeah, it is. But I checked with the airline. Still going be delays for another twenty-four hours. Might be Monday before I can get out."

"At least," she said, "you're comfy there at the hotel with room service, and the R-rated films they offer."

"And you're snug and safe in your Country Inn Motel with your cable TV and Snickers bars. Right?"

"Right."

As their conversation dwindled down, he said much the same thing as the sheriff had, "Tomorrow's Sunday. Just take it easy and rest. I'll find a way out of here Monday if I have to hire a dogsled."

ANDY WOKE EARLY, thought of Millie and how she greeted each new day with eagerness. Or was it afternoon in Zambia, and she'd already spent hours on her feet in a makeshift hospital? He never had quite figured out the time difference. He knew they didn't do surgeries on Sunday, but they did have to check on the post-op patients. It didn't really matter what time it was in the other continent as he knew Millie was keeping busy. And that's what he had to do—keep busy, so the loneliness didn't engulf him.

He started with a morning run. The park close to his apartment complex was intended for spring strolls, summer picnics and autumn leaf watching. In the winter it was mainly deserted. Last fall some avid runners had petitioned the city to keep one circular trail plowed out for their use; the council agreed. The fact that many of his running friends were either city or county police personnel or EMTs went a long way in getting an affirmative vote. Apparently the city fathers realized the benefit of keeping their employees fit.

As he made his way around the trail, he waved to the few brave souls who had come out while the temperature was still below freezing. There was nothing better, he thought, than a morning jog in brisk weather to get the heart racing, to clear the brain, and to cleanse the spirit. But even while he was doing all that good stuff, his mind was looking forward to breakfast at the Pancake House with enough cholesterol to clog his arteries and enough sugar to make him swoon.

Another thought was also going around in his head, and he hoped Allison would agree with it. He would wait a couple of hours before calling—give her a chance to get bored sitting around but not long enough for her to want to venture out on her own. He'd asked her the evening before if she intended to go to Leona's church and she'd shaken her head, said she wasn't up to seeing a lot of people yet. He hoped she was up to seeing him again, that he wasn't making a nuisance of himself.

When he did call, it was with a simple, "Hey, feel up to taking a ride?"

"Sure. Where to?"

"What I had in mind was checking out Cider Creek north of your farm. We might be able to get an idea of where the contamination is coming from."

"But Sam said his department wasn't going to investigate that."

"This won't be official. I'm off duty, and there's nothing wrong with you and me doing a little sight-seeing."

"What if you get in trouble with your boss?"

"I won't tell if you don't. However, it would probably be better if we drive your car. Someone might report a patrol car snooping around, and my personal car is in the garage being resuscitated."

Allison laughed. "So now we're going snooping instead of sightseeing?"

"Something like that."

"Good. I'm an A-1 snooper. You can pick me and my car up in about half an hour."

ENDING THE CALL, Allison glanced at the time—a little before eleven. She was delighted Andy had called because that solved her problem of what to do to fill in the hours. She'd lingered as long as she dared over her continental breakfast in the lobby, had chatted inanely with her three loved ones, had watched the weather channel until she was dizzy, and had done as much yoga as she could manage with her bum ankle. Now she had a little snooping to look forward to.

She limped only slightly as she went to the window, peered at the melting snow and the bright sunlight. It seemed to be turning into a lovely day. Her attention went to the bird feeder. The bright red male cardinals looked as if they were members of the royal guard while their mates dressed in dowdy brown coats appeared like poor relatives. She'd always figured it was Mother Nature's little joke to make the males of most species bigger, stronger, and prettier than the females. But when humans came along, the women tended to have their own ideas, especially in the beauty department—and most of the men never objected.

Forgetting her philosophical meanderings, she turned to check out her ankle. It was doing much better, and she was grateful. She took off the ace bandage, noted the swelling had gone down. She would probably be back to normal soon. She rewrapped the bandage, pulled on sweatpants, and eased her foot into her boot. It was a tight fit, but she thought it would be all right for a few hours.

When Andy knocked on her door, she was ready.

"You look great," he said. "How the ankle?"

"Good. Thanks to the excellent emergency care I received." She took a last swallow of coffee. "Let's get this adventure on the road."

Andy helped her into her car and took the wheel. When they turned onto Mount Vista Road, he glanced at her. "Want to stop at the farm to get anything?"

"Not now. But I was thinking I ought to get Leona's laptop, so I could go over her accounts. We could pick it up on the way back to town."

"Good idea."

"I thought we'd drive north and see if we come upon any place of business, factory, whatever, that might be a source of pollution."

"The only close-by place I can think of is the old Binken Paper Mill, but it was shut down years ago. When I visited here in the summers, we used to call it Stinky Binky."

Andy gave her a weird look. "I know the old paper mill. It's on the way to the ski slope, but I never heard it called 'Stinky Binky.'"

"Then you never lived near enough to smell it. When the wind was in the right direction, we could smell it clear to the farm. But that wasn't considered pollution—just part of the regular paper making process. Folks around here were glad when the mill closed, except, I suppose, the people who worked there."

When they passed the apple orchard, Allison turned to Andy. "Did I tell you Ted Kirkman wants to buy the place?"

"Nope. What does he want with an apple orchard?"

"He doesn't. Just the land. It connects to his Silver Lake condos up ahead. Guess he doesn't want any close neighbors."

It wasn't long before they saw a tasteful sign that

read *Silver Lake Park*. Beneath the name, it stated that two and three bedroom condos were available. To the right was a sprawling three-story complex with a circular drive. The buildings were painted a soft acorn brown, so they almost seemed a natural outcrop of the surrounding mountains.

"Nice," Allison murmured. "I hadn't been up this way since they've been built."

"You noticed they didn't put a price for the condos on their sign. That means they're way out of my price range." Andy slowed the car. "But since we're just sightseeing, we could go in and look around. Want to?"

Allison was amused at the idea. "Why not? You could be a nouveau riche looking for a vacation home."

"As if anybody would take me for a rich kid." He pulled the car into a visitor spot, walked around, and opened her door. "Come on, rich relative, let's see how the upper crust lives."

As they approached the front entrance, a tall, thin, young man in a blue uniform jacket came out and started sweeping snow away from the door. He gave them a cursory glance followed by closer scrutiny. He leaned on his broom when they came near and gave them a big grin. "Allison Aldridge, how nice to see you."

Allison was confused for a moment until she recalled his name. "Buddy Wilson, I hardly recognized you. I haven't seen you since you used to help with apple picking when I visited my aunt."

"Well, I've come up in the world since then."

"You're working here now?"

"Yes Ma'am" he said. "I'm the resident man-

ager, desk clerk, and snow sweeper." His grin widened. "Kind of a skeletal staff until we get more
residents. Mr. Kirkman says I've got a good future
here, though." His face became serious. "I'm so sorry
about your aunt. She was a nice lady."

"Thank you."

Andy stepped forward and broke the awkward
moment by introducing himself. "I'm Andy Cox, a
friend of Allison's. She might be interested in one of
your units. All right if we take a look?"

"Oh, sure. That'll be fine. Come on in." He ushered them into the lobby. Before Andy had a chance to
look around, Buddy turned back to Allison. "Do you
want to look at the same one your aunt did last week?"

Allison blinked, wondered if she'd heard cor-
rectly. "Leona looked at a condo here?"

"Sure did. Let me check the visitor's log book,
and I can tell you the number."

Buddy went behind the desk, pulled out a notebook, and flipped back a page. "I remember now. It
was 211. It was funny."

Andy edged up to the desk and studied the open
notebook. "Funny how?"

Buddy squirmed. "I don't mean funny—funny. Just
a little odd. Most people want to overlook the lake or
the flower gardens. The gardens will be really pretty
in the summer, but Mrs. Whitley wanted to look out
at Cider Creek. I told her the view was much better
on either the north or south side, but she said she liked
to see the sun come up in the east." The clerk looked
back at Allison. "Want to see at that one?"

Allison tried to respond to Buddy but couldn't make

any words come out. Andy answered for her. "Yes, that's the one we want to see. 211. Can you take us up?"

"I can't right now. There's no one else here to answer the phone. But I can give you the key. Go on up and look it over. The elevator's on your right. I'm sure you'll like it."

The key changed hands, and still Allison hadn't said anything else. Andy tossed the key into the air and asked Buddy, "Did Mrs. Whitley like it?"

"I don't really know. She let herself up, and I didn't see her when she came down. Left the key on the desk. Guess I was busy somewhere."

When the elevator door closed on them, Allison shook her head, "There's something terribly wrong here, Andy. Leona wasn't interested in buying a condo. She must have been doing just what we are—investigating the Cider Creek pollution."

"Seems like. She may have seen the contamination just like you did and wanted to know if it went farther upstream."

"But why didn't she report it?" Allison blinked back tears. Finally, here was a possible explanation for her aunt's death—for her maybe murder.

As the elevator rose, she tried to puzzle out how it may have come about. Leona had apparently first seen the pollution last fall and feared it may be run-off from the orchard. That's when she ordered the grass seed for the creek bank. Then when she went back to check, maybe the contamination was worse, and she knew it wasn't from her land. So she decided to investigate. Then what?

When Andy unlocked the door to 211, Allison

dashed in as fast as she could and went straight for the balcony on the east side of the room.

Andy opened the balcony door and helped her out. Cider Creek flowed serenely by several yards to the east and two stories below. A high wooden fence had been erected behind the condos that blocked any view of the creek from ground level. But it was visible from the second floor balcony. Even at a distance, though, she could see the water was murky and discolored.

"Leona stood on this very spot and saw the pollution. It may just look like dirty water to you, Andy, and perhaps to others, but I know, and she would have known, that it might be serious contamination. What were her thoughts? What did she intend to do?" Allison grabbed handrail. "If we knew that, maybe we'd know why she died." She jerked back and stared again at the creek. "We've got to find the answer."

"We will or the sheriff will. He doesn't say much, but he won't give up until he finds the truth."

"You mean, until he finds the killer." Allison closed her eyes, tried to calm her frazzled brain. This whole thing was a nightmare. When would it end? She forced herself to concentrate. "Did Buddy say what day she was here?"

"No, but I looked at the visitor log. The date and time by her name was Monday at eleven—the day before she died."

"Poor Leona. I guess she didn't have time to tell anybody about the pollution."

"I'm not so sure about that," Andy said as he paced the small balcony. "Think about it. Your aunt discovers Cider Creek is polluted. She comes up here to confirm that it doesn't start at her farm. She is probably upset about it, thinks something should be done to correct the situation. But the next afternoon, she's painting her fingernails, getting ready to go out on a date with Harry. I doubt if a woman would be calmly painting her nails if she was still upset. What do you think?"

Allison pondered the thought and slowly nodded her head. "You're right. So she did tell someone, and that someone told her not to worry about it, that he'd take care of it. She trusted him, and so she relaxed and didn't go any further with her investigation. That must be it."

"And now," Andy said, "we're back to the 'who'. Who did she talk to?"

Allison clasped her hand over her mouth after, "Oh, no!" escaped. She shook her head in dismay. "It can't be."

Andy stared at her. "You were thinking of Harry?"

She nodded. "It would have been the natural thing for her to do. He was the closest friend she had—her boyfriend. She would have called him for advice."

"That's what crossed my mind."

She grabbed the railing, leaned over. She was nauseated with the fear of what might have happened. The thought of Harry hurting her aunt was too much too bear. Gasping for air, she lifted up her eyes to the sky.

"I've got to know the truth—but what if the truth is too painful?"

TWELVE

ANDY TOUCHED HER SHOULDER. "Let's go. We can talk about it later."

They were silent as the elevator slid smoothly down to the lobby. Buddy stood by the desk with the visitor's log book open in front of him. "Well, what do you think of our little place here?"

"Lovely," she managed to say. "Lovely view."

Andy placed the key on the counter and they headed for the door.

"Wait a minute," Buddy called after them. "I need your contact info." His hand was poised over the log book.

Allison turned and stared at him. "My what?"

"Contact phone number. For the sales people. They contact everyone who looks at a unit."

"But," Allison stammered, "I'm not interested in purchasing a condo. I just wanted to look at it."

"That's what most people say, but they change their minds when they learn of all our amenities. So what's your number?"

Andy didn't wait for Allison to answer. He reached over the countertop, took the pen out of Buddy's hand, and crossed out her name that had been written in. "She said she wasn't interested." Taking her elbow, he guided her to the door.

Once outside, Allison peeked back, saw Buddy slam the log book shut and shove it under the counter.

WHEN ANDY PULLED out of Silver Lake Park, he swung right and headed further up the mountain. Allison touched his arm. "If you don't mind, I'd like to go back to town. I'm not up to any more sight-seeing today."

"I understand, but I want to go by the paper mill. I've driven by it many times but never really took time to look at it."

It was only a short while before a large, ware-house-like structure came up on their right side. Andy slowed the car. "So is this what you called 'Stinky Binky'?"

She bobbed her head. "Looks ghostly, doesn't it?"

His gaze fell from the building to the drive lead-ing to it. "Maybe the ghost is coming back to life."

"What do you mean?"

Turning into the drive, he stopped the car, opened his door, and looked down. "Tracks. Fairly recent. Not today since there's a coating of snow on them but not enough to cover them completely. I'd say they were made yesterday."

"Maybe the land's for sale, and someone is look-ing to buy it. It actually is a nice looking structure, has a certain character. They used to make industrial buildings that were pleasing to the eye and fit into their setting. This one might even pass for a hotel."

"Yeah, it looks as if it could be fixed up nicely. Just out of curiosity I'll check the present owner and status when I have time." Turning the car around,

Andy hesitated before exiting the driveway. "How about having a cup of Clyde's coffee before heading back?"

"Who's Clyde?"

"The man who owns Clyde's Coffee Cup. He caters to skiers coming and going from the lodge, but he's attracting a lot of locals, too."

"I don't know. I really don't feel like socializing."

"It's early yet, probably won't be many there. And he's got a great selection of Danish."

Allison managed a smile. "Another thing you have in common with my son. He has to eat about every two hours."

"Then it's a go?"

"Go. I could use a little caffeine and calories. Anything to clear my brain a little."

The parking lot held only a spattering of cars; and when they went in, Allison was pleased to find the atmosphere was inviting with dim lights and muted background music. "My kind of place," she whispered to Andy. "Quiet and peaceful."

Andy's lips parted and then quickly closed. Reading his face, Allison nodded. "You mean it isn't always this quiet and peaceful. We just happened to pick a good time."

"Well, it *is* Sunday. The churchgoers don't get rowdy until late in the day, and right now the skiers are too busy breaking their legs to carouse. But if you want, I can bring you back when the partying starts."

"Think I'll pass on that."

Andy took her by the elbow, led her to the counter, and pointed out the selections. She was suitably

impressed by the variety, but ordered a simple cin-
namon roll along with black coffee.

The young man behind the counter tapped a
few buttons and asked, "And what's for you today,
Officer Cox, mighty hunter of wrongdoers and
champion wrestler of over-imbibers?"

"It's good to know the grapevine from the ski
slopes is still intact and working well." Andy turned
to Allison, "This is Zach Deedledum, champion
gossiper and owner of this fine establishment. And,
Zach, this lovely lady is Allison Sawyer, a friend and
my surrogate mother."

"I'm pleased to meet you, Mrs. Sawyer. I take it
your job is to hold Andy together until Millie gets
back to the states."

Allison smiled and was amazed how two inane
guys could pull her out of her doldrums if only for
a short while. "Something like that. But he said you
were the owner here. What happened to Clyde?"

"That's me, too. When I was trying to come up
with a name, I couldn't think of anything that allit-
erated with Zach. So, I went with an alias."

"You could have called it Zach's Zingers."

"Oh, where were you, beautiful lady, when I
needed you?"

Andy waved his hands between his two friends.
"Enough chit-chat. Let me have two of your luscious
chocolate and pecan éclairs and we'll get out of the
way of all your other customers."

Allison twisted around, ready to step away, but
there were no other customers to be seen. "I give up.

I'm going to find a booth, Andy, and you can bring my goodies."

When they were seated in their booth, Andy turned their conversation to the upcoming Valentine's Day and how much he missed Millie. "It'd be easier if we could Skype or even email, but there's no internet in most of the places the team goes. She *has* been able to call a couple of times when they were near a city. Thank goodness, she only has two more weeks."

"That's good. I'm sure you'll hold together until she gets back." Allison finished her coffee in a gulp. "We'd better be going. My sweetie may be calling before long."

Back in the car, the pleasant diversion was soon wiped from her mind, and the scene from the condo balcony popped back in. They passed both the Binken Paper Mill and Silver Lake Park without comment. Her brain, though, was replaying everything they had seen, every word that had been said.

There were spots when her memory was a little blurred, and she had to go back over it again. One particular scene was causing her trouble, something odd about it.

What was it Andy had said about Leona telling someone of the pollution and then not being upset anymore? Something about painting her nails and getting ready to go out.

Jerking around, she cried out, "Andy."

Andy slammed on the brakes. "What? What's the matter?"

"How did you know she painted her fingernails?"

The deputy gaped at her as if she'd lost her mind. "I'm not sure," he answered slowly. "But can we talk about it when I get off this slippery road?"

Allison slid back around and didn't say another word but her brain was in overload. *The funeral home director said Leona's nail polish had been smudged and he had removed all of it. The funeral attendees who'd viewed the open casket would have seen Leona's hands folded across her chest and the nails would have been unpainted, so who could have mentioned it? How did Andy know?*

They pulled into the farm driveway and without speaking, Andy parked by the kitchen door, came around and helped her out of the car. She handed him the key. Once inside, he pulled out a chair, motioned for her to sit. Allison could tell from the look in his eyes that her friend was angry, and she couldn't really blame him. She'd spoken to him in a very accusatory manner.

Before she could say anything, he plopped down opposite her. "First, I really must remind you that it's not a good idea to yell at a driver when he's trying to maneuver an icy mountain road."

"Sorry about that."

"Okay, now about the nail polish. I remember now how it was. Deputy Roberto Flores told me. He was first on the scene. In examining your aunt's body, he noticed the polish of a couple of her fingernails was smeared. He didn't say anything at the time because both the coroner and the sheriff concluded the death was accidental."

She opened her mouth to comment, but Andy's

held up a hand to stop her. "You've got to understand about Roberto. One, he's a pretty shy guy, doesn't talk much. Two, he's fairly new on the force. Actually, he's been there longer than I have, but unlike me, he's not pushy. As a consequence, even though he thought it was odd for a woman to make a trip to the basement before her nail polish was dry, he didn't voice his suspicion."

"But he told you?"

"Only when I asked him if he'd noticed anything unusual when he responded to the 911 call. This conversation took place Friday night after we'd broken up the ski lodge fight. Since I was scheduled to be off Saturday and he was going to be working, I urged him to tell the sheriff about it. He said he would." Andy finished with a sigh. "There. Does that satisfy you?"

"Not completely. Did he tell the sheriff? And if he did, why didn't Sam say anything about it when we were there yesterday?"

"I don't know, but I assume Roberto reported it. And as to why Sam didn't mention it, again I'm assuming, probably because at the time we were discussing your stalker, not Leona's death."

"And Sam isn't obligated to tell me everything that goes on with the investigation. Right?"

"Right. Sometimes we lawmen like to keep certain information to ourselves." He smiled at her. "Makes us feel important."

"Is that why didn't you say something to me about it? We sat chatting at the diner for nearly an hour last evening. Seems like you could have brought it up."

"At the diner I was trying to get your mind off your anxiety, not add to it."

"Okay."

"Not okay. Now it's your turn. How did you know about her painted nails?"

Allison accepted the turnabout gracefully, and told him about the funeral home meeting with Mr. Albert Knotts. "I'm ashamed to say I didn't attach any significance to the smudged polish at the time. I knew Leona liked to dress up: do the girlie thing with polish and perfume and fluffed hair, but I didn't think about why the polish would be messed up."

Andy sat back in his chair, gave her a smirk. "Girlie thing? That sounds odd coming from you."

Allison bristled. "Why? Because I'm old enough to be your mother?"

"No. Because you seem like some a practical person with your short wash-and-go haircut, scant makeup, and neatly trimmed finger nails—with no polish."

Trying to hold back a laugh, she nodded in agreement. "You do have highly honed detective skills, Deputy Cox. You're right on every aspect. But there's one thing you don't know."

"That you lead a double life?"

"Exactly. During the week I teach physical education, otherwise known as 'gym.' I'm also the girl's basketball and track coach. Thus, the short haircut, short nails, and sparse makeup.

"Okay. That's one life. What's the other one?"

"Most evenings and weekends, I celebrate and become a lady who likes girlie things. I look good.

I smell good. And on occasions, I paint my nails Fire Engine Red."

"I see. I'd like to meet that lady some time."

"Invite me to your wedding and you will."

"It's a deal."

Andy's face became serious as he got up and started pacing the kitchen floor. "Now as much as I hate to return to the previous subject, I think we both agree that Leona would never have voluntarily gone down those stairs until her nail polish was dry. Which means she was either pushed down, or slipped when trying to escape from a threat."

"There's no doubt in my mind. And what I do have doubts about is why I'm being stalked. I know there must be a connection, but I can't figure out what it is. It's apparent he doesn't mean to kill me since he's had ample opportunity. It doesn't make sense."

"True. We'll keep working on that one. Right now, let's get that computer you wanted and get you back to town. If you tell me where I would find it, I'll get it for you."

"Leona's bedroom is the one on the left. It's probably under the bed."

He raised his eyebrows; she went on to explain. "She did a lot of her computer work in bed."

"Makes sense."

"While you're doing that, I'm going to get some more clothes out of my room."

Coming back through the den, she noticed the light flashing on the house phone. She was tempted to ignore it, but Andy came in at the same time, stared at the phone and then at her.

When she didn't move, he stated the obvious, "Looks like you have a message."

Giving in, she went to the phone and pushed the button. "Allison, this is Molly. I don't know when you're planning on going home, but I really want to talk to you before you leave town. Give me a call back, or come by the house. I'll be home all afternoon."

Allison frowned. "Strange," she said.

"What's strange?"

"For her to call here again. Ted has my cell number. Wonder why she didn't call me on that if she's so anxious to talk to me."

"Maybe Molly and Ted don't communicate much with each other. Or he doesn't want her to know he called you about buying the place. Some men are pretty secretive about their business dealings."

"It doesn't matter. I'll return her call when I'm good and ready. But tomorrow morning I'm having this phone disconnected. I'm tired of getting strange calls."

"You've gotten other calls?"

"One from Jerry Howe. He wanted to know if I had any work for him to do. I told him, 'No.'"

"Why? Jerry's a nice guy and a good worker."

"That's what I thought until Ted and Molly set me straight. They said he's gotten dangerous."

"Dangerous? That's ridiculous. I see him around town a lot doing odd jobs and I chat with him. I admit it's like talking to a six-year-old, but he's pleasant and he likes to help people. He even works for the hospital, keeps the snow shoveled off their sidewalks."

"Well, anyway, I don't have any odd jobs for him to do. Now let's get out of here."

The ride back to town was quiet. Allison realized she'd ended the afternoon on a testy note, but she had so much on her mind and not sharing it with Fred was tearing her apart. If he didn't get here by tomorrow, she was going to burst.

At the motel, Andy carried the laptop in for her, set in on the dresser. "You'll call me if you find anything pertinent?"

Allison didn't understand the question. "What do you mean?"

"You do plan on going through your aunt's accounts, e-mails, whatever, don't you? There might be clues to what was going on."

"Oh, sure. I'll get started on it right away. I'll call if I find anything that might relate to our case."

As soon as the door shut, Allison did two things simultaneously—turned on the weather channel with the sound muted and punched Fred's phone number. The sun shining on melting snow looked promising while the voice asking her to leave a message was frustrating. Afraid that she might sound like a shrew instead of a loving wife, Allison opted not to say anything. Instead, she gave her attention to the weatherman. With a slight smile he announced air traffic from the snow-stricken states was starting to move. However, he went on to explain, because of the many cancellations and delays it may be twenty-four hours before things got back to normal.

Allison wondered if she'd be able to last another twenty-four hours without her soul mate. Her mind went to the many lonely years after her first husband had left her with two little ones to rear on her own. It wasn't that she wanted him back, but she wanted someone to love, to confide in, to share the load. Fred had been that someone. Now she couldn't imagine life without him. But she needed him here—now.

The tears were just beginning to dribble down her cheeks when her phone rang. She picked it up warily as if it might be a snake that would strike out at her. Seeing the name, she swiped away the tears, put a smile in her voice. "Hey, Honey."

"I'm on my way."

She closed her eyes for a moment in thankfulness. "Now?"

"Now. The roads are cleared. I've rented a car. Got my bags packed and I'm leaving."

"But it must be about a thousand miles."

"What's a thousand miles to a man in love? I'll be there tomorrow."

"Oh, Fred. How wonderful. I feel like a kid waiting for Santa. I won't be able to get to sleep tonight." As she said that, her practical mind jumped to the forefront. "But it'll be dark pretty soon. You're not planning on driving all night are you?"

"Remember, I'm in a different time zone. I'll have more daylight than you do, and I'm going to drive as far as I can. Don't worry, I'll stop at a motel when I get sleepy, grab a few hours of shuteye."

"You don't know how much I've missed you."

"No more than I've missed you. I'm going to hold you so tight, I might break a rib."

She laughed. "It'll be worth it. And I'm going to give you a kiss that will set off the sprinkler system."

"Hold that thought. Got to go."

For a long time after talking to Fred, Allison was in dreamlike state, remembering his words, his promise that he'd be with by tomorrow afternoon. Until then, though, she decided she would either have to keep busy or go crazy.

Digging into her purse for some change, she hiked to the vending machines, got a cold Pepsi. After drinking most of the can, she figured she had the strength to make the call to Molly. After all, the woman had been a good friend to Leona, and Allison couldn't ignore her. Then recalling that Molly had left her number after her first call, Allison dug into all her pockets to find the paper she'd scribbled it on. It was a piece of newspaper she'd picked up from Leona's coffee table. She smoothed it out and noticed it was the part of the paper with the daily crossword puzzle. It was only half finished which seem odd to her. Leona was very good at puzzles and almost always completed them in record time. Something must have distracted her.

A low pitched, aristocratic voice answered the phone. "Kirkman residence." Allison could picture Molly in her "chairman of the committee" role—no causal greeting in case it was somebody important.

"Hi Molly, it's Allison. Sorry I didn't get a chance to call earlier. How are you?"

"Oh, I'm fine," Molly said, her voice now sounding like a friendly TV announcer. "I'm so glad you called. Where are you?"

Allison wondered what difference it made where

she was calling from, then Molly went on to explain. "I know you're not at Leona's house because I just called there again and left another message. I was getting worried about you."

Even though it was none of Molly's business, Allison answered the question. "I'm staying at the Country Inn Motel. Was there something special you wanted?"

'No-o-o. I was just concerned about you. Staying all alone on that big old farm."

"Well, now you know I'm not staying there, so there's no need to worry."

When Molly made no immediate response, Allison voiced what was on her own mind, "Ted's offer to buy that big old farm caught me by surprise. Has he been thinking about it for some time?"

Several seconds passed before Molly commented. "Well, you know. I never meddle with Ted's business affairs. I guess he offered you a good price."

"My realtor seems to think so. I told him I'd think it over."

"Don't wait too long, dear. Ted is apt to get impatient."

That sounds familiar, Allison thought. Brice Hauser had said almost the same thing. Who did Ted Kirkman think he was, issuing warnings that sounded a lot like threats? "Well, I'll let him know when I make up my mind. I've got to be going now. Talk to you later."

Allison stared at the phone in her hand, not knowing what to make of the weird conversation. And what if Ted did get impatient? He couldn't force her to sell. Or could he? Was Molly telling her, 'What Ted wants, Ted gets'? And she didn't believe for a minute about Molly not meddling in his affairs. She was known all over town as a meddler.

But as irritated as she was with Ted and his tactics, she had to admit his offer was a good one, and she really couldn't afford to ignore it.

Trying to put Ted out of her mind and not wanting to think of Fred making such a long drive, she got out her aunt's laptop. Thankful that the little imp inside the computer didn't ask for a password, Allison started going through the Leona's financial files. After a while the spread sheets began to swim before her eyes and she knew she wasn't making any progress. As far as she could tell, everything seemed to be in order. Leona had gotten as far as completing the December figures but hadn't compiled the yearly amounts yet. I guess that is where Wes would start if he were to do last year's taxes.

Putting the computer away, she took a long bath, went to bed and hoped to dream of Fred.

FRED HAD BEEN on the road only a couple of hours when he realized the news report of the main highways being cleared was an exaggeration. Steep snowbanks rose on either side of the interstate leaving only one lane in each direction for traffic. Fortunately, there was little traffic and the lanes that were opened had been scraped, but there were still patches of ice which mandated caution. As eager as Fred was to get to North Carolina, his common sense told him he had to take it slow and easy.

As he drove, his thoughts were on his reunion with Allison. She had put up a brave front, attending the funeral of her aunt with no family members there to lean on, seeing to business affairs, and perhaps the hardest of all, knowing she had to sell the farm with the apple orchard that held so many good memories for her. He needed to be at her side, to lighten the load, to ease her pain. Ever since Tuesday night he'd tried to think of any possible way they could keep the orchard in the family. He'd come up empty. They had their home, their jobs; the kids had their own dreams for their futures. Leasing the land and becoming absent landlords could, and probably would, open up a barrage of problems. But still they could discuss it; she shouldn't have to make all the decisions by herself.

It was nearing midnight when he gave in to his fatigue and heeded the lure of a flashing motel sign. He asked the night clerk to call his room at five o'clock.

MONDAY MORNING, fortified by a lukewarm shower and the worst coffee he'd had in years, Fred was again on the road. A few hours later, he was nearing Little Rock. Traffic was getting thicker with folks starting their work week and school buses transporting their precious cargoes while road crews were still spewing sand on some remaining slick places.

It was when he was looking for the sign to I-40 East that the crash happened.

THIRTEEN

ANDY HAD SPENT Sunday evening at his computer writing down everything he'd learned and could remember so far in the investigation of Leona Whitley's death and Allison's stalker. He used his own style of shorthand and didn't list them in any kind of order, so the resulting page could have been mistaken for a witch's brew recipe or a secret code. It didn't matter since he knew what it said and he planned go over it with the sheriff in the morning. He printed it out and studied each item.

Nail polish, apples in kit, no basin in base, cookbook out, door locked, desk, light off in base, pollution—chemicals?, condos, tire tracks at mill, footprints, slick tires, rats, Harry, Elmer, Ted wants farm.

Probably he was forgetting something but he could scribble other things in later. At least he had a starting point.

On the back side of the paper he made a list of all the things he wanted to do the next day. Andy hoped he'd be allowed to question Harry Roberson. He wasn't at all convinced the boyfriend had told them everything about the day Leona died.

A couple of the things would only take phone calls. He would check to be sure the exterminator took care of the rats in the Whitley barn, and he'd try to find out who owned the closed paper mill.

But come Monday morning, it took less than ten minutes for most of Andy's plans to go askew.

He went into the office with his lists in his pocket and a determined look on his face. He greeted Marie with, "Sheriff in yet?"

"Nope, and he won't be until late this afternoon. Remember that sheriff's conference in Charlotte? He was going to drive down last night and leave to come back right after the mandatory luncheon."

Andy had known about the meeting, but it'd slipped his mind. "Darn," he said as he headed for the assignment board. Nothing about following up on Mrs. Whitley's death. Instead he was instructed to go back to the Westside Apartments for more interviews regarding the gas station burglary. "What a waste of time," he muttered to Roberto, who'd just come in. "The kids are all in school—or should be, and the parents are either working or standing in the unemployment line. Who am I supposed to talk with? Besides, the only thing of value that was taken was a few cartons of cigarettes."

"A common form of currency among teens," Roberto said.

Jerking his head toward the other deputy, Andy asked, "What do you mean?"

"I grew up in those apartments. When kids runs out of cash, they barter with cigs, use them to play poker with. The cigarettes are usually pinched from their folks. If that doesn't work, they steal them."

"Interesting. Hey, since you know so much about it, why don't you take this assignment?"

"And have the sheriff on my case—again? No thanks."

"Well, do you still have contacts there? Someone who might give me a lead?"

"Try Mrs. Scapelli in 115. She's lived there forever and knows everybody. She spends her days looking out at the Dumpster. That's where kids gather to smoke, gamble, and other monkey business. She doesn't bother them unless she thinks one of them is heading for serious trouble. Then she tells the parents."

"She doesn't call the police?"

Roberto shook his head. "Not unless their folks can't or won't handle it." He paused. "She caught me smoking my first weed, told my Mom, and let's just say, my mother knew how to handle it."

Andy laughed. "I bet your mom and Mrs. Scapelli are both proud of you now."

"You better believe it."

"So," he said, "I'll head out that way and meet the woman who set your feet on the right path."

ALLISON AROSE MONDAY morning feeling better than she had in days. She had only one thing on her mind—her husband was even now speeding toward her. Correcting that thought immediately because she knew that Fred never sped anywhere unless he was in a police car chasing a dangerous criminal, she changed it to—driving as fast as the law and conditions allowed. In only a few hours he would be Upton and she would be in his arms.

And then after a suitable time had elapsed and they'd said all the sweet things to each other they'd been saving up, she would tell him of the investigation into Leona's death and of her stalker. At first he would be furious because she hadn't told him earlier, but then he would calm down and put his detective mind to work on the puzzle. Or maybe she would introduce him to Sam and Andy first and let the sheriff fill him in on what had been going on. It didn't matter. Either way, once Fred was on the case, she was sure it would soon be solved.

She snatched up her phone, anxious to hear his voice, to hear how his trip was going, to find out how close he was. Instead of his warm, loving voice, though, a cool, detached woman announced, "if you wish to leave a message…"

"You're darn tootin' I wish to leave a message," she said while waiting for the beep. She then modulated her voice to that of an aggrieved wife, "Honey, if you're driving, pull over immediately and call me back. But if you're lazing in a motel bed, then get up, call me back, and then get on the road." In a softer tone, she added, "I'm waiting for you."

Allison's message floated past the Smoky Mountains, did a square dance through Nashville, slipped into Arkansas, and landed in a snow-filled ditch next to a mangled Avis rental car.

The crash that had propelled the car into the ditch also ripped off the driver's door, tossed Fred's phone out into the cold, and left Fred dangling on his seat belt.

KNOWING FRED WOULD call back as soon as he could, Allison got ready for her day. Her appointment with Leona's attorney, Dewey Vernon, was for nine thirty, and she wanted to look presentable. Even though she hadn't brought many clothes with her from the farm, she picked out a decent pair of slacks and a light-weight sweater. Her parka, however, was the only warm coat she had with her. The dress coat that she'd worn to the funeral hung in the closet at Leona's.

She would never be able to think of the apple orchard and the farmhouse as her own even if that what the will said. In her memory it would always be Whitley's Apple Orchard and her aunt's home—no matter who bought it.

Trying to put the thought out of her mind her eyes went to the piece of newspaper with Molly's phone number. But it wasn't the phone number that caught her attention; it was the unfinished crossword puzzle. She scanned the clues. They didn't seem particularly difficult, and she wondered again why Leona hadn't completed it. But she didn't have time to think about it now.

She tried Fred's number again, left another message. It didn't make sense. If he'd been delayed or was having car trouble, he'd let her know. An icy fear started to seep into her being. Something was wrong. Just as she was about to panic, a possible explanation came to her. He might be in the high country of Tennessee where there was no wireless service. She knew there were many pockets in rural areas where cell phones were useless. That must be it. As soon as he reached a more populous place, she would be hearing from him.

With that comforting thought, she went to a

nearby restaurant for breakfast and then headed for her appointment.

Mr. Vernon showed her the will and stated that aside from some charitable gifts and a substantial donation to her church, the rest of the estate went to her. There was no mortgage and no outstanding debts except current utility bills. He explained the probate process and the waiting period in case any other bills for the estate came in. But, he said, that she could go ahead and list the property.

The signatures and the appropriate witnesses didn't take long and she was soon free to leave the office. It took a few moments for the reality to sink in. She, Allison Aldridge Sawyer, was the owner of a valuable piece of property. Actually, the apple orchard was also a piece of history. Sweet, luscious mountain apples were sold in numerous roadside stands, shipped to stores across several states, enjoyed by thousands.

One part of her psyche—the sentimental part— wanted desperately to keep the orchard intact, to keep the tradition going. At the same time, her practical nature understood the benefit of selling the land to whomever and for whatever.

She had struggled and pinched pennies for years to rear her kids alone. Then came the college years when all three of them took out hefty loans to pay the costs. Both Connie and Dave had gotten some scholarship money and had worked part-time jobs, but they would still face heavy loan payments upon graduation. And unknown to either of them, Allison had tied up most of her retirement money on their education. When she and Fred married, he'd wanted to help pay their tuition, but her foolish pride couldn't accept his offer.

By selling the farm and the equipment, she would be able to erase all their debts, and probably finance the remainder of their studies. It should have been a no-brainer, but she kept hoping someone would come along who wanted the orchard and not just a buffer zone for his ritzy condos. If she could get such a buyer, she would be willing to lower the price. It would be worth losing some money to preserve the heritage. This was also something she had to talk to Fred about once he arrived.

Back in her car, Allison tried Fred's number again. Tears sprang into her eyes when there was no answer, and she didn't feel up to leaving another message.

Vowing not to give in to groundless fears, she hurried back to the Country Inn Motel. Smiling to herself, she admitted she was growing a little fond of the name—and of her room. When Fred got here, she would take him out and show him the farm, but they would come back here for the night. It would be much cozier and more romantic than the big farmhouse. She called the desk and reserved the room for two more nights.

With nothing else to do except wait, she opened Leona's laptop and started going over more of her financial records. Was there anything here that might indicate a motive for her death?

BEFORE LEAVING THE station to go to the Westside Apartments, Andy thought of something else he wanted to do first. He headed over to the file clerk. "I'd like to see the coroner's report on Leona Whitley, please."

"That's not kept here. It's filed with the medical examiner reports."

"But it wasn't a medical examiner's case. It was determined to be an accident."

"Even so, that's where the report goes."

"All right. Then guess I'll have to go across town."

On his way out the door, he stopped at Marie's desk. "Please tell me the sheriff left instructions for you to call the state environmental department to report the Cider Creek pollution."

"Nope. Why would he? Pollution isn't in our job description."

"I know. That's what he told me." Andy rubbed his forehead. He was getting a frustration headache. "But he did say he'd have it reported."

"Than you'll have to remind him this afternoon. I'm sure there's no hurry about it."

He turned to go when Marie handed him a legal looking piece of paper. "What's this?" he asked. She read all the incoming mail, unless it was marked "private," so he knew she'd already digested its contents.

"One of the guys you arrested at the ski lodge is charging you with excessive force."

He stared in disbelief at the paper. "But *he* hit me. All I did was put cuffs on him so he couldn't do it again."

The dispatcher reached over and gave his hand a

motherly pat. "Don't worry about it. You'll be able to explain it all in court."

Andy groaned.

THE LITTLE ROCK first responders had the crash scene well under control. Traffic was detoured around the two cars involved; the EMTs had carefully examined the one unconscious victim, informed the officer that his vital signs were good, and stabilized his head as they strapped him on the gurney.

The other driver was upright and contrite. "I couldn't help it, Officer. I must have hit a patch of ice, couldn't control the car. I swear I wasn't speeding. Is that guy going to be okay?"

"He's breathing. If he wakes up, he might be all right."

"Know who he is?"

"Not yet. Rental car. Texas plates. We'll get his ID. But right now, I need to see your ID and insurance— and check for alcohol."

"Omigawd. You think I was drinking this early in the morning? I was just going to work."

Sergeant Silverman hoped the man was telling the truth. Accidents happen, but he and his partner would do a thorough investigation before coming to any conclusions, including interviewing the injured driver when and if he regained consciousness.

It took a while, but the uninjured driver was cleared of any violation. There was definitely an icy spot that the road crew had failed to sufficiently cover with sand. The driver hadn't been drinking and apparently not speeding. Dismissing him to go on his way, the officer urged him to seek medical help if he developed any problems and to get his car checked even though it didn't appear badly damaged.

Before driving off he asked, "Can I get the other guy's name and the hospital where he's going? I'd like to check and be sure he's going to be all right."

Shaking his head, Sergeant Silverman said, "No. We don't even know his name yet. Check on the news later. They pick up on all the accidents and when we know who he is, they will."

Turning to his partner, the sergeant sighed. "Let's find out who this poor devil is."

First they searched the car and his luggage, found no alcohol or contraband, and tossed the suitcase in their squad car to take to the hospital later. Knowing he could find the driver's ID on the copy of the rental agreement, the sergeant pawed around in the glove compartment.

"Fred Sawyer," he read aloud, "Holliston, North Carolina." He turned to his partner, "Ever hear of Holliston, Mike?"

"Nope. Probably a little burg. Phone number?"

"Just his cell."

"Come on, Tim, how can you tell the difference between a cell and landline number?"

Silverman shoved the paper in front of Mike's face. "Look. Home phone is marked 'NA' while Cell phone has his number. And I'm sure it's his phone because no man would dare put down his wife's number for a car he rented."

"Okay. So we go to the hospital. If he's not awake, we check his phone and you call the first woman listed and hope it's either his wife or current girl-friend."

"Hey, for a rookie, you're learning fast. And I'll give you the job of informing her of the bad news."

Mike shook his head. "I'm not that green. I think protocol states the lead officer calls the next of kin."

Tim shoved the rental papers at Mike. "Then you notify Avis that they have a wrecked vehicle and they can claim it at the impound site."

ANDY DECIDED TO take his time getting to Westside Apartments. Mrs. Scapelli might be a late sleeper, and he didn't want to disturb her. First he would get a copy of the coroner's report he wanted to read.

As he drove down Main Street, he passed the Rob-erson Hardware Store. Did he dare talk to Harry without Sam's approval? Better not. At this point, he wasn't feeling too kindly toward the store owner, and he might mess up the investigation. On the other hand, he thought, maybe I could just have a friendly chat with him—ask how Elmer was getting along. As appealing as that notion was, Andy knew it would not be a wise move. His common sense told him he'd better stay clear of Harry.

So he got on with his other work. He obtained a copy of the coroner's report with no problem. Dr. Franklin had written a thorough and professional report detailing the injuries and the position of the body. Mrs. Whitley had an open wound on her left forehead and a contu-sion on the left side of her head apparently resulting in a depressed skull fracture—both were consistent with falling down the stairs. The accompanying photos showed one of her feet twisted under her and the other one on the second step from the bottom. Her forehead rested on the cement floor where a splotch of blood had oozed around it. She had on jeans and loafers signifying that she had not yet gotten dressed for her evening out. Andy studied the visible shoe that was halfway off her foot. The sole looked well worn, maybe slick. The stairs hadn't been slippery, but maybe her shoes had been. By reading the report, it now seemed to Andy very possible that Leona Whitley had tripped accidentally at the top of the stairs, maybe tried to right herself and then tumbled forward hitting the side of her head on one of the risers and finally striking her forehead against the cement. Dr. Franklin did not specify which blow killed her. But since there was little blood at the scene, it was evident she didn't live long. He'd put the time of death between two and four p.m.

If it hadn't been for the smeared nail polish, and some other inconsistencies, Andy thought he would probably have reached the same conclusion the coroner had. Accidental death.

There was no mention of the nail polish in the report, but the fact of the funeral director mentioning it to Allison confirmed it in his mind. That, along with the desk drawers being rifled, and the undisputable fact that someone had stalked Allison afterwards, added up to a suspicious death. Legally, it probably couldn't be classified as a homicide yet, but Andy was sure it soon would be.

As he left the building, the question that had been niggling at his brain since last night came again in full force. Was Allison safe now that she was staying at the motel? What if her stalker knew where she was?

He tried to put his uneasiness about his new friend out of his mind and headed out to the Westside Apartments. He still had an assignment to do. He hoped this Mrs. Scapelli would be able to help him.

The elderly woman answered her door with her cane swinging and her eyes blazing. "What do you want, young man?"

Taking a step back from the door, Andy surveyed the woman in front of him, decided she wasn't going to hit him with her cane, introduced himself, and added, "I'm a friend of Roberto Flores. He used to live here. Do you remember him?"

A slight smile touched her lips, and her eyes softened. "Oh, yes. I remember Roberto. He was quite a scamp, but he got straightened out and made something of himself. Comes around to visit once in a while." She opened the door wider. "Come on in. You say, Roberto sent you?"

"Yes Ma'am." Andy stepped inside, carefully shut the door behind him, and at the same time, turned off his cell phone. He knew instinctively one didn't slam doors around this lady or let phone calls interrupt conversations.

Mrs. Scapelli led Andy into the living room and motioned for him to sit. He chose a wing chair even though the sofa looked more inviting. He was here on police business and didn't want to get too comfortable.

She sat in a rocking chair, started a slow rhythm, and waited for him to explain.

"You see, Roberto told me how you steered him in

the right direction when he was a kid. And I thought you might be able to help another boy before he gets into too much trouble."

She rocked and nodded. "Might. Who is he?"

"That I don't know, but maybe you do." He explained about the gas station break in, about the cigarettes being stolen, and then he showed her a picture of the lad in the gray hooded jacket. "You can't see his face, but maybe you recognize the jacket or something about him."

Mrs. Scapelli studied the picture and started bobbing her head. "Billy. Billy Kimmel. He wears that jacket everywhere. Doesn't have a winter coat. Lives with his mother. He has a father somewhere, but not around here. I see him hanging out over there," she said, pointing to the window and the Dumpster beyond. "Him and a bunch of other boys who don't have anything better to do, gather there after school. They pass those smokes around like they were pure gold." She shook her head. "They'll probably all end up in jail."

Andy agreed with her prediction, but his brain rebelled against the idea. There had to be some way to help, not only Billy, but the others who were drifting into dangerous waters. Andy had grown up with the advantages of close family, moral values, appropriate discipline, and enough money. But where would he be if those had been missing? In Billy's shoes? Maybe he could talk to the sheriff about their department sponsoring some kind of mentoring program. It was something to think about, but right now he had to think about the case at hand.

He rose to leave. "Thank you for your assistance, Mrs. Scapelli. I guess I'll go to the school and see Billy."

On his way to the school, Andy reminded himself an identification of a jacket was hardly enough to accuse Billy of any wrongdoing. He would only talk to the boy and see if he could elicit any further information.

At the school, he explained his mission briefly to the principal and asked him to stay in the room with him and the boy.

Billy entered the principal's office wearing his gray jacket. His eyes had a wary look like that of a cornered animal. Andy introduced himself and reached his hand out to the lad. It apparently took the boy a few seconds to realize he was expected to shake hands with the officer. Andy noticed Billy's hand was small and thin and cold. For just a moment, the deputy wished he could put his arms around the boy and offer him some comfort. Maybe another time and place. Now he had a job to do.

The three sat in chairs on one side of the room. Andy began by saying he was investigating the break in at Lou's Gas Station and wondered if Billy had any knowledge of it.

Glancing the principal, Billy asked, "Do I have to?"

"If you'd rather have your mother here first," the principal said, "we can call her."

Billy's head swung back and forth. "No. Please don't call Mom." He put one hand to his forehead and exhaled deeply. "Course she's goin' to find out anyway." He sat up straighter in his chair. "It was that nut Jerry that ratted on me, wasn't it? I was afraid he'd blab when he saw me in there."

Andy stared at the boy. Was Billy confessing? And who was this Jerry? The deputy tried to play it cool. "What makes you think Jerry told me?"

"Aw, when he's workin' around the apartments, he's always tellin' us kids to behave. Tries to scare us by sayin' he gonna report us. Mom says he's not all there in his head—what with the war and all."

It dawned on Andy that Billy was talking about Jerry Howe—the same Jerry that Allison and he had discussed the day before.

"So," Andy said, "when Jerry saw you at the gas station, you figured he'd report you?"

"Yeah. But maybe I should report him. What was he doin' there snoopin' around that time of night?"

Good question, Andy thought, and one he was going to ask Jerry when he had the chance. He remembered the shadow on the door in the surveillance tape and the car parked there. That must have been Jerry. Interesting.

He pulled his chair closer to Billy. "I'm going to advise you not to say anything else until we contact your mother. She may want to get you a lawyer. In the meantime, I'd like you to come with me to the county sheriff's office."

Billy shrugged. "Sure, why not?"

Driving back to the station, Andy made a detour to the drive-thru at The Biscuit Place. He ordered three ham, eggs and cheese biscuits—two for Billy and one for himself.

"Coffee for me," and turning to the kid, "What do you want to drink?"

"Man, I don't have no money."

"It's on me. I'm hungry and I didn't want to eat in front of you. So, drink?"

"How about a Dew?"

Reaching for the bag and drinks he handed them to Billy. "You hungry?"

"Yeah, a little."

He was sure Billy was more than "a little" hungry. He looked like he seldom had a filling meal. "Well, don't dig in until we get to the station.

They had barely finished eating when Mrs. Kimmel arrived. The school principal had called her at the local hotel where she worked as a housekeeper. She came in looking terrified, and her eyes filled with tears when she saw Billy. Wrapping her son in a hug, Andy heard her murmur, "It'll be all right. It'll be all right."

The sight of that hug was a big relief to Andy. He could see there was love in that home, in spite of whatever else it may lack. He knew now what he had to do and immediately called Lou at the gas station. After a long conversation he came up to the Kimmels with a grin on his face.

"Lou Vickery wants to talk to you. I'm guessing if you apologize, offer to work for him after school to pay restitution, and promise never to get into any more trouble, he'll be willing to drop the charges. What do you say?"

Mrs. Kimmel answered first. "That's wonderful.

I know my boy won't be in trouble again. I'll make sure of that."

The boy nodded. "Yeah, I'll do what Lou says."

"And one more thing," Andy said.

"What's that?"

"Stop smoking. It's bad for your health."

Billy sighed. "Man, you drive a hard deal."

When everything was settled, Andy decided this was one report he was going to enjoy writing up.

But not now. He had to go see Jerry Howe and then take care of some of his own business.

On his way out he told Marie his plans. "I've got to go to the ski lodge, get somebody there to vouch for me in court. I need witnesses to swear I didn't use excessive force with that pudgy drunk."

"That's my boy. You can even take some of my cookies if you need to bribe them."

"And send the whole lot to the hospital? No thanks. Be back by two or so."

"You'd better be or Sam will be looking for you."

FOURTEEN

IT DIDN'T TAKE Allison long to realize Leona's spread-sheets of income and outgo weren't going to be of any use to her. She wasn't an accountant, and if there was anything amiss with the files, she wouldn't know it.

Getting up, she paced the floor, squelched the urge to call Fred one more time, made another pot of coffee. She was sure he would call whenever he could or when he had cell coverage again.

She picked up the unfinished crossword puzzle and wondered again why her aunt hadn't finished it. Allison idly turned the paper over. On the reverse side was an article about a federal government cleanup operation of a big dioxin pollution area near a paper mill. Instantly interested, she read on. It told how dioxin was formed in the process of paper bleaching when chlorine was mixed with wood pulp. She read snatches of the article out loud to herself, "In animal studies, dioxins have caused nerve damage and birth defects," and, "There are a number of sources of contamination, but paper mills are the most significant source."

The words blurred in front of her eyes. Pollution. Paper mill. Dioxin. Is this what had interrupted her aunt's crossword puzzle? A puzzle of another kind? The article referred to an area in a different state, but had Leona connected the pollution in Cider Creek to the Binken Paper Mill? Was pollution possible even though the mill had been closed for years? She recalled driving by the mill yesterday, and Andy pointing out recent tire tracks. Was something going on there?

She needed to call the deputy and see what he made of it. But first she wanted to do some research, learn more about dioxin. Reaching for the laptop, she clicked on the internet.

Before typing in her search words, Allison decided to check and see what her Leona had been reading on the internet. Her fingers flew up from the keyboard in astonishment as she read the contents of previous searches. There was d*ioxinfacts.org* plus a Wikipedia and a government site about dioxin poisoning. The list went on including watchdog and sierra club sites. Her aunt had been researching exactly the same things Allison had intended to do. It was almost as if Leona was speaking to her from the grave, telling her to finish the job.

Clicking on each of the sites, Allison read all about the poison, learned that dioxin was similar to Agent Orange used in Vietnam, found out the many places that had to be cleaned up. She read that dioxin posed no danger to those exposed at low levels, but at high levels it was a deadly poison. Exposure to high levels of the chemical could lead to cancer, liver failure, and in pregnancy it could result in birth defects. She saw no mention of any pollution in the North Carolina mountains, but there was no doubt in her mind that Leona had suspected it.

Did this tie in with her death? Had her aunt told her suspicions to someone? To the wrong person?

Alison pushed back the computer, grabbed her cell phone, and punched Andy's name. She had to tell him this latest development. But again, the person she desperately wanted to talk to didn't answer. She didn't want to go into details on his voice mail and only left a brief message. "This is Allison. I've found something important. I think Leona suspected the pollution was coming from the old paper mill. Call me as soon as possible."

ANDY LEFT THE office in search of Jerry Howe and to hear his side of the story about seeing Billie Kimmel at the gas station—at midnight when both of them should have been home in bed.

He knew the vet lived with a sister and if Jerry wasn't at home, his sister would probably know his whereabouts.

He found Jerry hosing down his car in the driveway. Andy parked on the side of the road and walked on the grass. "Hey, Jerry, remember me?"

Jerry nodded, turned off the water, and dropped the hose. "You're that nice policeman who works for the sheriff. Officer Andy Cox. I'm good at remembering people." He looked back at his car. "Mud don't look good on a black car or a white drive. I try to keep things clean around here."

"You do a good job. I hear you're really good at doing odd jobs around town."

Jerry smiled. "I like to help people. You know what my best job is?"

"No. What's that?"

"Sweeping the sidewalks at the hospital. I go there early every morning and clean them up before people start coming in. Makes it look nice. And then I go back after lunch and pick up all the paper that people toss around."

"Yeah, I heard about that. They're really pleased with the good job you do."

A wave of sadness swept over Andy. Here was a man who went off to fight for his country and came back a wounded child. He wondered if the veteran was getting the benefits and help that he needed from the government.

But now was not the time to go into Jerry's problems. He came directly to the point of his visit. "Did you think you were helping Billy Kimmel when you didn't report him breaking into Lou's Gas Station?"

Jerry dropped his head a moment and scuffed his feet. When he looked up, his face wore a puzzled frown. "Did I do wrong?" He rubbed the back of his hand across his eyes. "Sometimes I don't know what I should do. I want to help people, but I don't always know how."

Andy put his hand on Jerry's shoulder. "I guess we've all had that problem. But, the fact is, if you see somebody breaking the law, you need to report them. Okay?"

"Okay." Jerry shifted his feet again. "Is Billy in trouble?"

"He'll be all right. He's going to work to pay back what he took."

"That's good." Jerry picked up his hose. "I'd better finish my job, or I'll get in trouble with my sister."

Andy turned to go when he noticed the tires on Jerry's car. "And you'll get in more trouble if you don't get some new tires. Those look mighty slick to me."

"I know. I'm going to do that as soon as my next check comes in."

It was only after Andy was several blocks away he realized he'd not ask Jerry why he'd been at the gas station so late at night.

Going back across town to get to Mount Vista Road, Andy drove pass the county sheriff department again and saw Roberto getting out of his patrol car. He pulled into the drive, called out, "Hey Rob, wait a minute."

Roberto waited as Andy got out and came over. "You hear about me getting sued?"

"Yeah, man. That sucks."

"Nothing's dropped on you?"

"Nope. My guys were actually apologetic once I got them in the car."

"Lucky you. I'm going need a witness to vouch for me. You know I didn't strong-arm that fellow."

"I know you, so I know you didn't use any more force than was needed, but I didn't actually see what went down. I was pretty busy at the time."

"Well, I'm on my way to talk to the lodge workers. They called in the ruckus. They had to be watching what went on. I need some help to fight this thing."

"Go for it. I'll back you up as much as possible."

"Thanks. Be back as soon as I can." Andy waved, got in his car and headed toward the mountain top. He slowed when he passed the Whitley Apple Farm. The sign would soon be gone, he thought. Would the orchard be gone, too?

He'd grown up in the eastern part of the state where peaches were the dominant fruit, and his teen spending money had come from various jobs in the peach orchards. It was hot, hard work, but he'd enjoyed it. It was satisfying to work alongside of Mother Nature to produce sweet, succulent fruit. He imagined apple farming would be much the same. An idea began to form in his head.

He and Millie had talked about buying a little acreage, building a house. They wanted to be fairly close to town because of their jobs, but they also wanted space for privacy and room for their intended kids to flourish. His folks, who already loved Millie like a daughter, had offered financial assistance to get them started. Would it be possible?

The idea of the Cox Apple Orchard stayed with him the rest of the way up the mountain. He barely noticed when he passed Silver Lake Park or the old paper mill, but when he drove into the ski lodge parking lot, his mind shifted to the legal summons in his pocket.

The staff at the lodge greeted him warmly. He wasn't only a cop to call in time of trouble but also a frequent skier on to the slopes. Two of the workers were more than happy to testify on his behalf. He began to feel much better about the lawsuit. In light of the evidence, his lawyer might be able to get the case dismissed. If not, Andy felt sure he'd be vindicated.

He left the lodge feeling much better than when he'd arrived. In fact, he was grinning as he rounded the curve by the empty paper mill. However, when he saw the fresh tire tracks in the melting snow and mud, he realized the old paper mill wasn't empty after all. He pulled off to the side of the road and got out. There was no car in sight, but there was a distinct set of new tracks leading into the parking lot and none leaving. If a car had come back out, he reasoned, the ingoing tracks would have been crisscrossed or smudged. The car was probably parked behind the mill.

He hesitated. Should he investigate or call it in and wait for instructions? Probably some kids had found a good place to hang out, drink a few beers, maybe play some poker. He decided to give them a good scare—send them home to their parents with a stern warning. He'd been a kid himself not too long ago. No need to make a big deal out of it.

To the left of the paper mill drive was a grove of trees with a lot of underbrush. Andy drove his car in there until it was nearly hidden from the mill and from the road. He walked up the perimeter of the parking lot, to what must have been the main entrance, and rounded a corner. A black pickup truck was parked by a loading dock.

He crept closer, keeping his head below the windows that lined the outer wall of the building. He got nearly to the dock when he heard voices—deep, rough voices. He paused. These didn't sound like kids.

Bending closer to the ground, Andy pulled out his gun as he came nearer to the dock. He couldn't make out what they were saying except for several cusswords. Their voices got louder each time one of them swore. He was certain there were only two men. He could surprise them and keep them covered while he called for backup. Whatever they were doing here, he was sure it wasn't legal.

He was at the bottom of the stairs leading up to the dock and he could see the tops of their heads. Cautiously and quietly he climbed the few steps. The two men came into view. They were each carrying a large pail that appeared to be filled with liquid.

"This crap gets heavier with every bucket," one of them grumbled. "I've about had my fill for today." They went to the end of the platform and lifted the buckets.

Andy could tell they were about to pour whatever was in the pails into Cider Creek that flowed below the dock. He sprang up the steps. "Stop right there. Put the pails down, raise your hands, and turn around. Slowly." He kept his gun trained on the two as they obeyed his orders.

They seemed surprised but not scared. And they didn't look dangerous. Two middle-aged men, dressed in decent jeans and jackets stared at him. One was tall and thin. The other was tall and muscular. He didn't recognize either.

Muscles spoke up. "What's going on here?"

Waving his gun at them, Andy said, "I'm the law, and I get to ask the questions. Who are you and what are you up to?"

The skinny one started to lower his hands. "We can explain."

Whatever was going to be his explanation, Andy didn't hear it. The back of his head exploded with pain; he felt his gun flying out of his hand and his body falling to the floor. He sank into an ocean of blackness.

FIFTEEN

AFTER SOME DELAY Sergeant Tim Silverman and his partner were at the hospital where the accident victim had been taken. They had hoped to find him awake and alert. It didn't happen.

Upon their arrival they talked to the doctor, was told the patient was not conscious, but his vital signs were good and he had no broken bones. She suspected Mr. Sawyer would awaken within the next few hours. If not, they would do an EEG to determine his brain function. "It's my opinion he'll come out of this with nothing more than a headache."

Mike asked, "But you did draw blood for alcohol and drugs?"

The doctor looked slightly insulted. "Of course. That's routine in cases like this."

The unit secretary gave the officers the inventory of the patient's personal property and stayed close by while they went through the items. There was no cell phone. "This is it?" Mike asked. "Where's his phone?"

"If it isn't listed, it wasn't there."

"But we searched the car. It wasn't in there."

She shrugged. Her message was plain, *Not my problem.*

"Did you get the name of an emergency contact?"

She studied the papers in front of her. "The only

info we have is what the EMTs gave us: name, address, date of birth. I guess they got that off his driver's license."

Mike spoke up. "Reckon we better go through his personal effects again, Tim?"

"Not now. It'll be simpler to wait until he wakes up. The doctor said it should be soon."

Giving the secretary a number, he said, "Please call as soon as he's awake."

ALLISON WAS SLOWLY going mad with worry, with frustration, with indecision. But it was the worry that topped everything. Something bad had happened to Fred. She knew it. Even if he hadn't gotten her messages, he would have called by now. It was nearing noon. If he'd kept to his original plans he should be close to the North Carolina border, probably less than a hundred miles from Upton. He would have called with excitement in his voice, telling her to get ready for an over-the-top kiss, or that if he got a ticket for speeding it would be her fault because he couldn't wait to see her. And if he hadn't been able to keep to his schedule due to car trouble or slick roads, he certainly would have called to explain his delay. Allison's brain had no choice but to conclude that she hadn't heard from Fred because he was unable to call.

Trying her best to conjure up benign reasons for his lapse, she imagined some pretty bizarre scenes: he'd been caught in a traffic jam and had to sit for hours while the battery of his cell phone ran down because he'd forgotten to pack his charger, or he'd pulled off on the roadside to rest his eyes when he was accosted, and his car, wallet and phone were stolen. After a bit, though, she knew she had to stop playing games, and she braced herself for the dreaded phone call from a hospital or a police station.

She deliberately forced her mind in another direction by wondering what Andy was up to that he couldn't answer his phone or return a message. Maybe, she thought, I should give my information regarding Leona's research into dioxin pollution from paper mills directly to the sheriff. No need to mention about her and Andy's little investigation yesterday.

If only she had someone to talk to: about her fears, her stress. She knew both Connie and Dave were in class, and even if she did talk to them, she wouldn't be able to share her concerns. Her kids had come to love Fred as their own father and she couldn't worry them about what might have happened to him. She hadn't heard from Claire, didn't know how the visit from her wayward husband had gone, and figured her friend might have enough trouble of her own to handle.

Allison crawled up onto the bed, propped pillows behind her back, pulled the spread up to her chin, closed her eyes. She went to the sacred place within her soul—halfway between meditation and prayer. Evoking images of peace, of beauty, of serenity, she slowed her breathing, remembered the words, "Let not your heart be troubled." Very slowly her fears ebbed, her trust returned: trust in the cosmos, trust in herself.

ANDY SHIVERED. He was cold. He hurt in more places than he could name. He stunk. Or maybe the awful smell didn't come from him, but his nose was right in it. Slowly the gears in his brain started to grind as he tried to figure out why he was lying face down on a linoleum floor that smelled like a chemistry experiment gone bad.

He slowly opened his eyes and could see a faint light that seemed to come from his left. He had to get up. But how could he stand when his hands and his feet had disappeared? He attempted to make sense of his situation. It was several seconds later when his memory kicked in. He'd stopped at the mill to roust some kids from their merrymaking. Instead, he'd been conked on the head and hauled into this room by two—make that three—men. The third man must have hit him while he held the other two at gun point. So much for being a hero.

They had tied his hands behind his back and trussed his feet together. He might as well forget about trying to stand, but maybe he could turn over. Maybe get a better look at his prison and his situation—a situation which he recognized as being perilous, if not dire. What had he walked into? And more importantly, what did his captors intend to do with him? He tried to push those questions out of his mind. As scared as he was, right now he had to concentrate on getting free and the first step was to turn over.

He tried rocking from side to side hoping to get enough momentum to flip over. It didn't work. On to plan B. He moved his hands up his back so his elbows were more at an angle. He might be able to prop up on one elbow and twist over that way. He hoisted his knees upward to use as a fulcrum. He had a lot of upper body strength; he could do this thing. With one mighty heave, he thrust his body onto one elbow and then over on his back. He'd done it.

Looking around, he could see he was in a small office. There was a desk, a rolling desk chair, and a tall filing cabinet. The light he'd noticed came from a transom over a door at the far side of the room. He saw a small, high window on the opposite wall but it was covered by a dark curtain. Around the edges of the curtain, slivers of sunlight slipped in, so it must still be daylight, but he had no idea how long he'd been here, how long he'd been unconscious.

Thankfully, he'd told Marie he planned to be back by two, and he'd also told Roberto he'd be back soon. So at some point in time, someone would start missing him, maybe start worrying about him, and maybe even start searching for him. He wondered, though, how long all those maybes would take.

But where would they search? He realized there would be no reason for anyone in the department to suspect he was at the old paper mill. And like a fool, he'd hidden his car amongst some trees and shrubs so it couldn't be seen from the road even if someone was looking for it. At the time, it seemed like a good idea—just like it seemed like a good idea to try to catch some kids goofing off at the mill. Dumb! Dumb!

The enormity of his problem nearly overwhelmed him. He was being held prisoner by men who, he was sure, had no intention of letting him go. He was a witness to their presence here and to their probable unlawful activity. He'd seen two men about to dump something in the creek that ran by the mill, the same creek that ran by the Silver Lake condos and past the Whitley apple orchard. It didn't matter that he didn't know what the substance was, it was apparent the dumping was being done secretly and that they would want to keep it that way. That fact made him a danger to them.

He was alone, and he had no idea how he was going to get out of this mess.

Closing his eyes to think, Millie's face swam into view. He blanked everything else out and thought only of the girl he loved—her blonde ponytail, her smattering of freckles, her greenish-blue eyes, her stubbornness, her faith. That was the message she was sending: he needed to have faith and to be stubborn. *Yes, Millie. I will get out of here. Somehow. Someway.*

A door slammed close by and loud voices floated over the transom. His captors must have been out of the building and now had come back in. Andy tensed expecting them to come into the room where he lay. He could pretend to be still unconscious, but surely they would notice he was on his back rather than face down as they'd left him.

However, there seemed to be no movement toward the door of his room. He listened intently. Maybe he could hear something of their plans. A voice Andy decided belonged to Muscles asked of the others, "Why doesn't the boss call? I don't want to sit here all night."

"We'll get a call. Don't get antsy." That voice didn't sound familiar to Andy—more guttural than either of the men who had been on the loading dock. It must belong to the third man, the one who had cocked him on the head. Thinking back on what he felt just prior to losing consciousness, he concluded he must have been struck him with the butt of a gun—which meant they were armed. Not a good thought.

The man had told the others they would get a call. That meant they were waiting for orders. That's good, Andy thought. The longer, the better. Give me more time to try to escape. He started working the rope on his hands. Maybe he could loosen it enough to slip one hand out.

"To heck with all this waiting," the man Andy had dubbed "Skinny" said. "I say we load this cop in his car and roll him off a cliff. They'll think he dozed off and went over the side. Happens all the time."

"Good idea," Muscles said. "Dumb cop like that deserves to run off the side of a mountain. Thinking he could hide his car from us and sneak up like we were a bunch of dodos."

Third man gave a deep laugh. "Actually, you two did look like a couple of dodos when I came out. He had you covered good. But it would be easier just to shoot him with his own gun."

A tremor went through Andy's body. These guys weren't kidding. His time was running out. He shut his eyes, worked his hands faster, and started praying.

"Yeah," one of them said. Andy stopped trying

to decipher who was saying what. It didn't matter. He just had to get away from here before they carried out any of the plans. "Make it look like he done himself in. Cops are always under a lot of pressure, and it got too much for him."

Andy shook his head. No way would anyone believe he committed suicide. He wanted to yell out to them that they'd better wait for orders from the boss—whoever that was. In the meantime the rope around his hands seemed to be loosening. He used all his strength to try to stretch it more.

"I've got his cell phone," a voice said. "I could call 911, disguise my voice, and say I'm ending it all." He cackled at his plan.

"Gimme that phone," Third man shouted. His deep voice was unmistakable and it was obvious he was the one in charge. "You ain't making no calls and we're not killing anyone—yet."

Hearing what seemed like a slight tussle, Andy wondered what was happening to his phone.

In a moment, Third man's voice, louder than ever, again came over the transom. "Hey, he's got voice mail. Let's see who's been calling him."

Andy froze. Voice mail! He'd forgotten he'd turned his phone off while seeing Mrs. Scapelli. Who had called him and would they keep trying? Someone who might know he was in trouble if he didn't answer?

"Put it on speaker, so we can hear it too," one of the others said.

Allison's voice came through loud and clear, "This is Allison. I've found something important. I think

Leona suspected the pollution was coming from the old paper mill. Call me as soon as possible."

So that's what got Leona killed, Andy thought, and since I now have the same knowledge, it's going to get me killed if I can't get these ropes off.

His attention was brought back to the men in the other room. "Who is this gal?" demanded Third Man. "And how does she know so much?"

"Reckon she knows it's us doing the dumping? Was that why the copper was snooping around?"

"Looks like we have more than one person to worry about," the head man said. "Better call and let the boss know we have another trouble maker."

Andy recoiled. This was Allison they were talking about. Another trouble maker to worry about? No, his soul cried out. She can't end up in the hands of these goons. Allison had become like a second mother to him, he couldn't let her be hurt.

He tried to calm himself. He had to think. They had heard her voice, her first name. That's all. They didn't know her last name or where she was. How could they get to her? Her telephone number was on his phone, but surely they wouldn't have the brains to call her and lure her out here. She would be too smart to fall for that trick. Wouldn't she?

A door slammed, and the light that had shown through the transom disappeared. Of course. It had been from a flashlight or a lantern since the old mill wouldn't still have electricity.

The near darkness of the room and the silence covered Andy like a funeral shroud. He dropped his head back, and for a moment, he felt defeated. But only for a moment. He couldn't give up. He'd never give up. Continuing his efforts to free himself, he inched his way up against the wall until he was in a near sitting position. His head swam dizzily as if he just gotten off a Whirly-Gig at the carnival. He'd been lying nearly flat on the floor for so long it took a while for his body to adjust. When his brain settled down, he went to work on his wrist restraints again. By leaning forward he had more room to work, and he thought he was making progress.

A short time later, he heard voices and feet tramping into the room next door. Then the door to where he was imprisoned burst open. An intense light shone on his face. He blinked his eyes and squinted against the glare.

"So you finally woke up? Now you can answer some questions."

It was the voice of Third Man that Andy hadn't gotten a look at yet, the one who had knocked him out. He tried to look around the light to the man holding it. All he could make out was a vague form, maybe shorter and older than the other two. Nothing about him seemed familiar. Who were these thugs? They weren't any of the local riff-raff he'd run into in Upton.

The man propped the flashlight up on the desk, came over to deputy, and kicked his legs. "I said, 'now you can answer some questions.'"

Andy decided to play dumb. He answered groggily, "Where am I? What happened?" The words came out slurred, and that wasn't pretending on his part. His throat was so parched he could barely move his tongue. "Water. Need water."

Third Man jerked his head at Skinny. "Get him some water."

"Ain't no water in here," Skinny said.

"The jug. Get some out of the jug in the back of the truck. Do I have to draw you a picture?"

Doors crashed opened and shut as Skinny went to carry out his orders. He was clearly unhappy. Maybe, Andy thought, he could play one against the other and gain some time. It was worth a try.

Skinny returned with a quart jar about half full and smacked it down on the desk. Andy eyed it longingly. Weren't they going to give him any? He wiggled his tongue around inside his mouth trying to work up some saliva so he could talk. "Hands. Hands tied."

Muscles let out a giggle. "Hey, man, we know your hands are tied. I did the job myself. Now you want me to untie them?"

He managed a, "Please."

"Hear that? He said, "'Please.'" Muscles stood over him and sneered. "Reckon he could say, 'Pretty please?'"

"Cut the crap," Third Man said. "Untie him and let him have the water. Then we'll see what else he has to say."

His hands loosed, his thirst quenched, Andy tried for one more prize. Ignoring the gun pointed at him, he said to Third Man. "I've got to go to the john."

"Fine. Untie his feet, take him outside. But know this, copper, if you try to run, I'll shoot both your legs."

Muscles was clearly unhappy as he yanked out a jackknife, slashed through the rope around Andy's ankles, and jerked him to his feet. Needles seemed to have pierced the soles of his shoes as his feet hit the floor and, at the same time, his head started to sway.

A string of curses filled the small room followed by, "Move it. I'm not here to play nursemaid to ya."

Andy gained enough equilibrium to move to the door, then to follow Skinny to another door that led to the loading dock. Third Man trailed behind. Even though he couldn't see the gun, Andy knew it was aimed at his back. There was no chance of trying to escape.

Squinting against the bright sunlight, Andy took a deep breath of the blessed fresh air. It was cold, but it sure smelled better that what he'd been breathing for the past hour or so. Skinny motioned him to the end of the dock. He complied, did what he came here to do, and turned slowly around. Taking his time, he studied the surroundings: the creek flowing by in back, thick woods on both sides of the open parking area, and the long driveway leading to Mount Vista Road. He decided that when he did make his escape, his only hope of not being caught would be either along the creek bank or wading to the other side of the creek. Neither seemed too hopeful, but he kept faith with his vision of Millie and his promise not to give up.

He glanced quickly at the sun, tried to gauge its descent. He figured it must be about three. That meant there were maybe two or two and a half hours before darkness would start creeping in. Then what?

Third Man came up to him, punched him in the ribs with the gun. "Now you better be willing to talk if you want to keep on living." He let out his bottom-of-the-barrel laugh. "'Course I won't kill you right away because I want to witness the reunion between you and your girl."

Reunion? Girl? Had they found Allison? Did they think she was his girlfriend? Or was Third Man bluffing? Andy tried to keep his voice calm. "What girl you talking about? I've got gals scattered all over the county."

"Sure you have. But I doubt many of them leave you messages about pollution."

This time they tied him into the desk chair. It was more comfortable than lying on the floor, but they crisscrossed the ropes in and out of the chair back and between its legs. His spirits plummeted even lower than they had been as he figured he'd have to be a Houdini to untie that maze of knots.

Andy endured several minutes of Third Man's questions, threats, and a few boot kicks. He stuck to his story of thinking some kids were using the abandoned mill for a hangout and only wanted to scare them into leaving. He had no idea of what else was going on.

He refused to tell them anything about Allison, and denied knowing anything about pollution. "As far as I know, you men were simply cleaning out an old building. Nothing wrong with that."

"You had your chance, copper," Muscles sneered at him. "I don't think you'll be so cocky when we bring your girl in."

They were bluffing, Andy told himself. There was no way they could get to Allison.

When they couldn't get anything else out of him, Third Man got up and left the room. Muscles took his foot and kicked the chair across the room, slamming Andy into the wall. "Have a good afternoon," he said.

As soon as his captors left the room, Andy again started working to loosen his restraints. He had to get loose to help Allison if these guys actually did find her and bring her here. The thought of his friend being held captive and perhaps harmed was unbearable, and he'd do anything to protect her just as he would his own mother.

He jerked up when he heard the outside door slam and then heard the truck start up. Were they leaving him alone, or was one of them staying to guard him? Not that it made any difference. No matter how hard he tried, he couldn't seem to loosen the ropes that bound him.

But he kept twisting and pulling and yanking on them. When he caught himself thinking about giving up, he'd bolt upright and start in again with renewed determination.

He gaze went to the old filing cabinet and he managed to scoot his chair closer thinking he might find some sharp edges that could be used to saw at his ropes. The curtain at the one small window kept out most of the sunlight so it was too dim to see much. Scooting the chair even closer, he bent his head over and ran his cheek up and down the edges, but he couldn't find anything sharp or jagged or movable. The cabinet may be old, but it wasn't rusted or falling apart. Where else could he look for help?

ALLISON'S MEDITATION WAS interrupted by the shrill ring of her phone. She opened her eyes, lifted them heavenward. "Thank you, thank you. I know it's Fred. It has to be him." She scooted to the dresser, snatched up the phone. Expecting Fred's voice, she let out a gusty, "Hello."

A soft female voice asked, "Mrs. Sawyer?"

As her world tumbled around her, Allison managed to reply, "Yes, I'm Allison Sawyer."

The voice sounded slightly familiar, but she wasn't concerned about who was calling, Allison only wanted to be assured that it wasn't bad news—that nothing had happened to Fred.

"I'm calling from Upton Community Hospital. We have Deputy Andy Cox in the emergency room. He's been injured, and he's asking to see you. He says it's important."

It took a few seconds for Allison's brain to respond to the message. It wasn't Fred. It was Andy. Her emotions went up and down like a yoyo: relief that it wasn't her husband who'd been injured, concern for her friend, and puzzlement as to why Andy was asking for her.

"What happened? Is he hurt badly?"

"I don't know any details, but his condition is listed as serious. I'm the unit secretary and was asked to call you. Can you come?"

"Of course I'll come. I'll leave right away. But how bad is he?"

Silence hovered over the phone for a few seconds and then the woman said, "I've got to go. I'll tell the doctor you're on your way."

Questions swirled around in Allison's head, as she grabbed her coat, purse, and keys. *Had Andy been hurt in the line of duty? How serious was his condition? Serious was better than critical, wasn't it? And why hadn't Sam called her instead of a secretary? Or was Andy just taking this mother substitute thing a little too far?*

She knew her questions would have to wait. The important thing now was to get to him. But if he'd asked her there just to hold his hand while the doctor stitched him up a little, she was going to put an end to this nonsense. She had enough to worry about without tending to a kid who missed his mama and his girlfriend.

In record time she careened into the hospital parking lot, skidded to a stop outside the emergency room, and jumped out of her car. Before she could get to the door, Molly Kirkman was by her side.

"I'm sorry, Allison. He's not here."

Allison's hands flew over her mouth; she gaped at the woman in front of her. *What was going on here? Had Andy's injuries been worse than the secretary had let on? Had he died before having a chance to tell her what was so important? And where were Sam and his fellow deputies?*

Molly grasped her arm. "He's being transferred to the medical center in Asheville. The ambulance just left with him."

The breath escaped out of Allison's lungs, and she planted a hand on her heaving chest. "Than he's alive?"

"Yes. He's alive. But…but his condition got worse. They had to move him quickly." She shoved Allison toward the passenger seat. "Get in. I'll leave my car here and drive yours."

Allison moved as in a daze. Things were moving too fast. What had happened to make them transfer Andy? The Upton hospital was small, but it was equipped with the latest technology, and their doctors were excellent. She climbed in and handed her keys to Molly before she thought to ask, "What are you doing here?"

Before answering, Molly started the car and drove out of the parking lot. "I'm on the hospital board and do some volunteer work. I was in emergency room when they brought the deputy in. He didn't look that bad at first and I heard him ask the nurse to call you. Frankly, I was surprised. I didn't know the two of you were such good friends."

"We're not. It's just… Oh, it doesn't matter. Just tell me what happened."

"I really don't know. As a volunteer, I just try to make myself useful to the patients and families in the waiting area—you know, bring them coffee and stuff. Then I heard the doctor talking about transferring him to Asheville, and I heard the secretary call you, so I knew you were coming." Molly shrugged. "That's why I got my coat and came out to meet you. I thought you shouldn't drive by yourself to Asheville."

Allison pulled herself together enough to smile at Molly. "Thank you. You were a dear friend to Leona, and now you're coming to my aid. That's so sweet of you."

Molly nodded, "Glad to do anything I can." She

reached over, took Allison's purse and tossed it in the back seat. "That will give you more room."

"But my phone. I'm expecting a call from Fred."

"Don't worry about it. You can reach it if it rings. Just sit back and relax."

Allison knew she couldn't relax. The calmness she'd achieved during her quiet session was completely shattered. Her nerves were a wreck, her mind was full of questions, her heart ached to think of Andy being seriously injured, and most of all, she was still in limbo about Fred's whereabouts and condition.

She dropped her head back and closed her eyes, but it only made things worse as her brain threw another question at her. *If Molly was in the waiting room fetching coffee for visitors, how could she have heard the doctor's plans to transfer Andy?*

Opening her eyes, Allison started to ask Molly that question when she noticed they were on Mount Vista Road. She leaned forward in alarm. "You said we were going to Asheville. Why aren't you heading for I-40?"

"We'll take the back road. It's shorter."

"But no one drives that road in winter. It's too dangerous."

Molly kept her hands clenched on the steering wheel and didn't look in Allison's direction. "It's fine. Snow's all gone."

"Well, okay then." Allison was uneasy about the road conditions past the ski lodge, but decided not to interfere with Molly's driving.

She leaned back and her eyes went to her side mirror. A small, black car was behind them. Molly was driving over the limit and this car was pretty much matching her speed, staying behind them but in view. She turned to Molly. "I think a car may be following us. He's been back there quite a while."

"Of course, he's following us. I'm going too fast for him to pass."

Allison nodded, but still it made her uncomfortable. She watched it for a few minutes and wondered why it looked familiar. Twisting around in her seat, she looked out the back window to get a better view. She gasped, quickly turned back around, and slid down in her seat. "Molly, that's the same car that followed me a few days ago. I'm positive."

Glancing in the rearview mirror, Molly said, "Plenty of black cars around. Nothing for you to be concerned about. Just forget it."

"You're right. I guess I'm so nervous I can't think straight."

When they sped by Leona's farm several minutes later, neither of them commented. Now was not the time to talk real estate. Soon they rounded the curve past Silver Lake Park and continued up the mountain. Allison rested her head again on the back of the seat, but she kept her eyes on the side mirror. The black car was still following.

She jerked up when Molly suddenly slowed down and made a quick right turn. Puzzled, Allison scanned the area. They had left the road and were driving toward a large brown building. Her throat went dry. They were headed toward the abandoned Binken Paper Mill.

The car slowed even more and Allison grabbed

Molly's hand on the steering wheel. "What...why are we stopping here?"

Molly knocked her hand away. "You'll see." The car stopped only a few feet away from stairs leading to a raised platform.

Allison watched in fear as two men ran down the steps toward them. One snatched open her door, seized her arm, and dragged her from the car. She turned her head to Molly. "Help me. Help...." Her plea was cut short when one of the men covered her mouth with a huge paw.

At that same moment, her phone rang from the confines of her purse in the back seat. *Fred. It has to be Fred. I've got to get it.*

She heard Molly call out to the men as the car was turning around, "Be sure you keep her out of the way so she can't mess things up."

Her car was gone. Her phone was gone. Her supposed friend was gone. What was happening?

She kicked, she clawed, she tore at their clothes—all to no avail. The men were bigger and stronger, and they had their marching orders.

SIXTEEN

AFTER THEIR LUNCH BREAK, not having heard anything from the hospital, the Little Rock police officers went back there. The nurse met them with a shake of her head. "Nothing yet. The doctor thought he'd be coming around by now."

"Might be worse off then anybody figured," Sergeant Tim Silverman said. "We really need to get in touch with some of his family. Let me see his wallet again. He's got to have some kind of info in there."

The nurse instructed the secretary to let the officers see Mr. Sawyer's personal effects again. They took the envelope to the waiting room and found two comfortable chairs. Tim started with the wallet. "Here we go," he said as he pulled a card out. "He works for the county sheriff's department."

"He's a brother?"

"Not exactly. It says, 'Fred Sawyer. School and Law Enforcement Liaison.' They ought to be able to tell us about his next of kin." He called the number on the card.

It took a while, but Tim explained about the accident, told what he knew of Mr. Sawyer's condition and their need to notify Mrs. Sawyer or whoever was listed as an emergency contact. He was given Mrs. Sawyer's number as well as the number of the school where she worked. The gentleman on the other end of the line explained, "If she's in class, she won't be able to take a call. Probably be better to call the office and they can get her a message."

"Thank you, I'll do that."

But when he called the office, the secretary informed him they didn't have a Mrs. Sawyer working there. Tim was too tired to be very polite. "She has to be working there; I was given this number for Fred Sawyer's wife, Allison."

After a pause, the secretary laughed. "Oh, you mean Allison Aldridge. She goes by her professional name here. Sawyer is her married name."

"Can you get her to the phone for me? I have an important message."

"No. That is, I would be glad to, but she's not here."

"Not there?"

"No, she had to go to her aunt's funeral. Somewhere in the mountains. Now, let me think a minute."

Tim let her think, afraid if he said anything, it might prolong his agony.

In a few moments, she said, "Upton. That's the name of the town. Upton, North Carolina. You can call her there. I'll give you her cell phone number."

"I have that number. Thanks so much for your help."

Tim quickly punched in the number and after several rings was told he could leave a message. Not wanting to shock the lady with the bad news, he left the hospital number and asked her to call regarding her husband.

Leaving word to be notified the minute Mr. Sawyer woke up, Tim motioned to Mike, "Lets get out of here before they have to admit me for severe case of frustration."

THE FAINT LIGHT entering the room from the small window was getting fainter, and the room was getting colder. What had happened to the sunshine a while earlier? Even though Andy had his heavy jacket on, he could feel the frigid air seeping in. Was there a cloud cover heralding another snow storm, or was it simply cooling off as late afternoon approached? As he kept working at loosening his bounds, he tried to keep his thoughts off from Allison. Surely, there was no way they could get to her? Or was there? Is this where her stalker came in? But that doesn't make a bit of sense. It wasn't until the men had heard her message that they knew she might connect them to the pollution. And what was this poison were they dumping into Cider Creek and sending downstream? Would it kill off the fish population, the wildlife that drank from the creek banks, the people who maybe played and splashed in its waters? Had Allison found the answers to questions such as these and had called to tell him?

It wasn't long before Andy heard the truck pull up to the building. His captors were back. What would happen to him now?

To his surprise no one came immediately into the building. He strained to hear any noise from the dock. What was going on out there? Had another vehicle driven in? Yes, there were slamming doors and faint voices, but he couldn't determine whose voices they were or what was said.

In a few moments, the outside door opened and shut. Footsteps headed in his direction. Andy sat up as straight as possible—ready to face whatever might be happening.

His door flew open, but no one entered. He stared at the vacant space. His heart beat faster; his breaths became shallower; he licked his dry lips. A blur of color appeared in the doorway, but before Andy could focus on who it was, the person was thrust forward into the room. She tripped and fell face down in front of his chair.

Andy wanted to scream as he recognized who it was, but no sound came out. Tears slid down his face as Allison looked up at him. "I'm so sorry," he said. "I should have protected you."

Skinny came up, grabbed Allison's arm, and heaved her to her feet. She pulled free and rushed to Andy. "They told me you were in the hospital, and I came to see you."

"Who told you?"

Third Man pounced on her, seized both her arms and pinned them behind her back. "We're the ones going to be asking the questions. She's going to another room where she'll be tied up until we find out what you two know about our operation here."

Allison tried to escape from his grip. "Let me go," she yelled. "I don't know what you're talking about. Why did Molly bring me here?"

Andy's brain did a double take. Molly? He recalled the tall, muscular woman he'd met at the Arts

Council event—much bigger and stronger than Allison. But she was supposed to be a family friend; what could Molly have to do with all this?

Before he could think further, Third Man shoved Allison to the door. He motioned for Muscles. "Come on. I need your expertise to get this gal settled."

"I'll get her settled all right. Nice and tight."

Allison struggled and kicked until Muscles drew back his hand and slapped her across the face. She let out a cry and dropped her head. Third Man yanked her out into the hall and the door rattled shut.

Andy squinted his eyes shut and clenched his fists. He had to stay calm. He had to think. Since he couldn't get loose, maybe he could do something to get their attention away from Allison. He eyed the filing cabinet again. It was four drawers tall but looked to be only a little more than a foot wide. If he could get it off balance, maybe he could tip it over and cause enough noise to get the men back in here. If they hadn't tied her up yet, Allison might have a chance to get away.

Thank goodness they'd put him in a desk chair with wheels. He pointed his toes down until they touched the floor. By pushing on his toes he was able to very slowly rotate around so the back of the chair was toward the side of the cabinet. Then by leaning back as far as possible and moving his toes, he moved closer to his goal. He told himself he could do this thing. He could create a diversion and give his friend a chance.

He stopped several inches from the cabinet, leaving space enough for him to rock back and forth.

Each time, the chair swung backward a little further. Now. This was it. He plunged the chair against the metal cabinet. It shuddered. It rocked. It settled back down with a muffled thud.

He moaned. It has to work. It just has to. One more time. He moved the chair into position again. He closed his eyes. He squared his shoulders. Using every bit of strength he possessed, he plowed the chair backward.

He heard the creak of metal. He heard the drawers crack open. The cabinet swayed away from him. Then it swayed back—and it didn't stop. It toppled over. But not in the direction he had intended.

The heavy metal cabinet fell on top on him—crushing the chair—crushing him—trapping him underneath. The top drawer fell out, making a resounding crash and spewing papers over the floor.

Andy had seen the flutter of papers. He'd heard the crashing noise. And he'd felt a searing pain—just before the blackness took him away.

SHERIFF SAM BABCOCK strolled into his county department, winked at Marie, and snatched a peanut butter cookie.

"What? They didn't feed you in Charlotte?"

"Not anything as good as you make."

"In that case, have another one."

He did, and asked, "Everything okay?"

"Of course. We missed you, but managed to struggle by."

"Good. Andy find out who did the gas station caper?"

"Sure did. Brought the kid in and then released him to his mother."

"Didn't book him? That doesn't sound right. Let me read that report."

Marie hesitated. "Well, you can't right now. Andy said he'd be back and do it later."

"How much later? Where'd he go?" Sam frowned. "Can't I go away for a few hours without people goofing off?"

Marie matched Sam's frown and did him one better. "Sir, people here do not goof off. Andy went to the ski lodge to interview witnesses of his scuffle Friday night with the inebriated gentleman, who turned out not to be a gentleman, because he's suing."

"I see. And when is he expected back?"

Marie glanced at the wall clock that was edging toward three-thirty. She grimaced. "Two."

"Better give the lodge a call. Maybe they started celebrating early."

FRED SAWYER'S EYES flickered open. He stared at the white ceiling, twisted slightly and stared at the white walls, lifted his head a little and stared at the bars on the side of his bed and at the IV running into his left arm.

His head was throbbing and in trying to find a reason for the pain, he used his right hand to explore the area. His fingers encountered what felt like a bandage.

Fred's thirty years experience as a detective had not been wasted as he immediately deduced he was in a hospital and that he had a head injury. Unfortunately, he had no idea of where the hospital was located or of what caused his injury. But he was determined to find out.

Locating the call bell tied to the side rail, he gave it a punch. Instead of a pretty young nurse rushing into the room to see what he needed, a husky male voice emanated from somewhere above his head with the question, "How may I help you?"

"Where am I and what's wrong with me?" The words came out sounding weak and wobbly to his ears—more like a lost kid than a grown man demanding answers. Thus he came to his second deduction. Whatever had happened to him must have been pretty bad.

The disembodied voice tried to reassure him. "A nurse is on her way in, Mr. Sawyer. She can explain everything."

He took comfort in the fact they knew his name. That probably meant they'd called Allison and if she wasn't already here, she would be soon. Maybe she'd just stepped out to get a Snickers bar. As far as he knew, her chocolate craving was the only vice she had. Otherwise, she was perfect: lovely, strong, funny, and she could make him feel twenty years younger. He hadn't yet figured out why she'd agreed to marry a crusty old bachelor.

As promised, a nurse hustled into the room, and she was, as he had imagined, young and pretty. In addition, she was smiling as if she'd won the lottery. She came up to the bedside, patted his hand, studied the monitor above the bed, checked his pulse and blood pressure, and said, "So glad you decided to wake up. How you feeling?"

"Like I lost a bout with a sledge hammer."

"According to the police, your car flew into a ditch. Your head must have hit the door or dashboard. The airbag softened the blow and, like a good boy, you had your seat belt fastened, so it wasn't too bad. A minor concussion."

"I hate to think how I would feel if it were anything major. Can I get anything for this monster of a headache?"

"Soon. I've notified the doctor of your return from dreamland. She'll want to examine you before we give you any medication. And the police, too."

Fred scowled. "What about the police?"

"They'll want to know what you remember about the accident."

"That's easily told. If I was in an accident, I have absolutely no memory of it. So they'll have to tell me what happened."

An older woman wearing a white coat, a stethoscope dangling out of one pocket, and carrying a chart brushed by the nurse, came to stand close to his head. "I'm Doctor Holliday, the neurologist. Tell me the last thing you do remember."

Brushing back some dark hair flecked with gray that had escaped from a thick braid and without waiting for his answer, she pulled an otoscope out of a pocket. Using its focused light, she checked his eyes and his ears. Apparently satisfied, she stepped back and said, "Well?"

Fred knew this was a woman who didn't go in for

small talk, so he answered her previous question. "I was coming into Little Rock, traffic was picking up, and I was looking for I-40 East." He shrugged. "That's it. I don't remember any crash or accident or being brought here. Am I still in Little Rock, or did they ship me someplace else?"

At that question, Dr. Holliday allowed herself a slight smile. "You're in the finest hospital in Little Rock and, for that matter, the finest in Arkansas. Patients get shipped in here—not out."

"That's good to hear, so how am I doing?"

"Let me finish my exam and I'll tell you."

"Fine. But in the meantime, can my wife come in?"

The nurse came up to the other side of the bed, gave him a questioning look. "I'm sorry, Sir. Your wife isn't here. I'm not sure if she's been located yet."

ROUGH HANDS HAD pushed Allison into an adjoining room and into a straight-back chair. Her arms were pinioned around the slats in back, her wrists quickly tied with a piece of coarse rope.

She fought back tears; her mind in a whirlwind. *Oh, Fred, you were right. You always said my snooping would get me in trouble. And not just me, but Andy, too. Did I tell you he reminds me of Dave? I've got to help him, but what can I do? If only you were here.*

One of the men bent in front of her and slapped another rope around her ankles. His hands and his head gave a spasmodic jerk when a thunderous boom reverberated through the room. "What the...?" He dropped the rope, leapt up, and followed the other two men out into the hall. No one bothered to shut the door.

Allison's body trembled. What was that? It didn't sound like an explosion. Definitely not a gunshot. Something falling? Someone falling? What was happening to Andy?

She could clearly hear the shouts of the three men. "What was the fool up to? Trying to kill himself?"

Then a mean laugh from the man who'd tied her hands. "Looks like he succeeded. What a mess."

Andy hurt, maybe dead? She kicked the rope away from her feet that her captor hadn't finished tying. She tried to pull her hands up over the back of the chair. That didn't work. She would have to take the chair with her if she went anywhere. After several attempts, she managed to stand on her feet and tip the chair up so it rested on her back.

The men's voices were still loud and unchecked. One man ordered the others, "Let's get this crap off from him. See if he's still breathing."

She heard scraping noises and a few cusswords. They apparently were absorbed in their task, and she doubted they would hear her. She took careful steps toward the open door and out into the hall. The door where Andy was held stood wide open, also.

As she reached the doorway and looked in, she saw the men heave a large object up and set it against the wall. Her gaze went to where it had come from. On the floor was a splintered chair. Under the snapped pieces of wood, was a crumpled body dressed in a brown uniform.

She gasped and fell backwards. The chair tied to her back smacked down on the floor, teetered for a moment, and then settled down on its four legs.

All three men turned toward her. The older one yelled, "Get her out of here."

The other two swooped down on her, each grabbed a side of the chair, and carried her out.

She screamed. "No. Let me be. We've got to help him."

They ignored her pleadings and plopped her chair where it'd been previously. The skinny man picked a rope from the floor and threw it at the other man. "Okay, Dan, how about tying her up good this time?" he said as he left the room and slammed the door.

Allison didn't make it easy for Dan who was left with her. When he knelt down by her feet, she kicked him in the mouth. He reeled back, rubbed his hand across his face, took a deep breath and tried again. This time her foot smashed into his nose. A spurt of blood spattered on the rope. He backed away and stood up. Taking a dirty handkerchief from his pocket, he pinched his nose to stop the bleeding. She could see his eyes above the handkerchief. They were filled with hate.

His voice was guttural as he came at her. "You asked for it." He balled his right hand into a fist and struck her chin with the force of a rock.

Her head snapped back, and her brain whirled around a few times before going blank.

When she opened her eyes, her assailant sat straddling a chair right in front of her. He sneered at her. "Want to try any other tricks?"

She knew her tricks were over. All her extremities were bound tightly to the chair. Her jaw throbbed with pain. She swallowed hard and asked the question she had to know the answer to. "Andy? Is the deputy alive?"

"For now." This came from the older man who seemed to be in command. "But he's in no shape to talk. So it's up to you."

She was all out of fight. She would tell these men whatever they wanted to know. Then maybe they would let her and Andy go. She knew that idea was ridiculous as soon as her mind formed it. Only a miracle would get them out of here. "What do you want?"

"I heard your voice mail to the copper. So, tell me, what did you learn that was important to the case?"

Her voice mail? He had Andy's phone. Was that why he hadn't answered her call? How long had he been here? She stared at the man waiting for her to say something. "I learned my aunt was researching dioxin pollution in water sources. She found out that waste discharge from paper mills could be poisonous. And I think that's why she was killed."

"Killed?" The skinny man jumped from his chair, his face a picture of shock. "We ain't killed nobody. What are you talking about?"

Allison studied the man who was obviously sincere. These men may be involved in the pollution but, she thought, maybe not in Leona's death. Who else could it be? Her mind scurried around, remembered Molly bringing her here and delivering her to these horrid men. But Molly was Leona's friend. Maybe it was Ted, and Molly was protecting her husband. If Ted was so anxious to buy the farm why hadn't he made an offer to Leona? Or maybe he did and Leona refused it, so he killed her thinking I would be easier to deal with.

Her inquisitor interrupted her thoughts. "And what did you intend to do with the information?"

"Report it to the EPA."

"But you haven't done it yet?"

Allison hesitated. If she tells him, 'No,' then he might kill her right now to keep her from blabbing. If she tells him, 'Yes,' then he might kill her right now in retaliation. She decided to go with the truth, although maybe not the whole truth. "I informed Sheriff Babcock about the pollution in Cider Creek. I would imagine that very soon this place will be swarming with state investigators, if not with the Feds."

The skinny guy again leapt to his feet. "No way. I'm not ending up in any lockup. Me and Dan just agreed to dump the stuff. We didn't know what was in it." He gaped at the men across the room. "I didn't sign up to poison nobody."

The older man slowly rose to his feet, drew a gun from his belt, and pointed it at the skinny one. "What you signed up for was to keep your trap shut. And I'm going to make sure you do it."

He stepped back, swung the gun around toward the other man's face. "You got a problem with following orders?"

The eyes of the muscular man bugged out, and he shook his head as if caught in a twister.

"Good. Grab the rest of the rope. Looks like you have another tying job to do."

"No! You can't do that to me." The terror stricken skinny man turned to run. He barely got through the door when Allison saw the gunman aim and fire.

She squeezed her eyes shut. She had little sympathy for the skinny guy, but he hadn't struck her or pushed her around like the others had, and she didn't want to witness a killing.

"Next time I'll aim better," she heard the man with the gun say. "Now get."

Allison cautiously opened her eyes. The gunshot had apparently been meant only to scare the skinny guy.

As they left the room, the man who had tied her up asked, "What about our prisoners?"

"They're not going anywhere."

ANDY TRIED TO lift his head. Had he heard a shot? Or was it his brain knocking around inside his skull? He opened his eyes, and a shaft of light made him blink. He turned his head, looked straight up, and saw a mottled, dirty ceiling. After thinking about that for a few seconds, he concluded he was lying on his back on the floor again. What had happened to the chair he'd been tied in? Soon the memories came rushing back. Him trying to knock over the filing cabinet to create a diversion so Allison could escape. The cabinet falling in the wrong direction. Then the blackness slowly enveloping him.

Had his diversion worked? The cabinet was again in an upright position, so the men must have come in. Had his friend been able to get out? He had to find out.

He shifted his weight, and a bolt of lightning seared up his left leg. Raising one hand, he covered his mouth to stifle a cry. He didn't want to attract his captors' attention now. It was then he realized his hands were no longer tied. Very slowly he boosted up his head until he could see his legs. The ropes were gone there, too. They'd untied him. Why? Did they think he'd been killed when the cabinet fell on him? Well, he wasn't dead yet. He would get out of here, and he would make sure Allison was okay.

He used his elbows to prop himself into a sitting position, waited until his brain stopped spinning, and started to pull up his knees so he could stand. The pain in his left leg stabbed him again. He fell back down. The truth hit him like a hammer. He had a broken leg. No wonder his captors hadn't tied him back up. It wasn't necessary. He wasn't going to travel far in his condition.

Staring at the ceiling, he contemplated just what his condition was. It might be his broken leg wasn't his worst problem. Every time he tried to move, he was overtaken with dizziness. His hand explored his forehead where he located a soft lump—probably from striking his head on the floor. His medic training told him it was possible he had intracranial bleeding. It was also possible he had other internal injuries. Although the back of the chair must have deflected some of the weight of the filing cabinet, he'd still been squeezed together like an accordion. Who knows what that might have done to his insides? He'd tried to ignore the pain in his abdomen, attributing it to hunger and dehydration, but now he wasn't so sure. He had to face the fact he might be in very bad shape.

Continuing to fix his eyes on the ceiling, Andy tried to forget his pain and willed his thoughts to come up with a plan. In a short while some of the cobwebs in his brain seem to part. He pushed himself up on his elbows. To his right side, he saw fragments of the chair that had imprisoned him along with tangled pieces of rope. A course of action took form. He slithered over to the wooden remnants, careful not to disturb his body any more than necessary, and snatched two of the wide slats that once comprised the back of the desk chair. He then snagged the rope. With his trophies in hand, he slid back until he was able to lean against the wall. Bending forward, he gingerly inched up his left pant leg. There was a definite outward curving in the middle of his lower leg, but fortunately, the skin wasn't broken. He glided his trouser leg back down. It would be the only padding he had for the splint he was about to make. Hey, if MacGyver, his TV hero from his childhood, could do it, so could he. Every week he'd watched the reruns where the hero got himself out of impossible situations. And since he seemed to be in an impossible situation, he might as well try.

Andy slowed his efforts from time to time to listen. He hadn't heard anything since the sound of a shot had awakened him from whatever dreamland he'd been in. He refused to think the shot may have been intended for Allison. But, he wondered, where were Skinny, Muscles, and Third Man? They may have left, although he hadn't heard the truck start up. What would happen if they came back in here and found that he was not only alive but in the process of escaping? For that was just what he intended to do. He didn't know how, but he going to get out of this room, find Allison if she were still here, and get them both out safely.

ALL THE LAUGHTER had gone out of Marie's voice when she reported back to Sam. "The guys at the ski lodge said Andy left hours ago, saying he had to get back to work."

Sam rubbed his chin, stared at the clock on his wall.

Marie went on. "Roberto's here. He spoke with Andy as he was leaving and that he intended to come right back from the lodge. Rob has no idea where he might be."

"Then we start looking. Get an APB out on his patrol car, call the area hospitals, the city police. You know the drill."

Marie nodded. "Yes Sir."

SEVENTEEN

FRED GLARED AT the nurse. "What do you mean, haven't located her? All you have to do is call her. Give me my phone. I'll call her and get her down here."

"You didn't have a phone with you, Sir."

The doctor poised her stethoscope above his chest and said one word, "Hush!"

Fred knew an authoritative command when he heard one. He hushed while giving the nurse a look that plainly indicated he wasn't through with her.

Completing her exam, Dr. Holliday gave Fred the tiniest of smiles. "Everything looks good."

"Then I can leave?"

"Maybe tomorrow. Head injuries require at least twenty-four hours of observation. Any questions?"

He waved toward the bandage on his head. "What about this?"

"You had a slight gash on your forehead."

"Feels like a mighty big bandage for a slight gash."

"We tend to be overly cautious. The nurse can change the dressing, make it a little smaller."

"Good. One more thing," Fred said, wiggling his left arm. "When can I get rid of this IV and have a decent meal?"

"We'll try the meal first. If that goes well, we'll DC the fluids, and you can get up—with help. Don't try to get too frisky. You're a lucky man, Mr. Sawyer, considering what the city policeman said about the condition of your car."

Fred sobered. "Yeah, I guess so. And believe me, I'm grateful to you and to the Good Lord."

The doctor's smile widened, "You're welcome—from both of us."

As Dr. Holliday left the room, Fred turned to the nurse, "Now about my phone. I always carry my cell. It has to be here somewhere. Where are my clothes?"

The pretty young nurse wagged her finger at him. "Not now. Sergeant Silverman from the Little Rock City Police is here to talk to you. I notified him as soon as you awaken per his orders. He was at the scene and can explain about your accident. I'll be back in a little and change that dressing on your head."

A blue uniform was in the room before the nurse finished her spiel. He approached the bed, held out a hand, "Tim Silverman. Glad to see you're awake. You had me worried for a while this morning."

"Yeah, I was kind of worried, too, when I woke up here. What happened? And where's my wife?"

The sergeant answered the first question as succinctly as he could, explained about the icy patch on the road, that the other driver escaped without harm, and that Fred's rental car was totaled. "Your airbag and seat belt prevented you going through the windshield, but when the car skidded into the ditch your head must have been slammed against the door." Silverman pulled up a chair, leaned back. "You don't remember anything?"

"Afraid not. I was looking for my turnoff when the lights went out."

"Where were you headed?"

"North Carolina. Upton, a little town in the mountains. That's where my wife is. And why haven't I heard from her? You guys did notify her, didn't you?"

"We tried. Got her phone number from your workplace, called and left a couple of messages. The nurses say she hasn't called here yet."

"That's crazy. She's expecting me. In fact I should have been there hours ago. She's got to be worried. Where's my phone? I'll call her."

"We didn't find your phone. Might have been thrown from the car."

"Then let me use yours. I've got to get hold of her."

The policeman shrugged, slid his cell through the side rail. Fred sat upright, reached for the phone, and the walls started dancing in front of his eyes. Flopping back down, he closed his eyes, took several shallow breaths, gasped out, "I guess I'm not quite ready for that yet. You'd better do the calling."

Fred called out the number and the sergeant punched it in, said, "That's the same number I've been calling. But we'll try again." He put the phone on speaker so the man in the bed could hear, "If you wish to leave a message…"

"Something's wrong. Something's terribly wrong." Fred turned worried eyes toward the cop. "Call the motel, have someone go to her room. If she doesn't answer, tell them to go inside. Something's happened to her."

"The name of the motel?"

"Country Inn."

"Address?"

"I don't know. Upton's a small town. Just find it." Fred shook his head, added, "Please."

Fred's insides were doing a hoodoo dance. It wasn't enough that he was banged up in a hospital hundreds of miles away from his sweetie and that she didn't know what had happened, but now she couldn't be found and he didn't know what was happening to her. He should have never let her go to Upton alone. Allison meant the world to him; he should always be by her side, protecting her.

His attention went back to the phone conversation. Silverman had identified himself as a police officer and was instructing the motel clerk exactly as Fred had demanded, and then added, "If she's not there, check her room for a cell phone and see if her car's there. Call me back."

Both men stared into space while waiting for the return call. The five or so minutes seemed much longer. When the call came, Silverman again put it on speaker. "She's not there, but everything seemed fine. Her purse and coat are gone, and I didn't find her phone so she must have that with her, and her car's gone. Maybe she just went out shopping—or something."

"Have you seen her at all today?"

"I don't recall seeing her today, but I don't pay any attention to who goes in and out. I think she's eaten breakfast here in the lobby a couple of days. We serve a very nice continental meal, but I don't think she came in this morning. I think she's been going out somewhere everyday, I don't know where. Sorry, I couldn't be of more help."

"Well, thanks, anyway."

Fred nodded, "The apple orchard."

"What?"

"That's probably where she's been going every day. That's why she's in Upton—to bury her aunt who owned the orchard. Allison was her heir."

"Would there be anybody there who might know your wife's whereabouts?"

"No." Fred raised his head again, this time more carefully, and waited a bit for the swimming to subside. "Call the county sheriff. Sam Babcock. He's the one who called about her aunt's death and he's a friend of the family. If he doesn't know where she is, he can ride out to the farm and check there."

"I'm on it."

Again, Fred noted that Sergeant Silverman was careful to identify himself, so the answering party would know the call was official. He explained it was important to contact Mrs. Allison Sawyer as soon as possible and that she wasn't answering her cell phone. He then put the phone on speaker so Fred could hear the response.

The dispatcher's voice was rather dubious when she asked, "What do you want us to do, Officer?"

Fred motioned for the sergeant to move the phone closer, and he called out, "Is that you, Marie?"

"Yes. Who's this?"

"Fred Sawyer, Allison's husband. We haven't met, but Allison told me about you and about how good you've been to her."

"Oh, right. It's good to talk to you, Fred. Allison told me you would be coming in today."

"That's just it. I was supposed to be there, but I had an accident and I'm in a hospital in Little Rock. The cops haven't been able to get hold of Allison to notify her and I'm worried something might have happened to her. Can I talk to Sam about it?"

"Well, Sam's pretty tied up right now…"

"Marie. Listen to me. This is important. Allison is missing!"

"Missing? Oh my, not another one. Hang on a sec."

Fred heard a buzzer sound in his ear and then Sam's bellow. "What?"

Marie apparently had connected him to the sheriff instead of relaying the message. That was fine with Fred. "Sam. This is Fred Sawyer and my wife is missing."

Silverman was waving a hand in front of Fred's face and shaking his head. Fred understood the sign language. *It's too early to report her as missing.* Ignoring the officer, Fred went on. "I'm in Little Rock, in the hospital, wrecked my car. I'm all right, but the police here have been trying to locate Allison for hours and she doesn't answer her phone and she's not been seen at her motel. I'm afraid she's in trouble." His voice weakened, "Can you look for her?"

Reaching for the phone, Sergeant Silverman, took over the call, but instead of trying to explain, he asked a blunt question, "What did the dispatcher mean by saying, 'another one'? Is someone else missing?"

"Yeah," Sam answered, all the bluster gone out of his voice. "One of my deputies seems to have disappeared. And the thing is he's been working with me and Allison on her aunt's case."

Fred blurted out, "Her aunt's case? What does that mean?"

The sheriff answered the question. "Fred, like I told Allison when I first called her, Leona's death was ruled accidental, but now some facts have surfaced that makes it look suspicious. With that, and the fact that Allison has been being stalked, we're looking at a possible homicide."

It was too much for Fred. Homicide. Stalker. He sank back into his pillows. "She didn't tell me," he said. "She never said a word about any problems, any suspicions of homicide."

Fred tried to still his pounding heart so he could continue to listen as Officer Silverman asked, "Do you think since we're not able to locate Mrs. Sawyer, it may have a connection to your missing deputy?"

"It might. We're searching for him, got a bulletin out for his patrol car. We'll add her to the search. I'll send someone out to her aunt's farm, see if anything shows up there."

"All right. Keep me updated."

"Will do. And tell Fred we'll do everything possible to find her."

ALLISON HUNG HER head down and fought back tears. Tears would only make her more miserable as she couldn't wipe her eyes or blow her nose. And tears wouldn't help Andy. She closed her eyes and again saw his crumpled body on the floor in the next room. She had to get out of here. She had to get help.

She stiffened as she heard a faint noise outside her door. Were those awful men coming back? What would they do to her now that she'd answered their questions? She braced herself for whatever lay ahead.

The door opened silently, slowly. Allison held her breath; this wasn't the way the three men had approached previously. Who was out there?

A large figure backed into the room, apparently surveying the hallway before turning and shutting the door. Allison gasped in horror as she recognized the man.

"Jerry Howe! What are you doing with this gang?"

Jerry put a finger to his lips to warn her to be silent as he came closer to her chair.

"Stay away from me," she screamed. She twisted violently at her restraints. She was alone with a dangerous mad man. She'd been warned about the brain damaged veteran being a time bomb. Was now the time he would explode?

ANDY WAS TYING the last piece of rope around his makeshift splint when he heard Allison scream. It sounded like it came from the next room. What was happening? He yanked the knot tightly and started sliding toward the door. If he could get that far, he could use the door knob to pull himself to a standing position. He paused just long enough to grab a leg of the chair that had broken off. He now had a weapon, and somehow he was going to rescue Allison.

His head whirled. His leg sent jabs of pain up through his body. His every muscle ached. It didn't matter. He had to get to the door.

He moved quietly, wanting to hear while not being heard. But there was nothing to hear—no more screams, no voices that he could pick up.

He reached the door, grasped the knob, hoisted himself up. He stood there fighting the darkness that threatened to overwhelm him. His mind called out to his friend that he was coming.

But his body betrayed him, and he crashed to the floor.

EIGHTEEN

JERRY WAVED HIS hands in front of Allison's face. "Sh-h-h," he whispered, "I'm here to help you. Be quiet so the bad guys don't come back."

Allison stared at the man. This wasn't the face of a deranged person. He had the eager eyes of a child wanting to help. She'd seen those eyes in her students asking if they could clean the board or run an errand for her. Her aunt had trusted Jerry to do odd jobs for her, and Allison felt as if she should trust him now. Besides, Andy had vouched for him, told her that the veteran was harmless.

She nodded her heard toward her bonds, "Do you have something to cut this rope with?"

He nodded, took a jackknife out of his pocket, stared at it for a few seconds.

Allison got an uneasy feeling in her gut, and asked, "How did you know I was here?"

Stepping behind her, he started cutting her wrist ropes before answering. "I was at the hospital picking up trash when I saw you drive up and than I saw Mrs. Kirkman get in your car. I don't like her. Sometimes she isn't nice. I thought maybe she wouldn't be nice to you, so I followed your car."

She could feel the tug on her wrists as the blade slid back and forth, and he continued talking as he sawed at the rope. As he worked his breaths became shorter and his words choppier. "She drove awful fast. Nice people don't drive fast. And she didn't put on her turn blinker. But I saw her turn in."

Jerry's attention seemed to alternate between cutting the rope and explaining his actions. Apparently it was difficult for Jerry to talk and work at the same time, so Allison solved that dilemma. "You can explain all that to me later," she said. "Just keep on cutting."

As soon as her hands were free, Allison grasped Jerry around his neck in a giant hug. "Jerry, you're wonderful."

He smiled at her. "That's what Leona used to tell me." A tear slid down his cheek. "But I wasn't there to help when she was in trouble. Maybe she'll forgive me if I can help you."

Allison closed her eyes against the pain in the man's face. Did he somehow feel responsible for Leona's death? But she couldn't worry about that now. She motioned to the rope still tied around her feet. "Let's get the rest of this rope off."

Jerry got to his job and soon she was free. He helped her to her feet as she wobbled a little.

"Now we've got to go," he said. "Those men who grabbed you are outside, but they might come back in." He opened the door quietly, looked out, motioned her to follow him. "We'll go out by the basement. I know the way; my dad used to work here and I came with him one time."

Allison grabbed his arm as he started out the door.

"We can't go yet. Andy Cox is here, too. We've got to get him out."

"Andy?"

"Deputy Cox. You know him. They have him in the next room. I'm afraid he's badly hurt."

"Yes. I know the deputy. He's nice. He came to see me. He said I should always report people when they do wrong things, but I didn't have time to report Mrs. Kirkman. I had to help you."

"Yes. You did the right thing. Now we've got to help Andy."

Allison peered out into the hallway. It was empty. She rushed to the adjoining door and tried to open it. It didn't budge.

Jerry came up and shoved against it. It opened a crack. "Must be something holding it shut. Maybe a chair." He motioned her out of the way. He stepped back and then hurled his shoulder against the door. It parted several more inches.

Allison peered through the opening and saw part of a brown uniform. "Andy. Oh, Andy." She knelt, stretched out her hand and touched his arm. It was if she were touching her son, Dave. In the short time she'd known him, she had become fond of this substitute son and she had to try to get him safely out.

He was lying prone with his face turned away from the door. She couldn't see if he was breathing, and she couldn't reach a place to check his pulse. Trying to stay calm, she instructed Jerry, "Shove the door just a little more, and I think I'll be able to can crawl in."

The child marine did as instructed, placed his

back to the door and pushed gently. The opening widened. "That's good," Allison said. "You keep watch while I pull him away from the door."

She maneuvered her way through, careful to avoid stepping too closely to the prostrate form. She tried not to think about how badly he may be hurt. Her only job now was to get him away from the door so Jerry could get in, and maybe together they could carry him out.

Once in, she dropped to the floor, placed her fingers on his neck and felt for a pulse. It was there—faint, but there. Thank God. His breathing was shallow, and his face drained of color, but he was alive. That's all that mattered. She called out softly to Jerry, "He's alive. He's alive."

Now to get him on his back, she thought. She gingerly lifted his head and turned it toward the door. Crouching by his side, she put one hand on his shoulder and the other on his hip. With all the strength she could muster, she turned him onto his back. It was only when she went to straighten out his twisted legs that she noticed the splint. "Oh, the poor boy," she moaned.

The door was now open enough to allow Jerry to slink in. He knelt down and examined his friend. When he stood up, Allison observed a subtle change in his features. He was no more the eager child. His face was now that of a soldier taking command of the situation. He gave his orders in a firm, confident voice. "Grab his feet while I take his head, and we'll lay him on the desk. Then I can get a better hold to carry him." She nodded. "And," he added, "be careful of the left leg."

After they had Andy on the desktop, Allison held her breath as she watched Jerry glide one arm under Andy's upper torso, and the other under his knees. Then holding his back straight, Jerry lifted his wounded buddy up and was ready to carry him from the battlefield. "Check for the enemy," he instructed her.

She gave him the all clear, and they left the room. "Close both doors," he said, "so when they come back, they won't see the empty rooms right away."

"Yes Sir." She didn't know how long his battle flashback was going to last, but it seemed to be just what they needed for now.

"The basement stairs are this way," he said, heading toward the back of the building. "You run ahead and open the door."

Allison did as she was told. In between marveling at Jerry's strength and watching for the enemy, she felt she was in a TV action movie. If only she could be assured that this movie would have a happy ending.

She opened one last door, and they were outside. Cider Creek was in front of them, and the loading dock was above them. "Where's your car?" she asked.

Jerry turned his head to the left. "In the woods over there."

The woods he referred to were a long way over there with an open parking lot between the trees and the building where they stood. He answered her unasked question, "I snuck along the creek bank so I wouldn't be seen."

Jerry looked like he was about to fall over. Allison knew there was no way he could carry Andy all the way to his car. There had to be an alternative. She spotted a bench along side of the building. She tugged at Jerry's arm. "Put him down here until we can figure out what to do now."

As Jerry laid Andy down, Allison thought she heard a door slam. The men must have come back into the building. How long before they would go into the closed rooms and find their prisoners gone?

Jerry's shoulders slumped as he stared at Andy on the bench. He sat down, buried his head in his hands, and sobbed, "I couldn't help Leona, and I can't help the deputy."

The child had returned. Allison went to comfort him as she would have one of her students if they were disappointed in themselves. "That's not true, Jerry. You saved both Andy's and my life. Leona would be so proud of you. And we're going to get out of here. I just have to think a minute while you rest."

She bent over Andy, touched his face, checked his pulse. His face was hot, his pulse barely perceptible. Putting her mouth close to his ear, she whispered as loudly as she dared, "Andy, can you hear me? Hang in there. We'll get you to a hospital soon. I promise." But she had no idea how they were going to do it.

As long as they were under the loading dock they couldn't be seen, but if the men discovered they were missing, the search would be on. Then there would be no place to hide. Besides, hiding wasn't an option. Andy needed medical attention and he needed it as soon as possible.

She sat down next to Jerry. "You have a cell phone?"

Jerry shook his head, "Sorry. My sister said I wouldn't know what to do with one if I had it."

When they got out of this mess, someone should have a long talk with that sister. Jerry had a lot of potential. He only needed the right training and support. But right now she was the one who needed support, and there didn't seem to be any around. She forced back the longing that erupted in her heart for Fred. She was on her own and she had to figure a way out of here. "Jerry, you rest while I look around. You may have to carry Deputy Cox again. Okay?"

"Okay."

She got up and wandered under the loading dock. The dock extended down the entire south side of the mill ending with steps that led to the ground. A picture flashed into her mind. When she was brought here, Molly had driven up close to the steps and two men had come down, grabbed her arms and hurried her up. But before they hustled her inside, she saw a truck parked alongside of the dock. A black pickup truck.

She rushed to the outer side of the dock, bent her head down and looked to the right. The truck was still there. It was facing toward the road, and the bed of the truck was empty except for a few boxes. Here was their getaway vehicle and Andy's ambulance. Running quietly under the dock until she came alongside of the truck, she scanned the steps and the parking lot in front of her. She neither saw nor heard anyone. The truck was parked about three feet away from the loading dock. That meant that she would have to leave her protective place and expose herself in order to peek in the truck window. She wasn't overly concerned about it since it was doubtful any of the men would be looking out of a mill window in that direction.

She briefly wondered if the skinny guy was still adverse to killing. She hoped he was. In case they were spotted making their escape that would leave only two men to contend with—however, it would probably be two men with guns.

She kept her head down and crossed the few feet to the truck door. Holding her breath, she stood up straight and looked through the dirty window. Oh, the trials of being short. This vehicle was made for off-road travel, and her eyes only came about halfway up the glass. To make matters worse, there was a wadded up coat in the passenger seat blocking her view. She stood on tiptoe trying to get a peek at the ignition. She extended her vision by hopping up a few times. Finally her efforts were rewarded with a glimpse of a rabbit's foot dangling from the dashboard. And where there was a rabbit's foot, there had to be keys. Ducking back down, she returned to where Andy laid unconscious and where Jerry was resting.

She whispered her plan to him. As she went on, his head nodding became more vigorous and his grin wider. He was still the little boy eager to please, but his body was that of a strong warrior.

He bent down and lifted Andy up. If the maneuver taxed his strength, he gave no indication of it. He motioned for Allison to lead the way.

At this point there was no turning back, and Allison was so intent on getting Andy to the hospital, she didn't have time to be scared. They came to the tailgate of the truck. It would have to be lowered in order to slide Andy in. Allison slipped out from under dock, hoped the gate wouldn't stick or squeak, and very carefully lifted it up. The gate came up and out with no hesitation and no noise. So far, so good.

She helped Jerry position Andy's head on the gate and then she scrambled into the back of the truck. Kneeling by his head, she placed her hands under his arms and tugged him back until his hips cleared the gate. Jerry then climbed up and, being careful to protect Andy's injured leg, hauled him the rest of the way into the bed of the truck.

Allison rested Andy's head in her lap and waved Jerry off. Before he jumped to the ground, Jerry removed his jacket and tucked it around the patient.

"Now drive like fury, Jerry," Allison whispered.

Dropping to the ground and not bothering to raise the tailgate, Jerry opened the driver's door, started the truck with a roar, and flew out of the parking lot.

They were nearly to the road when two figures appeared on the loading dock. One of them raised a gun and fired, but either his aim was lousy, or the truck was too far away to be hit. The tires squealed onto Mount Vista Road as Jerry sped toward Upton.

EIGHTEEN

JERRY TORE INTO the emergency room drive, left the engine running as he raced through the double doors. In a few seconds, two men in white wheeled a gurney toward the truck.

Allison breathed a quick prayer as Andy disappeared into a treatment room. She then darted to the desk. "That's Deputy Andy Cox. You need to call the sheriff immediately and get him over here."

"Cox?" the clerk echoed. "They've been looking for him all over the county." She started punching numbers and relayed the message as soon as someone answered. She listened a moment and looked over the counter. "She wants to know who you are."

"Allison Sawyer."

Before she could say anything else, the clerk let out a squeal. "Sawyer? They're looking for you, too."

"I was kidnapped, and—let me have the phone." She reached up and the clerk dropped the phone into her hand. "Marie? Andy's unconscious. We were held captive at the old Binken Paper Mill. Three guys there. We stole their truck. Get someone out there to arrest them."

She paused for breath and the dispatcher tried to get her to repeat what she'd just said. "Just get the sheriff here. I'll tell him all about it. Got to see about

Andy." She handed the phone back to the clerk. "I can't answer questions now."

Jerry came in after parking the stolen truck, his face stricken in fear. "Where is he? Is he going to be all right?"

Allison led him to a chair. "You wait here, and I'll see what I can find out." She rushed down the hall and peeked through the curtain where several people were working on Andy. He was being attached to a monitor, oxygen, and IVs. She backed away, not wanting to interfere. She knew someone would come out with information of his condition when they had a chance.

She heard sirens approaching the hospital. Being such a small town it didn't take long to get from one side to the other. Soon Sam Babcock came bursting through the door.

"Where is he?" Sam belted out. "And are you all right?"

"Number four, and I'm fine." As the sheriff disappeared down the hallway, she wondered how he knew she'd been in trouble, too.

The sheriff made it into the treatment room in a nanosecond, ripped the curtain back and stalked in. Allison followed him, but stayed in the hallway.

"Is he going to make it?" the sheriff asked, his voice quavering.

One of the doctors answered. "I think so. His heart's strong. When we get him stabilized, we can do CT scans for other injuries and set his fractured leg. It's going to be a while before I tell you anything definitive."

"Okay. Keep me posted." He whirled around, left the room, and collided with Allison. He enveloped her in his massive arms. "Thank goodness you're all right. You're hubby's been having fit trying to find you." He dropped his arms, pushed her back a little and stared at her. His fingers went to her swollen jaw. "Looks like you had better be examined, too."

"Never mind that. Where's Fred? I've got to see him. Is he all right?"

"He's fine, and I'll fill you on him, but first let me put his mind at ease about you." Sam pulled out his phone, punched a number, barked out an order, "Marie, call that cop in Little Rock and let him know we've found Mrs. Sawyer, or rather, she found us, but anyway, she's okay. And he can inform Mr. Sawyer of that fact. Get the number of the hospital and she'll call him in a little bit."

Allison tugged at the sheriff's arm. "Little Rock? Hospital? What's going on?"

Very briefly Sam told Allison what little he knew of Fred's accident and echoed what he'd said earlier. "He's fine, but was worried because he couldn't contact you. Now we've got to talk about what you and Andy were up to. And get a doctor to look at you. Someone beat you up?"

She shook her head. "I'm okay. It's just that one of the men took exception when I bloodied his nose and he socked me, but other than that, they didn't hurt me. You do have men on the way to the mill to arrest those dudes, don't you?"

"They're on their way, but I want to hear your

story before I order them in. Let's go to the lobby, and you start from the beginning."

"There isn't time. You've got to stop them before they escape. There are three of them and they have guns."

Sam pushed her into a chair and sat down beside her. Jerry, who had been sitting a few seats away, came up and sat on her other side. "They won't get far. We've got their truck."

The sheriff stared at Jerry. "What are you doing here?"

Before Jerry could answer, Allison spoke up, "He helped me escape, carried Andy out, and drove the truck to the hospital." She patted Jerry on his arm, gave him a huge smile. "He's my angel."

Sam reached over and gave Jerry a handshake. "Thanks for your help, man."

The man dropped his head and murmured, "I like to help people."

Sam radioed the car he'd sent to the mill, warning them the men were armed, and ordered them to wait for backup before going in. Then he called for the backup. "Now we wait."

"No," Allison said and waved her hands in front of her face. "There's something else. Molly. You've got to arrest Molly. She kidnapped me, stole my car, my purse and my cell phone."

Sam gaped at Allison as if she had gone stark raving mad. "Molly Kirkman?"

"Yes. She took me to the mill and turned me over to those horrible men." Allison grabbed the sheriff's hand. "And she may have killed Leona—or maybe

Ted did. I don't know how he fits in, but you better arrest him, too."

"Think what you're saying, Allison. Molly and Ted Kirkman are two of the most respected people in the county—in the state. They have connections in Raleigh. And you want me to arrest them?"

Jerry nodded. "She's right. Mrs. Kirkman isn't a nice person. I saw her take Allison away."

"You saw her? Where?"

"Here at the hospital. I was picking up trash when I saw her get into Allison's car and drive away. I followed them to the old mill."

The sheriff rubbed his forehead as he made another call to his office. "Listen carefully, Marie. Send a car to Ted Kirkman's—no sirens, and have Mr. and Mrs. Kirkman brought to the station for questioning. Tell the officer to be nice to them. I'll be there as soon as possible."

Allison watched his face grimace as Marie apparently told him what she thought of the order. "I know it's crazy, but just do it. And pass the word that the doc thinks Andy will make it." He turned to Allison with a deep sigh. "I sure hope you appreciate what a dangerous limb I just climbed out on."

He stood up, reached for her hand. "You and Jerry are coming with me back to the station. On the way you're going to tell me why you're accusing the Kirkmans of kidnapping and possible murder."

"But I can't go. I have to stay here with Andy. And I have to call Fred. I've got to talk to him." She stopped, put her hand to her mouth. "Oh, I forgot. I don't have my cell phone."

"You can call him from the station. And the doctors here will keep us notified of Andy's condition. They'll call us when they know more or when he comes to."

Sam stopped at the desk and gave the clerk a card. "My personal cell. Please have the doctor call as soon as he knows anything more about Deputy Cox."

"Yes sir."

When they exited the hospital, Allison noted darkness had fallen and the parking lot lights were illuminating the area. She'd lost all track of time during her ordeal and escape. Now her stomach reminded her it had been a long time since she'd eaten anything. Her brain chided her stomach. *How can you think of food when you have criminals to catch and a hubby to check on?*

Sam interrupted the thought when he turned to Jerry, "Where's this truck you said you stole to transport Andy?"

Jerry pointed it out and grinned as he handed the sheriff the key with the rabbit's foot attached. "I guess this brought *us* luck instead of them."

"Looks like. You lock it?"

"Yeah. Didn't want anyone else to steal it."

The three of them walked together to the truck. Unlocking the passenger door, the sheriff reached into the glove compartment, and pawed through some papers. He read the registration card. "Fred Racine. Mean anything to you?" he asked Allison.

She shook her head. "From around here?"

"Nope. We'll have it impounded and find out about him." He slid the papers back in and relocked the truck. "Let's go."

NINETEEN

SERGEANT SILVERMAN RECEIVED the call from Upton, North Carolina and sighed in relief, glad that this scenario seemed to be heading for a good outcome. He drove to the hospital to give Mr. Sawyer the news in person.

When he arrived, the patient was sitting up in bed with a tray in front of him and was slurping loudly. Fred lifted his head, grinned. "Never thought chicken soup could taste this good." Then his face immediately sobered. "Any news?"

"The best. Got a message from Sam the Sheriff. Mrs. Sawyer has been found, and is all right."

"Thank God." Fred dropped his spoon, covered his eyes, whispered again, "Thank God." Then the questions started pouring out. "What happened? Where was she? Are you sure she's not hurt?"

"No details. But she'll call you here later this evening."

"She's okay. That's all that matters. Except that now I have to figure out a way for me to get there or for her to get here."

Silverman smiled. "Well, since that's not my department, I'll let you muse on it." He stepped forward, shook Fred's hand. "Best of luck."

AS THEY CONTINUED across town, Allison asked, "Are you sure it was a good idea to let the Kirkmans have time to talk to each other? They may be hatching up lies to tell you and will make me look like a fruitcake."

"And if I hadn't known you for years, I might believe them. But I have to know the whole story of what happened before I confront them. Now, start with why Andy was at the mill."

"I don't know. He was already there tied up in a chair when they brought me in." She paused, again seeing her friend unconscious, injured. "Sam, Andy will be all right, won't he?"

"Sure he will. He's a tough kid. And you're tough too. Did you really give one of those guys a bloody nose?"

"Sure did. With my foot."

"So tell me all about it."

Allison went on to tell the whole story starting with the call from a hospital secretary who she now thought must have been Molly. She told of hearing the terrific crash and then seeing the filing cabinet on top of Andy. "That must have been when his leg was broken. They hauled me out of there immediately so I don't know what happened to him after that."

Jerry piped up from the backseat, "The deputy put his own leg in a splint. Ain't that something?"

"That so, Allison?"

"He must have. When we found him his leg was splinted with broken slats and tied with rope. I doubt those men would have done it for him."

"Well, I'll be. That's going to make a good story around the station."

Allison finished her account of their escape just as the sheriff pulled into his parking space.

When they got out of the car, Jerry sidled up to the sheriff. "Could you call my sister? She'll be worried 'cause I didn't come home from my hospital job."

"Sure. And I'll have someone drive you home after we get your statement down. We'll let you know how Andy gets along."

"You'll get my car back?"

Sam nodded. "We'll try. You've been a big help, Jerry."

Allison gave him a hug. "When Andy wakes up, I'll tell him just how brave you were." Jerry left them to accompany an officer who would take his statement.

Sam shook his head as he tramped down the hallway. "Now I have to go face the Kirkmans." Marie motioned him to a room down the hall. "Together?" he asked.

"Nope. Roberto said there was no sign of Mr. Kirkman, and that she's blaming everything on him. She's alone in there now. Refused to call an attorney." Marie fingered a paper on her desk. "We've got Ted Kirkman's car info. Want to put out an APB?"

"Let me talk to her first."

Sam turned to Allison. "While I'm questioning Molly about her activities today, I'll have someone else take your statement. I know you've already told me, but make it as detailed as possible. And in order for me to hold her, you'll have to accuse her of kidnapping."

"Well, she did kidnap me. I mean I went with her willingly but only because she lied and said she was taking me to the hospital to see Andy. That's still kidnapping, isn't it?"

"Just tell how it happened. We'll figure out the charges later." He motioned to a female deputy and introduced her as Donna Worley. "Donna is going to keep me company in the lion's den."

A smile played on Donna's lips. "I'm supposed to be your bodyguard?"

"Something like that."

Allison sat in the hallway and watched as Sam and Donna entered the room to question Molly. Before they had a chance to close the door, the enraged woman screeched at the sheriff. "Instead of locking me up in here, you need to be out looking for that scumbag."

The sheriff took a step forward, but the door remained ajar. "And what scumbag would that be?"

"That louse I call my husband. He made me do it."

"Before you say anything else, Mrs. Kirkman," Sam said, "I must remind you of your right to have an attorney present and of your spousal privilege."

Allison couldn't hear Molly's reply as Donna quickly pulled the door shut.

Jerking her mind away from the drama unfolding in the next room, Allison went up to Marie. "Sam said I could call Fred from here. Is there somewhere private I could talk?"

"Sure, Honey. You can use the phone in the break

room and I'll put up a sign to keep everyone else out. That way you can relax and sip some coffee while you're talking."

The next several minutes consisted of tears of relief, terms of endearment, shudders of horror as each told their stories, and plans for their reunion. The reunion plans were sticky.

"Even if the doctor releases you tomorrow, Fred, you won't be able to drive, and I doubt if you would be allowed to fly. Head injuries can be tricky, you know."

"But you might be needed there so the sheriff can go over all your evidence."

"Right. And I don't really want to leave until I know Andy is going to be all right."

They left that point to discuss again later.

Sam was still in with Molly when a deputy took Allison's statement. Afterwards, she hurried to the dispatcher's desk. "Heard anything from the hospital?"

Marie shook her head. "Not yet. I'll let you know when they call."

Returning to the hallway and staring at the door behind which Molly was still undergoing questioning, Allison wished she could be a fly on the wall and hear all that was going on.. What was she telling the sheriff? Would he arrest her? What was Ted's role in her and Andy's captivity? What was going on in that old paper mill?

After a while, the door opened, and Donna came out. Seeing Allison, the deputy came over and plopped down. "The lady wants a drink of water, but I'm going to take my time getting it for her."

"What's her story?"

"It's all Ted's doing. According to her, he made her call you, disguise her voice, and lure you to the hospital. Then he told her to drive you to the paper mill because he wanted to talk to you. She swears she doesn't know anything about the guys who held you captive."

"But why the paper mill? What does that have to do with Ted?"

"Sam asked her that," Donna said. "Molly told him Ted had bought the property and planned to covert the building into more luxury condos like the ones at Silver Lake Park, and he was in the process of having it cleaned up."

Allison was trying to process this new information with the newspaper clipping about dioxin and Leona's internet research about it. Ted had bought the closed paper mill and in the process of cleaning it up, had he accidentally polluted Cider Creek? Had Andy found the source of the pollution and been seized to prevent him from talking? But why? None of it made any sense. Surely the sheriff would find out more answers.

Her mind took a sudden turn, and she asked the officer, "What about my car?"

"Says she ditched it in the Walmart parking lot. She gave me your keys. Tell me the make and model of your car. One of the guys can pick it up." Donna jotted down the information, gave it to Marie, and headed for the drinking fountain. "Guess I better get her majesty's water and return to my post."

Allison mulled over what she'd just heard. In some of their phone calls, Leona had occasionally mentioned being on a committee which Molly chaired and how she strictly controlled the agenda. It was hard for Allison to believe that Molly would blindly take orders from anybody, even her husband. Make that *especially* her husband.

Marie came over to where Allison sat. "You look beat. There's a lounge in back. You could go lie down for a few minutes."

"Thanks, but I can't relax. Not until I know Andy's going to be all right. You know, I told him he reminded me of my son and now I almost think of him as being one of my kids."

"I know what you mean. Most of the deputies here under thirty are like my kids, too." Marie reached down and took her hand. "Come on. Join me in a cup of coffee."

Allison was on her second cup of coffee and her third cookie when Sam came out to the dispatcher's desk. "Heard anything from our boys at the mill?"

"They're there," Marie said, "but the place is empty. If the culprits are on foot, they must be hiding in the woods."

"Or they got Jerry's car. He said he left his keys in it. Get a bulletin out on it."

"Will do."

Sam turned to Allison. "Thought I'd give Molly a little think time before continuing our conversation. She's starting to clam up."

"Does she know where Ted is?"

"Just says he took off after he got a phone call

But she's holding something back. I can sense it." He poured coffee, dumped in two heaping spoonfuls of sugar, and took a long swig. "We should have heard from the hospital by now. I'll see what I can find out."

Allison watched the sheriff's face as he talked to someone at the hospital and felt her tension lessen. It didn't look like bad news. He turned to her. "Andy's stable. He's getting his CT scan now, and then they're going to fix his leg. We can see him in about an hour."

"That's wonderful."

He sighed. "As much as I hate to, I'm going back in and see if I can pull any more information out of Mrs. Kirkman. Since she's pleading ignorance, it shouldn't take long."

Allison went to the restroom and tried to freshen up. Her brush and makeup were in her purse which was in the backseat of her car. Marie brought her a towel and soap from the locker room and loaned her a comb. It would have to do for now.

A few minutes later, Sam, Donna, and Molly came out into the hallway. The sheriff's voice was loud and harsh. "Deputy Worley will see you to your cell while I write up the charges against you."

"What charges?" Molly demanded.

"We'll start with kidnapping and obstruction of justice."

As she was led down the hall, Molly called back, "But Ted made me do it."

Sam's face was a mask of fury as he came up to Marie's desk. Allison came closer to hear what he said. "You can put out that APB now on Ted Kirkman's car. He's wanted for murder."

TWENTY

ANDY'S EYELIDS TWITCHED, slit open, gradually widened. He studied the ceiling. It was much cleaner than he remembered. And the room was lit up more than it had been. Maybe Muscles or Skinny had found another flashlight. The smell was different, also—like someone had been scrubbing with disinfectant. He listened for his captors' voices, their footsteps. All he heard was a slight beep, beep, above his head somewhere. He didn't know how he had ended up on the floor again. The last thing he remembered, he was going to find Allison. Allison! Yes. He had to get to her—help her.

He tried to push up on his elbows, but one arm was tied down. He managed to sit halfway up. Pain streaked across his back. His head whirled around. It didn't matter. He had to get up. "I'm coming, Allison," he shouted, but his throat was parched; he could barely hear his own voice.

The men must have heard him though because they started to wrestle with him, tried to push him back down. "No," he cried, doing his best to shake them off. "I've got to help her."

They were trying to tell him something, but he couldn't understand. Strong hands pinned him back down. Then a pleasant voice spoke into his ear.

"Allison is all right. She brought you to the hospital. She'll be here soon to see you."

Andy did his best to focus on the face in front of him, to take in what she'd said. It was too much effort.

He dropped his head, and his eyes fluttered shut.

WHEN THE SHERIFF said that Ted Kirkman was wanted for murder, both Allison and Marie gaped at him and echoed the word, "Murder?"

Sam put his arm around Allison's shoulders. "Molly told me how Ted killed Leona."

Allison's head was spinning, her legs trembling, her throat dry. She managed to gasp, "But why?"

He led her into his office, motioned her to a chair. "I'll tell you pretty much the way she told the story if you want to hear it." He paused. "It's not pretty."

She closed her eyes and drew in gobs of air. After a few moments, Allison composed herself, nodded her head. "I need to know."

"When I went back in, I asked her if she knew anything about Leona's death. Not that she was a suspect, but what with your abduction, I couldn't rule out a connection between it and your aunt's supposed accident."

"And?"

"And she wanted to know if she could testify against her spouse. I explained she couldn't be compelled to testify against him, but if she wanted to, she could tell what she observed that might have a bearing on the case."

Allison held her breath. What had Molly seen? What had really happened?

Sam went on. "She said that she was through protecting the louse. Her word. She said the Monday afternoon before Leona's death, she'd dropped in for a visit. That much we knew, but what we didn't know was what was discussed on that visit. Molly said your aunt told her she had proof someone was polluting Cider Creek, maybe with a deadly poison. Leona wanted to report it, but didn't know who to call."

Allison sat up straighter. So it did involve the pollution just as she'd suspected. She waited for the sheriff to continue.

"Molly told Leona she would call the proper agency. Since Molly has connections with many local and state authorities through her volunteer activities, that satisfied Leona. But instead of reporting it immediately, she first told Ted. She said Ted seemed very upset about it, wanted to know what proof Leona had. When Molly couldn't tell him, Ted insisted that both of them go see her the next afternoon. He said he wanted to get more details before reporting to the EPA. But, she said, when they got there and Ted started questioning Leona, Molly knew something was wrong. Ted told your aunt she should forget about it. Then he offered her an extravagant price for her farm and told her he would see about the cleanup. She said she wouldn't sell the farm until she was sure all the pollution was cleaned up, that she suspected it might be leakage of dioxin from the old paper mill."

"That's why he offered to buy the farm from me,"

Allison said. "So the pollution wouldn't be noticed by anyone else."

Sam jerked his head up. "You never mentioned that."

"I didn't think it was relevant. And I haven't the chance to tell you about Leona researching dioxin poisoning from paper mill waste. I found it on her laptop. It all fits in now."

"Molly said that Ted was determined the pollution wouldn't come to light."

"But why? If it was accidental, he might have had to pay a fine. Would that have been so bad?"

"But maybe it wasn't accidental." Sam rubbed his chin in deep thought. "Maybe he dumped the chemical purposely to avoid a costly cleanup. As I told you before, your farm is the only other residence down creek from the mill so it was unlikely anyone else would notice it."

"And he had built a wooden fence behind his condos at Silver Lake to hide the creek from close inspection."

"But he knew if Leona reported the pollution to the EPA he'd not only face a stiff fine but possible jail time."

"So he pushed Leona down the stairs to keep her from talking?"

The sheriff shook his head, "First he hit her on the head with the butt on his gun."

"Ted had a gun?"

"Molly said he'd had one for years, but she didn't know he had it with him that day." .

Allison put a hand over her mouth and caught a

sob. "I never really liked Ted, but I had no idea he was violent."

"Neither did I, but Molly said he would threaten her if she didn't go along with his schemes." Sam paused, inhaled deeply. "She went on to say the blow didn't kill Leona because she was still breathing, but that she looked really bad." Sam leaned across his desk and reached for Allison's hand. "I'm sorry. But it gets worse."

She blinked back tears. *How could it get any worse?* "Go on."

"When I asked Molly why she hadn't called 911 to get help for Leona, she said she was afraid for her own life. She said Ted was furious, tore through the desk drawers looking for the proof Leona said she had, but didn't find anything. I guess he didn't see her computer."

"She usually kept it under her bed."

"Good. Anyway, Molly said Ted told her to help him make the death look like an accident. That's when they hauled her to the top of the stairs and tumbled her down. And Molly opened up the cookbook so it would seem that she'd had gone down to get apples for a pie. Then they left, locking the door behind them and leaving her to die at the bottom of the stairs."

Allison could no longer stop the avalanche of tears. "It's too horrible. Molly was Leona's friend. And she's been protecting the killer all this time."

"She claims she had no choice. I doubt a jury will buy that."

When Allison had her emotions under control, she

gave Sam a weak smile. "Suppose we forget about murder and check on Andy?"

"Good idea. I'll drive us over there."

As they neared the dispatcher's desk, Marie called out to Allison, "Roberto's on his way with your car. Said it looked in good condition."

"I hope my purse is still there. Molly threw it in the backseat."

"We'll check it out," the sheriff said. "Then if everything is all right, you can have your car back."

"Good. I really need to go back to the motel, change clothes and put on some makeup. I don't want go back to the hospital looking like this." And she thought to herself, I need something to eat besides cookies.

Roberto drove up in Allison's car followed by another deputy in the department car. Allison verified her purse, wallet, cell phone were all there. She told Sam to go ahead to the hospital, and she'd be there soon.

Later after a quick shower and a quicker hamburger, Allison returned to the hospital. The sheriff was coming out of ICU when she arrived. "He woke up some, but they had to give him more pain med, so he's getting groggy again now."

"But he's doing all right?"

"Doctor says so."

"Can't keep a good man down," Allison said. She was anxious to see him—see for herself that he was doing well. But Sam kept on talking, and she couldn't walk away.

"He was pretty alert when I first went in, so I

brought him up to speed on what we learned this morning. Needless to say, he was as shocked as we were about Ted. Then he told me how he happened to be at the mill."

"How was that? I never could figure it out."

"Just a fluke. He thought he'd be rousting some kids and ended up in a hornet's nest."

"Did he remember everything that happened?"

"Everything except how he got out of there. I played you and Jerry up as real heroes. I promised I'd bring Jerry over later to see him." Sam grinned at her. "Well, what are you waiting for? Get in there and get your hero's welcome."

Allison made a dash for the nurses' station.

"He's sleeping now," the nurse said. "Don't stay long."

Allison studied the young face under the bandaged forehead, thought of Dave, and touched his hand lightly. She felt his fingers move and jerked back. Had she awakened him? His respirations remained slow and steady, but she thought she detected a momentary smile.

The nurse came up and tapped her on the shoulder. "He should sleep for a couple of hours. Why don't you come back later?"

She nodded, rose, decided as soon as she left here, she was going to give both of her kids a call. She wouldn't tell them yet about her ordeal or anything that led up to it, but she had to hear their voices, assure herself that her babies were okay.

Back in her motel room and after three phones calls, Allison felt as if her life was getting back on track. She'd kept the conversations with both Dave and Connie focused on their lives, their studies, their social calendars, and of course, the latest basketball scores. It was just what she needed. Then she told them very briefly about Fred's accident, where he was and that he was doing fine. They both said they would give him a call.

The call to Fred was different. On his end, it was a celebration of good news. He told of his doctor's evening visit and that she was pleased with how well he was doing. "She said I might be able to be discharged tomorrow and if so, it would be all right for me to fly. And one of the nurses here, learning that my phone had been lost, volunteered to buy me another one."

"I hope you didn't give her your credit card."

Fred laughed. "You know me better than that. I gave *him* some twenties, asked him to go to Walmart and buy the cheapest one he could find along with enough minutes to last a few days. When I get home, I'll get a decent one again. In the meantime, I can call you all I want without tying up a hospital line. How does that sound?"

"Good. Now give me your new number so I can call you anytime."

After giving her the number, Fred asked, "So, what's going on at your end?"

"First and foremost, I told the kids about your accident and gave them the hospital number so you can expect calls from them. Secondly, the doctors say Andy is going to be all right. I haven't had a chance to talk to him much because he's still on pain medication, but I'll check on him again tomorrow." It was then her voice broke. "Oh, Fred. It's been terrible here. I didn't tell the kids, but I can't keep it any longer. Leona *was* murdered and it was Ted who did it."

"Ted? The guy who wants to buy the farm?"

"Yes. Molly confessed to lying and covering for him. She was there, and she told Sam everything." Allison tried to go on, finally gave up. "I can't talk about it anymore. You'll learn all the details later."

"Sure, Honey. You don't have to talk about it. But is he under arrest?"

"No. Molly is, but Ted's on the run."

"Listen, Hon, don't talk about it. Don't think about it. Just let it go and know that we'll be together tomorrow, and everything will be all right."

AFTER HE ENDED the call, however, Fred couldn't let it go, and he wasn't sure everything would be all right. He didn't know the details of what had happened, but he did know murderers. This Ted guy might be on the run, but he could still be dangerous. If he thought Allison was responsible for him being found out, he might want revenge. Did Ted know where she was staying? Was Sam providing protection for her?

Fred knew his fears were probably groundless— that his wife was safe, and soon this nightmare would be behind them. If only he could make his heart believe what his mind was telling him.

It was the calls from Connie and then from Dave that finally brought him some comfort. Allison hadn't told them anything about what she'd been going through, so they were upbeat as usual. He assured them he was doing well and would be joining their mother tomorrow. He'd never imagined becoming a father at his age, but these two young people had become an integral part of his life and he was so thankful for them. He told them both to make plans on coming to Holliston this weekend. "We're going to have a celebration."

"Of what?" they'd asked.

"A celebration of being together."

They probably thought he was still a little woozy from the bop on his head, but that was all right. A few more days and his little family would be together again.

Allison's thoughts flitted from her family to her aunt's supposed friend. Molly's whining voice echoed in her head, "But Ted made me do it!" Did the woman actually think that excused her? What kind of person could watch a friend die and not try to help her?

Allison wondered if Leona knew she was in danger before the blow struck. Probably not. She would have trusted Molly and her husband. They'd known each other for years—even did some volunteer work together. How did a person go from being a friend to a betrayer?

Knowing such speculation was useless, she tried to do what Fred had instructed—to let it go. She pushed her questions and her anger out of her mind and replaced them with pictures of her laughing children and loving husband. After a bit, the effort worked and she drifted off to sleep.

In the morning, she jerked awake with a sharp

pain from lying on the left side of her face. She sat up, rubbed her cheek, her jaw, and tried to figure out why she was hurting. Crawling slowly out of bed, she went over to the mirror and stared at her swollen cheek where a dark bruise was beginning to form. She remembered then the man who had socked her in the jaw after she'd kicked him. He'd really packed a punch, she thought, and winced as she touched the tender area.

Since she intended to go to the hospital and visit Andy, she took great care applying her makeup. When she was satisfied the bruise was sufficiently covered, she practiced smiling. She could only do up to a half-smile without grimacing. "I hope he doesn't try to make me laugh," she said to the mirror. "That would really hurt."

She made a quick call to Fred, told him about her swollen and bruised face. "Good thing you weren't here, or folks might thing we'd been in a brawl."

"Good thing you told me. I'll be extra gentle when I kiss you."

"And when will that be?"

"About five-thirty. My plane gets into Asheville at four-thirty and I have a rental car waiting."

"That's a long time."

"I know. Asheville's not the easiest place to get to. Now if you were in Charlotte, I could get a non-stop flight. As it is, I have a two hour stopover in Nashville."

"Don't you want me to meet you at the airport in Asheville?"

"No. I just want you to be at the motel waiting for me."

After they'd said their goodbyes and exchanged phone kisses, she recalled his remark about Charlotte, and that brought to mind her friend, Claire. Claire had never called with an update on her reunion with her wayward husband. Guess I'll have to call her, Allison thought. She can't leave me dangling like this.

She finished getting dressed and headed to the hospital. When she approached the ICU desk and asked for Deputy Cox, the secretary informed her that he wasn't there.

Allison caught her breath and felt a rush of panic. "What do you mean? Did his condition worsen?"

"No, much to the contrary. He was doing so much better we transferred him to a regular room." She glanced at the sheet in front of her. "You'll find him in room 220."

She gave a long sigh. "Thank you. Thank you so much." She hurried back to the elevator and pushed the second floor button.

The door to 220 was ajar, so she knocked gently and slowly pushed it open. Andy was sitting up in bed with a grin big enough for Christmas. The bandage on his forehead had been reduced to a small patch, and his sheet was turned back to reveal his short leg cast.

Allison stopped about a foot from the bed. "You're looking great."

"Nothing wrong with me that a little food and plaster of Paris can't cure. I'm already back on my feet." He pointed to a pair of crutches in the corner. "I'll probably get to go home when the doctor makes his rounds. Pull up a chair and sit a spell."

She did as he suggested, placed the chair so they faced each other and rested an arm on the bed.

"Sorry I slept through your other visit. The nurse told me you'd been in, and Sam told me how you and Jerry rescued me. How embarrassing is that? You know, the guys at the station are going to give me a hard time. I intended to save *you* from the bad guys—not the other way around."

"Jerry's the real hero. Have you seen him yet?"

"Not yet. Sam is supposed to bring him by this morning."

"You know, Andy, I saw a lot of potential in Jerry when we were making our escape. I think, with the proper help from the Veterans' Administration and others, he could make real progress. He certainly doesn't get any encouragement from his sister. Jerry said she told him he wasn't smart enough to use a cell phone. That's ridiculous."

As if on cue, Sam Babcock tramped into the room followed by a hesitant Jerry Howe.

Waving his hand to the visitors, Andy greeted them with, "Good to see you both. Anything new to report on the fleeing culprits?"

"Not yet," Sam said. "Haven't had a sighting of Ted's car yet. We've notified all neighboring states. Most likely Ted is holed up somewhere. But we'll get him."

Sam closed his eyes, rubbed his neck. Allison guessed he hadn't gotten much sleep the night before and probably wouldn't get much until the murderer was apprehended.

He went on, "We did recover your patrol car where you'd stashed it in the bushes. Thank goodness the guys who held you and Allison captive didn't drive off in it. They probably figured we would be looking for it. But Jerry's car is gone, so I guess that was their getaway car."

"That would be Skinny, Muscles, and Third Man," Andy said.

The sheriff frowned. "Who?"

Andy chuckled. "That's what I named them in my head. I can describe each one in detail if you want to broadcast their descriptions."

"Good. I'll have you write it down before we leave."

"The skinny one wasn't too bad," Allison said, "but those other two were mean ones."

After giving Andy a timid smile, Jerry slipped to the far side of the room. The deputy now motioned him to come closer. "Jerry, I never did get a chance to thank you for getting me out of there. The sheriff told me what a hero you were. I think you deserve a medal."

Jerry hung his head. "I've got a medal. It never did me any good."

Allison felt moisture come into her eyes as she stared at the war veteran. Jerry had been a hero for his country, been awarded a medal for his bravery, and then had been forgotten.

Rallying to the moment, Andy reached out to grasp Jerry's hand and said, "Then I'm going to give you something better. I'm going to buy you a smart-phone, the best cell phone on the market, and teach you how to use it. That way we'll be friends for life, and anytime you need me, you can just give me a holler, and I'll be there to help."

Jerry nodded solemnly. "That's what friends do—help each other—like Leona and me. That's why I wanted to help Allison, for Leona's sake. I didn't want anybody to hurt her so I kept looking out for her."

Andy sat up a little straighter. "Wait a minute. You mean you kept watch over Allison other times than when you followed her from the hospital?"

Both Sam and Allison stepped closer to the bed to hear Jerry's answer.

He nodded. "I watched her house so no one would go in and hurt her."

"Sam," Andy said, "remember those slick tire marks we saw?"

"Yeah?"

"Jerry has slick tires on his car. I told him he needed to get new tires."

Allison pushed back her chair and jumped up. "Jerry, did you follow me through the orchard, too, and down to the creek?"

Jerry cowered back, "I didn't mean to scare you. I wanted to be sure you were all right. I'm sorry you hurt your foot."

"And," she continued, "you followed my car when I left the farm?"

The questioned man gave a barely perceptible nod

and turned imploring eyes to Andy. "Did I do wrong? I just wanted to help."

Sam came up and pounded Jerry on the back. "You didn't do anything wrong. You were acting as Allison's bodyguard, and we all thank you for it." The sheriff's eyes shifted to the other two. "Aren't we all grateful to Jerry for his watchful care?"

Allison nodded, went over and gave Jerry a hug. "Absolutely. If it hadn't been for you watching me and following me to the paper mill, we never would have gotten away."

Andy grabbed Jerry's hand again, "Thanks, Buddy, for everything you've done." Jerry was all smiles when he and the sheriff headed out.

"So that solves the dilemma of my stalker," Allison said. "Who knew he was actually my guardian? And now that we know who the real culprits are, I won't need anyone to watch over me. Molly's in jail and I'm sure Ted soon will be."

"So what are your plans?"

"I'm going to the farm and do a little cleaning before Fred gets to town."

TWENTY-ONE

On the way up the driveway to the farm, Allison stopped at the rural mailbox, extracted her aunt's mail, and found a few bills she would send over to the attorney.

As she got out of her car at the back door, she took a moment to breathe in the warm, spring-like air. The sun was bright, the snow was nearly gone, and a tiny crocus blossom was peeking out from the rock garden by the kitchen door. Another season was approaching, and soon memories of the harsh winter would fade. In the coming months Allison knew she would be able to remember Leona's joyous life and not be haunted by her awful death.

She felt the need of a cup of tea and put a tea-kettle of water on to heat while she started cleaning out the refrigerator. All the uneaten food from the church ladies would have to be discarded, the dishes washed and returned. She figured she could put all the dishes in a box, take them to the church kitchen, and let the ladies claim what was theirs.

The tea was steeping when her cell phone rang. It was Harry. "Allison, I heard of your harrowing experience yesterday. Are you all right? Is there anything I can do for you? The news about Ted and Molly is almost unbelievable."

"I'm doing fine, and I appreciate you calling. But, Harry, how did you hear about it? The write-up won't be in the paper until this afternoon, and there wasn't anything on the Asheville TV news last night."

"Sam called me. Thought I ought to know about Ted's involvement. He knew Ted and I were friends."

"I know how hard this must be for you. But I only hope they catch him soon."

"Well, I have an idea where he might be. I'm at the sheriff's office now. I came in when I got to thinking about my hunting cabin. Ted and I went up there a lot, and I gave him a key. Since his car hasn't been spotted anywhere and no sign of him at any airport, I think he might be hiding out there. The cabin's well stocked with canned goods and firewood. Someone could stay there a long time."

"I remember Leona mentioning your cabin, but she said she'd never been up there. Is the sheriff going to check it out?"

"He's getting cars ready now. I'm going with them as a guide, but I don't intend to get into any line of gunfire."

"You think there'll be a gun fight?"

"I don't think Ted is going to give up easily. Gotta go. Talk to you later."

Allison stared at her phone long after Harry disconnected. A possible gun fight. She fervently hoped none of the sheriff's men would be injured. Thankfully, Andy was still in the hospital, so she didn't have to worry about him.

In between sips of tea, she went on with the distasteful job of dumping food. The garbage disposal hadn't had this much to eat in years.

As she worked, her mind wandered over the happenings of the last week. This was Tuesday and it was last Tuesday evening her safe little world had been shaken with the news of Leona's death. Since then, she buried the woman who'd been like a big sister to her and then had learned her aunt had been murdered by a man she trusted and betrayed by a friend. Fred had been injured in a serious accident and she hadn't been able to be with him when he needed her. Her friend, Andy, was in the hospital with a broken leg. And she'd been stalked, kidnapped, and threatened. Not the kind of week one would ever want to remember.

But at least, she comforted herself, the worst was over. Ted would soon be captured, Fred would be in Upton this afternoon, and life would get back to normal.

Thinking of Ted reminded her that she'd lost the buyer for the farm, and she needed to talk to the realtor about it. She doubted the word had gotten to Brice Hauser yet, and she had no intention of filling him in on the details. She would merely tell him Mr. Kirkman had withdrawn his offer. He'd find out soon enough what really happened.

It took a while for Mr. Hauser to understand he had lost the easy money he'd been counting on and would now have to work for his fee. She was in the middle of instructing him to advertise the farm as a working apple orchard when he interrupted.

"Just a minute, Mrs. Sawyer. You haven't yet

signed a contract with me. Until you do, I can't start any advertising."

Allison felt like she'd been slapped in the face. Mr. Hauser hadn't let a lack of a contract stop him from lining up a deal with Ted Kirkman. The realtor was all ready to grab at the easy money and apparently had no doubt that Allison would sign the necessary papers. Now, all of a sudden, he was implying she couldn't be trusted and wanted a contract up front. She knew correct business procedure, but was insulted with his attitude.

She kept her voice civil and businesslike as she replied. "I understand completely, Sir. I certainly want to do everything in the proper order." Without any further platitudes, she ended the call.

And the first part of the proper order, she thought, is to never call Hauser Realty again. There had to be other agents easier to deal with—or she'd just advertise it herself. It was not a decision she had to make now. Thank goodness, Fred would be here this evening and she could discuss any further business decisions with him.

With that out of the way, she made the call to Claire. She didn't know what to expect but her friend owed her an explanation. If the reunion had gone badly, and if Dale was gone for good, then Allison would be ready with words of comfort. If the two of them had decided to try again, then she would find just the right words of encouragement. As Jerry would say, "Friends help each other."

Claire answered on the forth ring and her voice

sounded like it was coming from the bottom of a barrel. Not good.

"Hey, Claire. It's me."

"Hi, Allie, sorry I haven't called. Just haven't felt like talking."

"I guessing since you sound like you're drowning, things didn't go well with Dale."

"You could say that."

"Well, you don't have to say anything more because I've got plenty to talk about. You wouldn't believe what's happened to me in the last few days and the scandal that will hit Upton when the paper comes out tomorrow."

"I'm not sure I'm up to hearing about any scandal. I feel as if I'm living one."

"Not that kind of scandal. We're talking *Murder Most Foul*." Allison couldn't believe she had practically made a joke about Leona's death, but she had to do something to get Claire out of the hole her friend had sunk in. "Come on out, and I'll tell you a story that will make your troubles look like a rose garden."

Allison thought she detected a touch of humor in Claire's voice when she answered, "You always did try to top me, Allie. It sounds like it might be worth getting dressed for."

"You better believe it. Get dressed. Brush that gorgeous hair of yours. Put on some makeup and get your butt out here. I'm going to cheer you up." Allison softened her voice and added. "I'm all alone and I need a friend."

"Give me an hour. I'll be there. And knowing

you, there's probably nothing in the house to eat except stale crackers, so I'll stop and pick up a pizza."

"That's my girl."

Dropping her phone on the table, Allison clapped her hands. "I should have been a therapist."

She looked around the kitchen. Everything looked in order except for the trash can where she'd emptied waste baskets, dumped paper plates, napkins, and used plastic utensils. Pulling out the bag and tying a knot in it, she headed for the door and the backyard trash can. As soon as she opened the door, though, the cold wind reminded her it was still winter and she needed to put her coat on. She hurried to do so, went out and dumped the bag, and scooted back into the house.

As she hung her parka back up, something slipped from the pocket and fluttered to the floor. She picked it up and noted it was Wes Snyder's business card. She recalled he'd given it to her last week and had urged her to let him do her aunt's taxes. At the time she was suspicious about his motives. Now she felt ashamed that she hadn't trusted him when he was only trying to be helpful. She decided to call and tell him she would accept his offer. She picked up her phone, punched in the number on the card.

When she told Wes her decision, he was delighted. "You won't be sorry, Allison. I'll be able to save you from paying more than necessary on your aunt's estate. Like I said, I have a lot of important clients, and they're pleased with my work. I spent a whole afternoon last week with Ted Kirkman going over his books. We were going to meet again a couple of days later, but we had to cancel because of Leona's funeral."

Allison gave a slight gasp when he mentioned Ted's name. Wes doesn't know yet, she thought. Most of the people in Upton probably don't know that one of their most prominent citizens is a murderer on the run, and that his wife is already in jail. She wasn't going to say anything about it. He would find out soon enough that he'd lost one of his best clients.

She kept her voice calm as she went on, "I'll be on spring break in March, and I'll meet with you then with all her accounts. Will that be all right?"

"That'll be fine. I look forward to working with you."

Something niggled at Allison's brain after she ended the call. She replayed the conversation with Wes over in head. Something was wrong, but she couldn't quite put her finger on it. The calendar on the wall caught her attention. Wes said he'd spent an afternoon with Ted and then cancelled another appointment a couple of days later due to the funeral. Did he mean "couple" as in "two"? She grabbed her phone, dialed his office again.

With no preliminaries, she demanded, "Wes, what afternoon was it you said you met with Ted Kirkman?"

"Last week. Why?"

"Never mind why. Look at your appointment book, and tell me the exact day and time. It's important."

"Sure, just a sec."

Allison felt her heart racing and her head spinning. She slumped down in the nearest chair and held her breath until Wes came back on the line.

"It was on Tuesday at two, and he stayed until nearly four."

"Are you positive? Tuesday was the day my aunt died."

"I know, but we weren't aware of her accident until the next day. Then, like I said, we cancelled our Thursday meeting because of the funeral. What's this all about?"

"I can't explain now. I'll talk to you later."

Allison's head was about to explode. Ted couldn't have killed Leona! The time of death was estimated between two and four, and he was in downtown Upton discussing his tax situation with Wes. But Molly had described the scene perfectly. She knew about the cookbook, about the rifled desk drawers....

She slapped her hands over her mouth and closed her eyes as the horrible truth penetrated her mind. It was Molly! She hadn't come here with her husband. She'd come alone—to kill her friend.

And the sheriff was even now on his way to find and arrest an innocent man. She had to stop him before someone got hurt.

When Marie answered the phone, Allison's words tumbled out in torrents. "It wasn't Ted. It's Molly. You've got to tell the sheriff. Ted has an alibi."

"Allison? Slow down. You're not making any sense."

She gulped some deep breaths and tried again. "Tell the sheriff that Ted has an alibi for the time of Leona's death. Molly is the one who killed her."

"Are you sure?"

"I'm sure. So call Sam and tell him. I don't know

why Ted ran, but he isn't a murderer. Thank goodness, Molly's already in jail."

"But she's not." Marie said.

"Not what?"

"Not in jail. She walked out of here a few minutes ago. She got an attorney from Raleigh, and he arranged bail."

"What? Then get her back. Send someone to re-arrest her."

"I don't have that authority. I'll try to call the sheriff, but sometimes it's hard to make contact in the dense woods where they're going." Marie paused, "And, Allison, you'd better be right about this."

ANDY'S FACE LIT up as Roberto slipped into his room. He lifted his hand for a high five. "About time you got here to visit this poor old wounded soldier."

"A broken leg hardly counts as being wounded—especially when you did it to yourself."

"Hey, that bit of info doesn't need to be broadcast. I'd like to retain a little dignity in the community." He pushed himself up higher in the bed. "So, what's the news? Caught any of the bad guys yet?"

"Nothing new that I know of. I worked a fender bender out by the high school this morning. Headed out to the highway now. Maybe catch a few speeders."

"Looking for some Brownie points, are you?"

The door opened before Roberto could respond, and a doctor in a white lab coat marched to the bedside. "Mr. Cox, looks like you've making a good recovery. Going to send you home. Stay on your crutches for now, but come to my office on Monday and we'll give you a walking cast. My assistant can give you a time. Any questions?"

"No sir."

"Good. You can leave whenever you can arrange transportation home."

"I already have that. My buddy here is going to drive me." Andy grinned at Roberto. "Aren't you?"

"Sure. No problem. I'll even carry you upstairs and tuck you in bed."

But Andy had no intention of going home or to bed. He asked Roberto to split one leg of his soiled uniform pants to fit over his cast, then he finished getting dressed and took a practice spin on the crutches. "Now you can drop me off at the station before you go off on your ticketing mission."

Andy lurched into the office while Roberto sped away. The place seemed empty except for Marie at her post. Her back was turned away from the door, and she looked as if she were battling with the phone and the radio at the same time. Andy hopped up to the desk with the intention of surprising her, but her anguished voice stopped him. "Answer me," he heard her say, "doggone it, answer!"

"What's wrong?"

She jerked around, her eyes wide, her hands trembling. "I can't get through to Sam . He's...." Her eyes abruptly tore away from the phone and focused on Andy. "What are you doing here? You're supposed to be in the hospital."

"I escaped. Now, tell me what's going on. Where are Sam and everybody else, and why do you need him?"

It took a few tries, but Marie finally explained about

Sam going to the hunting cabin to arrest Ted, and then about Allison's call saying Ted was innocent and Molly was the murderer. "But Molly is out on bail and may be skipping the country this very moment. And I can't get Sam or any of the cars with him."

"Call Roberto. Get him back here. And I'm going to call Allison." Since his cell phone hadn't been recovered from the mill, Andy darted as fast as he could to the nearest empty desk and grabbed the phone.

Allison paced from the kitchen to the den as Marie's words echoed through her brain, *You'd better be right about this.* She had to be right. There was no other explanation. Molly was a killer—and she was free. Now what? Was Molly escaping as Marie had suggested, leaving Ted to take all the blame?

Dropping down on the couch, Allison cradled her head in her hands, tried to quiet her mind and her heart. A door opened and shut. The sound of footsteps floated in from the kitchen. She sprang up, remembering she hadn't locked the kitchen door after taking out the trash. There had been no need to since she no longer had a stalker.

She called out in a trembling voice, "Who's there?"

A soft voice answered, "It's just me. The door was unlocked. I had to see you."

Allison gaped at the figure in the doorway. "Molly," she gasped, "what are you doing here?"

TWENTY-TWO

"I CAME TO APOLOGIZE. I know you must hate me, but hear me out." Molly came into the room, her big black purse grasped in front of her. "You've got to understand. My lawyer says I was acting under duress. That I'm not really to blame. Ted has always been domineering. Well, you know him, Allison. You know how demanding he is. I've never been able to stand up to him."

Allison listened in amazement to Molly's monologue. *She doesn't know that I know the truth. She's still blaming Ted for everything. I have to play along with her.* "You want to apologize?"

"Yes," a hopeful smile crossed her face. "And to ask you not to press kidnapping charges against me. My lawyer says he can get me off for the other charges if you drop the kidnapping part." Molly stepped closer. "Actually, I didn't kidnap you, you know. You came along willingly. I didn't lay a hand on you. Isn't that right?"

Allison nodded, her mind spinning to come up with a plan. "I guess, technically speaking, that's right."

"Of course. You know I never meant you any harm. So you'll drop the charge?"

"I think that might be the right thing to do. In

fact, I'll call the sheriff right now and tell him." She picked up her phone, pushed the redial button. She hoped Molly didn't notice the speedy dialing. The phone rang three times before Marie answered.

Allison tried to keep her voice calm and business like. "This is Allison Sawyer. I need to talk to the sheriff about the charges against Molly Kirkman."

Marie sounded like she was about to the end of her rope. "You know Sam isn't here and I can't get up with him."

Allison didn't care what Marie's reaction was, she wanted to be sure Molly thought the call was legitimate. "Then will you please take a message for me. Molly is here with me, and she has apologized for her actions. So I'm dropping the kidnapping charge."

"What? Have you lost your mind?"

"I said that Molly is here with me now. Please tell the sheriff as soon as possible. I'm going to drop the charge against her."

Allison could hear the dispatcher catch her breath. "Molly's there? Are you all right?"

"Yes. Give the sheriff my message. Bye."

BEFORE ANDY HAD a chance to dial Allison's number, Marie started yelling at him. "Allison's in trouble. Molly's there and she made Allison call in to drop the kidnapping charge. Roberto's the only one I can send out there."

Andy made it to the dispatcher's desk in two steps of his crutches. "Hand me the keys to my car. I'm going."

"You can't go like that."

"Are you going to give me the keys, or do I have to dive over your desk to get them?"

She flung the keys at him and at the same time called Roberto.

In a few seconds Andy was racing up Mount Vista Road.

ALLISON SLIPPED HER phone into her pocket and smiled at Molly. "Well, now that all is forgiven, how about a cup of tea?"

"No, I've got to go. I'm meeting my attorney in a few minutes." Molly headed for the kitchen.

Allison moved past her. "Please, stay a little. It won't take but a minute to reheat the water; I just had a cup not long ago." As she talked, she grabbed the teakettle and flipped on the burner. "I know Leona would want us to be friends again. And she always said that sharing a cup of tea with a friend is one of life's greatest pleasures." Allison didn't know where that nonsense came from. Leona had never said any such thing, but she had to keep Molly here until help arrived. She was sure a patrol car would soon be coming up her drive.

She reached into the cabinet for cups. Planting herself between the cabinet and the table, she effectively blocked Molly's escape route to the kitchen door. Allison waved one of the cups in the direction of a cabinet on the other side of the sink. "I stopped at the grocery store this morning and picked up some macaroons. They're in that far cabinet. Could you bring them over?" Molly didn't move. Allison kept on chattering. "On the second shelf. You'll see them. There's nothing like a macaroon to go with tea."

"But I can't stay. We'll have tea another day— soon." Molly made her way around the other side of the table toward the door.

I can't let her get away, Allison thought desperately. What do I do now?

The teakettle started its shrill whistle announcing it had reached the boiling point. "Oh, grab that thing off the burner for me, will you, Molly? That noise drives me crazy."

Molly hesitated, then gave a shrug and went back around the table to the stove, moved the teakettle. It gave a last little tweet and subsided into silence.

The next noise Allison heard was a car coming up the drive. She smiled inwardly. It must the cavalry arriving to save the day.

Molly must have heard the car, too, and her reaction was very different.

"Who's coming?" Molly demanded.

"I guess more company for tea."

"I don't think so," Molly said. "You called the police. Pretended to be my friend, and then turned on me. Just like Leona." Her hand dove into her purse and came out with a small revolver. "This time I'm really going to kidnap you. You're going to put your hands up and march out that door. And if a cop tries to stop us, you're dead."

Allison still had two tea cups in her hands, but they were no match for a gun. She dropped them on the table. As she did, the car came into to view, stopped, and its door opened.

When she saw who exited the car, Allison stopped breathing and her pulse skipped a couple of beats. She'd forgotten all about Claire coming. She tried to move to the door to stop her friend.

Instead, she was stopped by Molly's menacing command. "I said, 'hands up!'"

Allison did as directed, but at the same time, she explained, "It's not the police, Molly. It's just an old friend. Let me get rid of her and then we can talk some more."

Before Molly could reply, the kitchen flew open, Claire entered with a pizza box in her hand and a perplexed look on her face. "Allie, I thought you said you were alone."

Allison saw Claire's eyes grow bigger as she stared at the two women, one with her hands in the air and the other one with a gun. "What...?"

"Run," Allison shouted. "Run!"

Dropping the pizza on the floor, Claire turned, but before she could go any further, a sound exploded.

Claire crumpled to the floor.

Ignoring Molly's gun, Allison ran to her friend, saw blood oozing from her right shoulder area. She grabbed a dish towel from the counter and pressed it against the wound. "It's okay," she whispered. "You're going to be all right."

Claire blinked her eyes, blinked again. "Allie, look out!"

Allison felt the barrel of the gun at the back of her head. At the same time she heard another car roar up the drive. That had to be the help she'd called for.

Molly must have heard the car, too. "On your feet, hands up, and out the door. We're leaving."

Allison raised her hands as she stepped out of the house. The patrol car was only yards away, but the late afternoon sun was in her eyes, and she couldn't see the driver's face. Why didn't he get out? What was he waiting for?

ANDY CRACKED OPEN the car door but froze when he saw Allison with her hands in the air and a gun to her back. What could he do now? He had no gun, no phone, no cuffs, and a bum leg. Was he going to mess up this rescue like he had at the paper mill? No way. Somehow he was going to save Allison.

He reached over, snatched one of his crutches that he'd tossed into the passenger side, and opened the door only slightly more. He didn't want Molly to get a good look at him. He slid the heavy cast to the ground and propped himself up. He saw the shock on Allison's face when she realized who her rescuer was, but he had no time to reassure her.

"Move another inch," Molly shrieked at him, "and I'll shoot her. She's going to drive me out of here, and you can't stop us."

"Not a good plan," Andy said. "Because I'm coming after you, and while you're shooting her, I'll be shooting you." Maybe a bluff is as good as a gun, he reasoned. "So drop your gun, and we can all leave here alive."

"I've got a better idea." Molly seized Allison around the waist and thrust her around to face the deputy. "Now you'll have to shoot your friend to get to me."

Andy stared into Allison's eyes. He could tell that she trusted him, but she didn't know either that he was bluffing about having a gun. She expected him to save her from the demonic fiend behind her. And he would.

He inched out to the edge of the door keeping most of his body covered. He smiled at Allison, then quickly dropped his head forward for a moment, hoping she would get the message. She answered him with a slight nod. Now was the time for action.

Andy flung the car door all the way open. Allison dropped to the ground. Molly wildly fired her gun. Andy stepped out on his broken leg and struck Molly's gun hand with the end of the crutch. The revolver spiraled to the ground. Molly and Allison both scrambled for it.

Andy raised the crutch again and smashed it against Molly's skull. She whirled back, hit her head on the kitchen step.

He toppled forward. His cast pounded on a jagged rock in the flower bed. Searing pain raced up his left leg.

Molly struggled to sit up as Allison quickly retrieved the gun and pointed it at her. "Don't move. I know how to shoot, too."

Holding Molly at gunpoint, Allison bent her head toward Andy. "You all right?"

"Not exactly. I think I broke my leg again."

She sidled over to him. "I hate that, but can you keep Molly covered while I see about Claire?"

He nodded, even though he didn't have the faintest idea who Claire was.

Allison handed him the gun, but before she could make it into the house, another patrol car raced up and Roberto sprang out.

Allison called out to him. "We need two ambulances here ASAP—and some handcuffs."

BEFORE FOLLOWING THE ambulances to the hospital, Allison checked the time, realized Fred must have landed at Asheville, and called his new cell phone number. Without saying one word about what had just transpired, she assured him she'll meet him at the motel at the appointed time.

It would take more than a killer with a gun, blood on the kitchen floor, and two friends in the emergency room to stop their reunion.

Allison barely had time to check in the ER to make sure Claire and Andy were going to be all right, and told them both she would be back later. Hightailing back to the motel, she pulled into her parking space and had just gotten the door unlocked when she eyed another car drive in and head her way. She quickly opened the door, stepped in, but kept the door ajar. When the incoming car came to a halt next to hers, she threw off her parka and came out with a wide smile and wider arms.

"Hi, Hon," she said, trying her best to make her voice light. "I've been watching for you."

His embrace and tender kiss nearly did her in. Allison wanted nothing more than to collapse in his arms and spill out all the turmoil she'd been in. She didn't. Her brain told her that he deserved a better welcome than her tears.

She pulled back, swept her hand toward the door. "Come on in, Big Boy."

FRED WASN'T FOOLED. Something was wrong with this picture. In the first place, she couldn't have been watching for him from the window because the blinds were drawn tightly. In the second place, one side of her jeans was torn and dirty, her shirt was spotted with food stains, and her hair was a mess. Not exactly the way one would greet a long awaited lover. And finally, she'd called him by his playful nickname in a voice that was anything but playful.

He followed her into the nearly dark room where she perched on the edge of the bed and patted the space next to her. Instead of accepting the invitation, he turned on the bedside lamp, pulled a chair up and sat down facing her. Taking her hands in his, he said softly but firmly. "Now tell me what's going on."

It took several minutes and several tissues, but she did exactly what he asked. She told of being at the farm to clean out leftover food, of Ted's alibi followed by the revelation of Molly's guilt and then of her showing up. She told of Claire's arrival, of her friend being shot, and of Andy breaking his leg again. The narration of events was spotty and greatly abbreviated, but after many interruptions with questions, Fred finally had an understanding of Allison's terrifying afternoon. No wonder she looked as if she'd been through a war.

A bunch of hugs later, he suggested she take a

nice, long shower, and then they would check on her friends in the hospital. "After which," he announced, "I'm taking you out to a celebration dinner."

ALLISON EMERGED FROM the bathroom feeling like a new person—her husband was here, her aunt's murderer was under arrest, and life could now return to normal.

The first person she saw upon entering the emergency room was Sam Babcock. He apparently had noticed her at the same time and they headed toward each other. They met in the middle of the waiting room where he enveloped her in a bear hug. "Thank goodness you're all right." He stepped and took another good look. "You are okay, aren't you? No injuries you failed to report?"

"No injuries for me. Claire and Andy were the unlucky ones. Have you seen them? How are they doing?"

"Just came from seeing both of them and they're going to be fine." Sam looked over Allison's shoulder and spied Fred. Stepping toward him, the sheriff thrust out his hand. "Fred Sawyer, I presume. I'm Sam. Talked to you on the phone. Glad to finally meet you."

Fred's took Sam's hand, gave it a hard pump. "And I'm mighty glad to meet you. Seems that it's been a rough week for a lot of people here."

"Is it finally over with?" Allison asked. "Did you catch up with Ted? Why did he run if he wasn't guilty? What will happen to Molly now?"

Sam held up his hand. "Whoa. I'll tell you both

everything later. But right now you need to go see your friend. Claire's been admitted. Room 206. She was pretty woozy when I was there from the pain meds, but the doctor said it was a flesh wound and the bullet went straight through. And they're keeping Andy here until his cast dries some more. He's in the snack room. After you see Claire, come find us in the snack bar and we'll talk."

She nodded, took Fred's hand and aimed for the elevator. When they reached Claire's room, she appeared to be sleeping. Allison stared at the ace bandage that covered her friend's left shoulder, extended down her arm and across her chest. It seemed like a mighty big dressing for a little flesh wound. She would have to get that clarified tomorrow. But not wanting to disturb Claire tonight, she left a short note, saying she'd be back in the morning. She drew a smiley face and signed it, *Allie.*

As she and Fred neared what was called the snack bar, although it only consisted of vending machines, two tables and a few chairs, she heard rounds of laughter. Poking her head in the open doorway, she waved to Sam, Andy, and Roberto.

Pulling Fred forward, she said, "Hon, I want you to meet the best crime fighting deputies in Upton, or for that matter, in this part of the state. The handsome one is Roberto Flores and the banged up one is Andy Cox." She snuggled closer to Fred. "And as you boys might have guessed, this is my husband, Fred Sawyer."

Handshakes all around were followed by chairs being moved to make room for the newcomers. When everybody was settled, Sam coughed, cleared his throat and asked, "Anyone want to know what I've been doing today while these youngsters were catching the real criminal?"

The heads of the two youngsters bobbed obediently; Allison gave Sam a thumbs-up; Fred slid down in his chair and relaxed.

Sam began. "Ted was at the cabin. Gave up without a whimper. He admitted to hiring the men to dump the chemicals from the mill into the creek. Seems that when the paper mill shut down, they left a lot of chemicals and sludge behind. Claims he didn't know the material was poison. And actually, we don't know if there was anything toxic in the waste or not. The stuff left may have been harmless, but that's up to the proper authorities to determine. The EPA can arrange for testing the chemicals as well as the water in Cider Creek. And then they'll determine how to dispose of the waste safely and how much clean-up needs to be done. Ted said he simply wanted to save a little expense. He bought the mill because Molly wanted to convert it into more luxury condos.

"He was flabbergasted when he found out Molly had fingered him for Leona's murder. He said he was with Wes Snyder that afternoon, which we know now is true. We had a hard time convincing him that Molly was the murderer. Until then, he still thought the death was an accident."

The sheriff shook his head. "Not sure I believe him on that point, but that's his story. And he claims he didn't order Allison's kidnapping. Says that was all Molly's idea. He got the call from the men about

Andy being there and about Allison's message. When he told Molly, she thought news of the illegal dumping would spoil her plans, and she'd lose a lot of money. She told him she had to shut her up."

Allison swiped a furrow of tears from her cheeks. "Like she shut up Leona."

Sam nodded and went on. "Ted said it was also Molly's idea for him to run. She told him he'd spend the rest of his life in jail if he was caught, and he believed her. But once he got to the cabin, he decided he couldn't stay on the run and was ready to turn himself in. He'll spend the night in a cell, but I suppose a lawyer will get him out until his trial comes up."

Allison had been quiet as long as she could stand it. "I can't believe he was as ignorant as he claimed. Think he'll do any jail time?"

Sam shrugged. "But I think it's a sure bet that his business career is over. He'll probably be forced to sell most of his holdings to cover the legal fees for himself and Molly.

"And as for Molly, she'll be charged with murder and a host of other crimes. And I doubt if any attorney is going to be able to help her much—and she'll definitely not get out on bail this time."

"If there is any justice," Andy said, "she'll never see the outside world again."

"Oh," the sheriff said, "but that's not all. "Skinny, Muscles, and Third Man are also in custody—in a little town in Tennessee. Seems like one of Jerry's slick tires had a blowout, sent them into a ditch. Some kind motorist called 911. The police responding recognized them from our APB, arrested the trio, and they're awaiting extradition."

Sam leaned back. "Well, that's all my news. Anybody have anything else to add?"

Andy sat up straighter in his wheelchair and a jack-o'-lantern grin lit up his face. "I have an announcement to make."

Sam put a hand to his waist, stared at his deputy. "If you think you're getting a vacation, you're crazy. I've got plenty of paperwork for you to do until that cast comes off."

"Farthest thing from my mind. In fact I plan to be working two jobs for the next several years."

The remark was met by silence and blank stares. He laughed and then hurried to explain. "Sam got my phone back earlier, and the first thing I did was to call Millie. I figured with the time difference, she was either ending her work day or starting it. At any rate she answered on the second ring."

Roberto grimaced. "You couldn't wait to tell her you'd broken your leg—twice?"

"Didn't say a word about my leg. I simply asked her if she could consider helping me run an apple orchard."

Allison bounced out of her chair. "What? You want the farm?" She turned to Fred. "Did you hear that? He wants to buy the farm!"

Fred gently tugged her back to her seat. "Let him finish."

If possible, Andy's smile got larger. "She said it sounded like a great idea."

Sam excused himself while the others discussed

the possibility of the Cox Apple Orchard. It wasn't until the nurse came in, pronounced Andy's cast dry enough for him to be discharged, that Fred could pry Allison away.

Roberto loaded Andy up to take him home while Fred and Allison headed out for dinner. They decided the rest of the discussion about the apple orchard could continue over long distance phone calls and by email.

BEFORE STARTING FOR home the next day, Allison and Fred visited Claire who was making a good recovery. Upon her discharge, the doctor would arrange for home health nurses to check on her and change her bandage. Allison assured her she would be back in a few weeks to have that long chat they'd intended.

After showing Fred around the farm and visualizing the young couple keeping the orchard producing delicious mountain apples, Allison was content to leave.

Harry met them at his place to return Elmer to his new owner.

Their last stop was the cemetery. "Now you can rest in peace, Leona. And thank you so much for being in my life."

EPILOGUE

Elmer barked his usual announcement of the mailman's arrival and Allison thanked him with a pat on the head. The expected wedding invitation was accompanied by a letter. Although she talked to both Andy and Millie from time to time, the letter was an update of events. Jerry Howe was working out very well as their resident manager of the orchard. The renovation of the old milking parlor for his bachelor apartment was completed. He'd come a long way in the past months with proper psychiatric counseling and independent living classes. He loved the cell phone Andy had given him and kept his boss informed of any problems that came up during the day.

Another plus for the couple was that they would never have to worry about extra hands during peak work periods in the orchard. The members of the recently formed Westside Apartments Teen Club were only too willing to help out. The club, consisting of both boys and girls, met monthly in Mrs. Scapelli's apartment with their mentors from the county sheriff's department.

And as part of their sales agreement, Andy reminded Allison she would have a steady supply of their delicious mountain apples.

* * * * *

REQUEST YOUR FREE BOOKS!
2 FREE NOVELS PLUS 2 FREE GIFTS!

 HARLEQUIN®

INTRIGUE

BREATHTAKING ROMANTIC SUSPENSE

REQUEST YOUR FREE BOOKS!

2 FREE NOVELS PLUS 2 FREE GIFTS!

ROMANTIC suspense

Sparked by danger, fueled by passion

YES! Please send me 2 FREE Harlequin® Romantic Suspense novels and my 2 FREE gifts (gifts are worth about $10). After receiving them, if I don't wish to receive any more books, I can return the shipping statement marked "cancel." If I don't cancel, I will receive 4 brand-new novels every month and be billed just $4.74 per book in the U.S. or $5.49 per book in Canada. That's a savings of at least 12% off the cover price! It's quite a bargain! Shipping and handling is just 50¢ per book in the U.S. and 75¢ per book in Canada.* I understand that accepting the 2 free books and gifts places me under no obligation to buy anything. I can always return a shipment and cancel at any time. Even if I never buy another book, the two free books and gifts are mine to keep forever.

240/340 HDN GH3P

Name	(PLEASE PRINT)
Address	Apt. #
City	State/Prov.	Zip/Postal Code

Signature (if under 18, a parent or guardian must sign)

Mail to the **Reader Service:**

IN U.S.A.: P.O. Box 1867, Buffalo, NY 14240-1867
IN CANADA: P.O. Box 609, Fort Erie, Ontario L2A 5X3

Want to try two free books from another line?
Call 1-800-873-8635 or visit www.ReaderService.com.

* Terms and prices subject to change without notice. Prices do not include applicable taxes. Sales tax applicable in N.Y. Canadian residents will be charged applicable taxes. Offer not valid in Quebec. This offer is limited to one order per household. Not valid for current subscribers to Harlequin Romantic Suspense books. All orders subject to credit approval. Credit or debit balances in a customer's account(s) may be offset by any other outstanding balance owed by or to the customer. Please allow 4 to 6 weeks for delivery. Offer available while quantities last.

Your Privacy—The Reader Service is committed to protecting your privacy. Our Privacy Policy is available online at www.ReaderService.com or upon request from the Reader Service.

We make a portion of our mailing list available to reputable third parties that offer products we believe may interest you. If you prefer that we not exchange your name with third parties, or if you wish to clarify or modify your communication preferences, please visit us at www.ReaderService.com/consumerchoice or write to us at Reader Service Preference Service, P.O. Box 9062, Buffalo, NY 14240-9062. Include your complete name and address.

REQUEST YOUR FREE BOOKS!

2 FREE NOVELS
FROM THE SUSPENSE COLLECTION,
PLUS 2 FREE GIFTS!

READERSERVICE.COM

Manage your account online!

- Review your order history
- Manage your payments
- Update your address

> ### *We've designed the Reader Service website just for you.*

Enjoy all the features!

- Discover new series available to you, and read excerpts from any series.
- Respond to mailings and special monthly offers.
- Connect with favorite authors at the blog.
- Browse the Bonus Bucks catalog and online-only exculsives.
- Share your feedback.

Visit us at:

ReaderService.com